FED UP

with the

FANNY

Franklin White

Simon & Schuster

SIMON & SCHUSTER
Rockefeller Center
1230 Avenue of the Americas
New York, NY 10020

SIMON & SCHUSTER and colophon are registered trademarks
of Simon & Schuster Inc.

Designed by Elina D. Nudelman

Manufactured in the United States of America

ISBN 0-684-84491-5

Acknowledgments

I would like to introduce the Supremes who made this happen. (Clap your hands everybody and give them a round of applause!!! Yes. . . . Yes. . . .) You ladies are wonderful and make beautiful music together! I can't wait until we do this all over again. Standing on the right, styling so fashionably in Dolce & Gabbana from head to toe: My manager, confidante, and best friend, Miea Allen, who has been with me from the beginning. Thanks for your support, honest opinions and advice—you are one of a kind! Keep doing what ya do! Standing on the left, laced in Gucci: my editor, Laurie Chittenden, who is point blank the best in the business. Thanks for seeing when I could not and helping me to get my point across. Your insight and knowledge only made it mo' betta and pressure free. I like your Stello! Last but not least, standing in the middle, draped in Versace, my agent, Victoria Sanders. Your commitment and expertise made this entire experience not only painless but fun. No wonder you're so much in demand! Take a bow, divas. . . . You all are fabu'!!!!!! **(Standing ovation)**

To the one who has never failed me.
God the father, God the son, God the holy spirit.

When situations become complicated and decisions have to be made they should be carefully analyzed throughout and prayed over. But lately that has not been the case for those in my life.

—KAHLIL

Everyday Thang

Even though I still had to finish up my last eight hours for the man I felt good about the beginning of my day. My new Volvo 960 put me in the right frame of mind by passing any and everything on the road as I cruised to work. Through the sunroof I could see the beautiful blue skies that covered the city, but the heat outside was ridiculous. When I planted my feet on the pavement in the parking lot, I felt like dropping straight down to my knees and asking God to take back this wicked, thick, humid air and return the cool breezy air that I love about my hometown of Detroit in early September.

It was so hot out that the coffee vendors weren't parked in their usual spots along the sidewalk for the first time all week. And without the vendors I didn't get to scan for the groups of women who make a habit of gathering around in clusters, drinking their coffee, tea, Slim Fast, and juice, while peepin' the few brothers who have jobs downtown. When these ladies see a brother, they get so excited you would think that Laurence or Wesley had been sighted with signs on their backs saying, TAKE ME, I'M YOURS! I could tell they were really trippin' as they tried their best to position themselves for their morning look over without it being too obvious.

"Hi," one of the ladies said as I approached them with a smile planted on my face. She easily stood out because she was the tallest of them all. I noticed the sister started to drink whatever she had in her cup as she seductively batted her long eyelashes at me, then grinned at her girlfriends waiting for them to tease her about how bad she'd been.

This attention was definitely a first from this group of young women. There are so many cliques on Woodward Avenue that I have memorized each one for acknowledgment's sake. I'd walked past this particular group every day on my way into work, but this was the first time anyone had spoken to me. As I walked directly into the gang, I thought about all the how-to guides in the bookstores that brothers and sisters are writing on how women can lure men. They must be selling big time, and these young ladies must have read every line and talked about it in a literary club because when I slowed down to speak to them, I felt like they were trying out a can't-miss example from the latest book on me. No doubt these sisters were fly, I had to give them that, and I kind of felt sorry for them because of the lack of brothers around to compliment them on their good looks or to do whatever we do to just make them smile. I knew they were up to something, so I just hoped their intentions were good. But I was prepared to encounter any type of game that they were planning to throw my way because in a gang bang you never know the flavor of the day. I had my fingers crossed, hoping one of the sisters hadn't stopped short of reading all of her chapters, because I didn't want to have to take anyone back to school. I have five sisters, and growing up in our house, you said good morning to the attitudes before anyone else in the house. So I was sure that I could handle these sisters if need be. "Good morning, ladies," I responded, making sure I looked at each and every one of them so I wouldn't offend anyone without breaking stride. I could feel their eyes on my backside and, to tell you the truth, I enjoyed the hell out of all the attention.

"Excuse me?" a tender voice sang out.

I stopped and turned around, then looked at the young lady who said hello and smiled.

"Are you a professional basketball player?" she asked.

They all waited intently for an answer. "No, I'm sure not." At six feet five I receive that question a lot. I'd been considered by a couple of NBA teams back when I played basketball at Central State University, and I made it a point to continue to work out over the years and keep my body in shape. At that moment I was glad that I did.

"Then you must be a professional model," a different sister said, as she slowly stirred her drink and looked around at her girlfriends to show them how much spunk she had. Smiling and slightly blushing, I told them, "No, not a model either, just a hardworking ad executive at the Houston Corporation who better get himself to work so that he can prepare for a very busy day. Nice meeting you all."

Waving good-bye to the ladies, I turned around and continued to walk to work. I overheard their comments.

"Hum, an ad executive. Not bad," one of the ladies said.

"Is that what he is?" another blurted out. "All I heard him say, is . . . he was hard." They burst into laughter.

Still grinning from their comments, I remembered when—and it was not that long ago—a brother of my complexion, deep-down chocolate, was not looked upon favorably by the majority of women. It used to be, if you didn't look like anyone in the Debarge family, you most likely had to settle for whatever came your way and hope and pray that she wasn't blacker than you. But the days of being called spook, black knight, tar baby, and crispy critter by your own people are gone. Women nowadays seem to want nothing but a chocolate mocha, radial-tire color black man.

While riding on the elevator to my office, I thought about what my father had told me about the corporate world and all the foolishness I would encounter in the workplace. So much of what he said has occurred like Scripture, and I am just thankful that God gave him to me as long as he did. Before my pops passed away he was always there for me, and one thing is for sure, working as the head of plant maintenance in the automobile industry for thirty-five years taught him a lot about people and what they will or will not do. When he died it hurt me so bad because he was so brokenhearted. Love and respect were always in abundance in the Richardson household, and with six kids to raise there was never a dull moment. My parents went the extra mile for all of us until the day Pops was rolled down the church aisle in his casket. His dream of raising six strong, independent children had evaded him, and he died worrying about my sister Leandra.

My sister Leandra, the eldest of five girls and myself, is the most irresponsible person I have ever known. And the most irritating thing about that is that she happens to be in my family. Everyone seems to have a problem with her and her know-it-all attitude, which has really turned my close family into a thing of the past. Since my father died, four of my five sisters have moved back in with my mother, to the house that he built for their retirement. He always joked that they were going to move out of the ghetto where the drugs and guns were sold to the place where everything is manufactured—the suburbs—and that's exactly what he did. After he passed, Toni, Kim, and Pam slowly moved back in with Mom. Michelle is the only one who doesn't live with my mother but still, she's always there.

In the beginning it really didn't bother my mother that she had a houseful again, but I can see that it's taking its toll on her. I'm sure she's grateful that she isn't there with Leandra by herself, and everyone works to keep her mind at ease as she misses my father dearly.

Fed Up with the Fanny

As usual I was the first one in the office and to my surprise the very important contract revision for the sneaker ad had not been done. It was still sitting on my desk. I wish my boss, Mr. Gales, would ensure that the office secretary, Danielle, would do my work as quickly as she takes off her panties for him after everyone has left for the day. When I first heard that she and Gales were fooling around I really couldn't believe it. I mean this girl looks like she could have her face plastered on all the white magazines if she wanted to—*Mademoiselle, Vogue,* or some shit. What could she see in Gales? But one evening I returned to the office to get my keys that I had left in my desk drawer, and after hearing for myself the two lovebirds getting their Jones on as I walked past his office door, I realized the rumors about them were true. While I didn't care if she and Gales were freakin' on their free time, this was my money that she was messing with and her lack of professionalism was about to piss me off. It was obvious I was going to have to get on her ass to get the work done before the ten o'clock appointment that I had scheduled with my client.

The first thing that I usually do in the morning is prepare for the customary morning meeting. But this was Friday and the first of the month, which means payday and I just had to ensure my money was deposited into the company's matching savings plan before I did anything at all. This is my bread-and-butter. Come December, I'm going to kiss this drive-you-crazy place good-bye and start my own company. God willing, when it matures I'll roll that money over, take a loan out on it, and pay myself back with interest. The balance in my account was so pleasing, the early morning phone call that took my eyes off my computer screen didn't bother me one bit.

"Good morning, Houston Corporation, Kahlil Richardson speaking," I said in my payday voice.

"Hi, Kahlil. Guess what? Your sister be trippin'!"

Why now? I thought to myself. I was in one of my better moods

15

all week and I could tell my sister Pam was ready to start talking about all of the confusion over at my mother's house. She calls me three, maybe four, times a week to keep me up-to-date on the madness. I settled into my leather chair, swiveled around to where the photos of my family are placed, and began going over my notes for the morning meeting. I was half-ass listening to what she was saying because I had about twenty minutes before I had to be in the boardroom.

"I just thought I'd call and fill you in, before you get a call from your sister Michelle. She came over last night and told Mama that she's thinking about moving in here with us because she and Terrance are having problems again. I overheard her say that she's tired of him and she's found herself a new man and get this—she's already been sleeping with him and Terrance asked her about it and she told him to stay out of her business and smacked him in the face. I'm sure she's going to ask you to help her move again. So be on the lookout for her call," Pam cautioned me. She always makes sure I knew everything that was going on, if I want to hear about it or not.

That was definitely bad news. I had moved Michelle back and forth at least four times in the past year and a half and I just didn't have the time to drop what I had going on in my life, especially this weekend, to go help her move, then turn around and move her back into the apartment with Terrance when they made up. I don't know why they don't leave well enough alone and accept that things aren't going to work out. I've tried to convince Michelle to just get a divorce and let that be the end of things, but she enjoys the drama of it all. They both do.

"Pam, do me a favor and tell her not to do anything before I talk to her, okay?" I said in a hurry, putting my paperwork in order. "Now I have to go, I have a meeting. I'll call you later on when I get home. Good-bye."

"Be sure to call me now," she said quickly, "because that's not all I have to tell you." For some reason, I really did believe that.

Everyone else had arrived at the office now, and, as usual, they were talking about their upcoming weekend game of golf. I swear the majority of these assholes think they are the authority on golf. I wonder how many of them would quit the game all together if they found out the tee was invented by a black man. I thought about sharing this fact, but after seven years at the office I know them too well. They would say some stupid shit like, "He made it because he was tired of bending down while our forefathers took their shots off his head," and piss me off. Plus they are still getting over the fact that Tiger Woods beat that ass in the Masters. I think they like to rationalize that he isn't really a black man, just something really special.

Those are the kinds of things I have to put up with at the office. I know how to golf, and I play with some of the brothers from church quite frequently. But I will never play a round with this bunch of disrespectful suck-ass white boys. A sister who worked in the production department and quit about three years ago told me about a brother who worked for the firm a couple of years before I was hired. He took these fools up on their offer to go out and play a round. What he didn't know was that they secretly videotaped the outing, then showed cutouts of the video at a diversity seminar at the downtown Hilton. The seminar went over with great success for the company. Unfortunately there was no mention whatsoever that those people my brother played with called him nigger while he was drinking beer with them in the clubhouse. He was never asked to play again, and I am determined not to be played like a sucker by these fools. Nor would they try me because they know that I'm well strapped.

Everyone here is aware that I sit on the board of the Urban Coalition, which is the strongest grassroots organization in the city of Detroit. All of our members on the board have a keen interest in the community. We are committed to making sure that the black community is well represented both in the workplace in the city and in the decision-making process regarding issues that affect the community.

I love the work that I do at the Coalition. I truly care about what goes on in the community, and I decided a long time ago that I wasn't going to succumb to the pressures of my job or luxuriate in my success without giving back to where I come from. I thrive on making a difference and helping my own people.

I'd already made up my mind that I was only going to answer questions directed at me during the meeting rather than play the political game. I decided to sit back and watch Mr. Gales, an overly large white man who loves to wear three-piece suits, belittle anyone that let him get away with it. He actually tried it on me once, but I set him straight so damn fast he was left speechless. Mr. Gales was the cause of one of the funniest things that has happened since I've been here—something that verified that these white-boy graduates of Harvard, Columbia, and West Point are not the shit like they think they are.

One morning, Mr. Gales sat and listened to an argument between two Ivy League, well-paid, hundred-thousand-dollar-a-year advertising executives that got out of hand. The boss made one of the reps recount his own words as though he was his father. The rep was told by the boss to say I'm sorry in front of the entire staff. The apologetic rep said "I apologize" instead. This was not acceptable. Mr. Gales stood up and slammed his fist on the conference room table and told the rep to do exactly as he said and say "I'm sorry." With tears in his eyes the stupid asshole said it. He virtually demolished his own self-respect, First Amendment rights, and the corporate toughness that he professed he had. Instead of tough he sounded like a three-year-old boy who had been corrected by his daddy for throwing a rock in the neighbor's front window. He quickly lost the respect of everyone in the office.

I know for a fact that they don't like me and I could care less. They look at me as though I'm just an affirmative-action disciple who has no right to be in the same workplace with them. I don't give a damn about their lack of enlightenment because for the past three years in a row I've led the entire company in advertising sales. I can back my shit up, and I never let them forget that fact. Quite frankly, I used to get upset and inflamed when they only talked about white current events and movies during and before luncheon meetings. They don't have a clue about black America. Even if I wanted to comment on a black event or activity I wouldn't because there were no other blacks around to back me up. I understand that they think everything and everybody revolves around their world because they were born into that way of thinking. I stopped becoming upset, and now I school them on movies by Bill Duke, Carl Franklin, and Julie Dash, just to let them know that there's a bigger world out there. And when I really want to piss them off I tell them that my favorite song is "Paint the White House Black" by George Clinton.

The meeting ended without a hitch, and they all started to talk about their plans for the weekend. I slid out of the conference room and went back to my office to finish what I had to do.

Messages

◇

The imported rum, a present from a client after his trip to Guyana, had never tasted any better. I normally drink it only on special occasions or use it as a conversation piece, but that hadn't even crossed my mind with the special night I was planning with my better half. I'd thought about entertaining at my place, but I am renovating and the awful odor of the treatments that have been put on my hardwood floors fills the entire house. I am trying my best to be patient as the work is being finished, but it is going on three months. As it gets closer to completion, I keep thinking how well the house is going to look with all of the Afrocentric art I've collected hanging on my walls.

No one could believe that I wanted to buy this house from my father and remodel it instead of moving out to Southfield like so many other folks have done. I don't have a reason to leave. This is where I was born and raised. I knew the house had potential, but all I heard when I started the project was how much money I was wasting because the house is right in the middle of the inner city where most of the home owners don't take care of their homes. I wasn't listening to shallow minds.

Since I started renovation the idea has spread like wildfire. Four of my neighbors on this block alone have already begun to do the same, and these all-brick beauties are going to be something to see when they're complete. Most of my furniture and appliances are still covered with sheets to protect them not only from the workers' spills, but from my 155-pound German rottweiler, Nite, who loves to sit his big ass straight up like a human in the chair he picked out for himself in the family room.

The sounds of Erykah Badu coming from my Sony Surround Sound system definitely put me in the right frame of mind. I could feel all of the pressure of the week beginning to lift from my shoulders. I was determined to spend some quality time with my lady, Cece. I'd been thinking about her the entire day, and as the rum started to hit me I thought about how over a year life can completely change. It seemed like yesterday that I was still against committing to one woman, but I think all men go through this. I didn't think I was ready for commitment, until I saw there was going to be a lot less drama involved if I stepped up to bat and took my chances.

Cece McCoy was one of the two ladies I was involved with and she'd known about the other relationship that I had been involved in for the past three years. I didn't keep anything from her. Both ladies knew about each other, but I could have easily kept my situation hidden from both of them if I wanted to. I was sure, however, that if I told the truth both ladies would understand. I knew they would respect me more for telling them the truth instead of finding out later that I had been lying to both of them and sleeping with them at the same time. I didn't want the situation to end up in a bloodbath.

I just laid it out. If anyone didn't like the situation, they could have gotten out. I guess Cece didn't mind because at least she knew who the other woman was and understood that I wasn't ready for a one-on-one commitment. Although she wasn't seeing anyone else, I don't think she was ready to commit herself, and she told me that she wanted to weather the storm. She said she knew one day we would be together, and I cherished her understanding. I don't think sisters understand that when all a man hears from a woman is "When are we going to settle down? I want to get married. Where is my ring?" it does nothing but put unwanted pressure on him. When brothers want to commit they will. Personally I think if more brothers had enough balls to be truthful in their relationships instead of sneaking around lying to sisters, we wouldn't be in so much trouble with the women we care about.

I met Cece at Central State University during the beginning of my senior year. She's a beautiful, petite, deep midnight black, slenda sista who stands about five feet five inches and weighs somewhere around 125 pounds, dripping wet. Her charisma, along with her engraved dimples and deep, dark eyes, set me off the very first day I met her. She reminds me of a very small, black, baby doll. She is eloquent and sophisticated and has the features of an African queen. Cece makes me feel as if there is not another brother in the world that she would rather be with. Her love for me is untouchable and, as time went by and I continued with both relationships, I began to feel more and more awful about not committing to her. But I wanted to be sure, because when I commit it's all or nothing. Cece understood that, and she's the same way. She let me know that she was in my corner, and that she was willing to wait without feeling like she was letting the entire black women's strength struggle down. Cece is definitely one in a million.

Tonight we are planning to meet and I have been looking forward to seeing her all day. I just hope that Kelly is prepared to keep her loud and obnoxious self quiet long enough so Cece and I can get our romance on. I don't know why I let Cece talk me into meeting those two out tonight. I mean I will do anything for my baby, but when it comes to Kelly appearing in our painted picture that's when I have to draw the line.

Kelly and Cece met at CSU and Cece has yet to realize that Kelly is a master of persuasion. She convinces Cece to do and think any way Kelly wants her to. My dislike for Kelly had surfaced way before she stuck her head into our personal business. It goes back to when Kelly manipulated Cece into thinking she was the reason Kelly got raped at a party during my senior year, when they were freshmen. Cece left Kelly at the party because she had to prepare for a test and Kelly was raped by four frat brothers who were all acquitted of Kelly's charges after a very highly publicized trial. The way that I saw Cece react to that situation was not appealing and left me concerned. Throughout the whole case Cece simply believed or did whatever Kelly said, and it's been that way ever since. I understand in all cliques there is always a leader of the pack and Cece wanted to stand by her girl, but there's a limit. If Kelly would only use her skills in a more productive manner I wouldn't have a problem with her. I just wish Kelly would learn that her abilities to persuade are dangerous and one day they could get her in trouble.

As I inspected the work that had been done in my family room I could see that my answering machine was blowing up with calls, but I didn't want to push the play button because I already knew what was on my schedule for the night. The sight of the blinking light made me wish I'd kept my old answering machine that worked when it wanted to, but I had to get a new one after I missed a couple of important messages concerning the Coalition. I took another sip of my rum and sat back to listen.

"Kahlil. It's me, Pam. I called you back today at eleven, but you weren't in. Guess what? Your sister be trippin' and I'm talking about the oldest one now."

This is just what I need, I thought. I was seriously thinking about turning the damn thing off and erasing everything.

"You're not going to believe what she did after I hung up the

phone with you this morning. I was making the kids some breakfast and Leandra came into the kitchen with my dress on. I've
only worn it once since I've had it. Can you believe that shit? She
said she bought the dress and has had it up in her closet for
months. How can she tell a lie like that? I'm telling you if the kids
hadn't been in the kitchen I would have beat her ass. You better
get over here because when the babies fall asleep I'm going to tell
her there's something I want to show her in the backyard—*then*
beat her ass. Call me, okay. . . . I like your new answering machine. How long can you talk before it turns off?"

"Too damn long," I screamed. I don't know how many times
I've asked Pam to stop calling me with simple-ass problems. I was
determined not to get upset. This one they were going to have to
solve on their own. All I wanted to do was finish listening to the
messages and then get into my tub to soak.

"Hello, Kahlil, it's Sonje. Where are you? I thought we'd made
plans to meet at Points for happy hour. Well I'm here and you're
not so . . . what's the problem? I'll wait here for twenty more minutes and then I'm going back to the station. I can't believe you . . .
bye."

I had no idea what Sonje was talking about. I hadn't promised
to meet her for happy hour. I told her when she called my office
complaining about how much she needed to see me that I
couldn't meet her. I had to remind her that our relationship was
over because of Cece and I. It has been nine months and I have
definitely gotten over the fact that our sexual escapades have
ended. To tell the truth, after I'd gotten over the glamour of
sleeping with the most powerful woman in Detroit, I began to
look at her as she really is. Sonje is a power-driven animal who
throws her weight around in the boardroom as well as in the bedroom. After all of those years I thought she was bigger than that. I
guess our relationship was more than just sex to her, as she loved
to say back in the day. The way she's been acting these last couple

of months I can tell she isn't accustomed to being told no, and she obviously doesn't like it. But it is just too bad because the only thing that I want to talk to Sonje about is the offer that the Coalition has extended to her to become a board member, which is still on the table.

Sonje Davis is the host of the *Women Only Show,* a regional talk show that is about to debut on the national scene. I've been trying to persuade her to join the Coalition because I am lobbying for the upcoming opening for the executive director position. I hope that her membership will benefit the Coalition and strengthen the board members' faith in my ability to bring in top-notch talent. I took another sip and listened intently.

"Hi, Kahlil, it's me, your mom. I know your sister has called you already to let you know that she and Leandra are at it again. I don't know what I'm going to do with these girls and their children—especially Leandra. She told me last month that she was going to pay me for staying here. And here it is one month later and she's walking around here like I owe her some money or something. This is just getting out of control. Pam told me that you were coming over. I'll fix you a plate and see you when you get here . . . bye."

Now they had pissed me off. I don't know why Pam told Mama that I was going over there. I didn't tell her that and knowing how my mother likes to cook she'd probably already started a meal for me. I really wish they would grow up. As much as I love them, I try my best to stay away because every time I go over there I leave exhausted from all of the counseling sessions and ass-whippings I have to perform on my sisters' kids. I quickly changed my plans and decided to see what was going on. Mama's house is three exits from where I plan to meet Cece anyway. As I stood up to take off my shirt I heard a very welcome voice on the machine.

"Hey baby . . . you know my voice. At least you better. I'll meet you at the Comedy Club around nine. I'll be with Kelly. Her boyfriend, Deric, is dropping us off so if you don't mind you'll have to take Kelly home. I'll see you . . . love you."

She was right. I did recognize that voice. Instead of the bath I was going to take I decided to jump in the shower because I definitely don't want to be late for my special night with my baby.

Gettin' Ready

Both Cece and Kelly were in moods that were untouchable and festive. They were bobbing their heads up and down to the beat of the music that was playing over the radio, enjoying their weekly after-work happy hour in Cece's living room.

"Did you see where I put Deric's cell phone number? I thought I left it right here on the table," Kelly yelled over the music to Cece.

"If you didn't have so many other men on your mind you'd be able to keep up with your own man's cell number," Cece said flipping through her *Essence* magazine and looking out the corner of her eye. Cece enjoyed seeing her girl scramble for the number.

"I don't know how many times I'm going to have to tell you, Cece, Deric is not my man. He's my fool. Every woman should have one. What's the name of yours? Here it is," Kelly said, holding up the number. "Up under all your shit." Kelly scattered the neatly organized magazines across the table. Cece looked at Kelly bright-eyed and decided to give it right back to her.

"That's right, up under all *my* shit, on *my* table, in *my* house that *I'm* renting, and am in the process of buying." Cece reminded Kelly that she didn't live there anymore. Looking from the outside in, one wouldn't have realized that, because Kelly was over at the house almost as much as when she actually lived there.

She and Cece were virtually inseparable. They met at freshman orientation at CSU and from the moment they found out they were both from Detroit, and very much liked Coach, Fendi, Chanel, and Donna Karan, they'd hung around each other like Siamese twins. Kelly is what they call a B-Girl. She's only interested in brothers with BMWs or Benzes, that have Big Bank who are able to buy her Bangles without (she claims) ever having to give up the Booty.

Kelly looked at Cece knowing her girl was in rare form tonight. She couldn't help but notice. Cece had been quiet all day long, and Kelly had known her long enough to recognize that when Cece got quiet, Cece wanted very badly to see Kahlil.

Cece walked into the kitchen and started to mix another pitcher of daiquiris while Kelly talked to Deric on the phone.

"Listen. I told you already, Cece and I are going out . . . is that clear? It's just one of those days, can't you understand?"

Kelly walked into the kitchen and sat her glass down, waiting impatiently for Cece to finish mixing the strawberry-flavored drink.

"Just because we talked about getting engaged don't mean shit . . . and if I do decide to wear your ring, I'm still going to come and go as I please, whenever I want, like it or not." Cece narrowed her eyes and looked at her girl as though she could not believe what she was hearing.

"Look, Deric, I have to go. Like I said this morning, nigga, I don't need you. Whenever you're ready to end this shit, just let me know and I'm out. Now, where are you, because we're sitting here and will be ready for you to pick us up about forty-five minutes before the show starts . . . and the Land Rover better be spotless, because you know how I like to roll." She paused. "I know that's how you keep it. I'm just letting you know."

Kelly slammed the phone down. Cece looked at her as she held the refrigerator door open with the pitcher in her other hand.

"Girl, you know you shouldn't be treating Deric like that . . . he's cool."

"Cece, please, don't start, because he likes that shit. Pour me a little more." Kelly held out her glass. Cece filled the glass up and they sat down at the kitchen table.

"See, look . . . he bought me this Barclay tote yesterday at the Coach shop and it was three hundred eighty-five dollars."

Cece wasn't impressed. She'd seen Kelly get expensive gifts not only from Deric, but from the many other men that she had hidden in her stable. It was just another day at the office for Kelly because she truly believed that all women should take anything they could get from a man. Kelly had really become ruthless, and it seemed as though each experience made her more malicious. She'd even thought about giving a six-part seminar for women that would teach them how to take from the men in their lives without feeling guilty. Ultimately she decided against it because flooding the city with women as devastating as she was would cut down on her prospects.

Kelly's attitude about men and what they were to be used for disgusted Cece, but by the same token it interested her. Cece couldn't believe that the men Kelly had in her life let her get away with the things she did. It was truly amazing.

"Cece, let's watch the tapes of *Style* that you made. I like how those models dress and how they work it walking down that runway. Tyra and Naomi are just fashion divas and I love how their clothes sit on their bodies. And give me a piece of paper so I can write down who these designers are so I can get laced right along with my girls."

Kelly grabbed her new Coach bag and followed Cece into the living room. As Cece put the tape into the VCR she thought about how Kelly was the last person that needed to be thinking about clothes. She had all of the latest perfumes, shoes, wigs, hair tracks, all types of clothes, Prada and Chanel to name a few, and she wore them well on her Flo Jo–look-alike body. Kelly swore up and down that she looked like Toni Braxton and Cece had to agree with her on that, except she was a little taller. Kelly's muscular thighs were definitely her best asset and she let everyone see them by wearing her tight-ass hoochie-mama shorts in the summer. Kelly had been participating in a fanny lift class at the gym that she didn't need, but she explained to Cece that when she was finished it was going to make her ass look So Damn Important.

As Kelly and Cece watched the tape, Cece picked up Kelly's new bag and ran her hand across the soft leather.

"This is nice. I think I'm going to buy me another Coach just like this, but I want mine in red." Kelly smirked and looked at Cece with attitude, then picked up her drink.

"Why don't you make Kahlil buy you a bag, girl? With all the money he makes I know he can buy you a four-hundred-dollar bag. There's absolutely no reason you should spend *your* money on it."

Cece could tell that Kelly was going to start telling her how to become just like her and go off on one of her tantrums about how and what she makes her men do for her. Cece didn't want to hear about it. All she wanted to do was see the man that she loved, so she just turned the sound up and tuned Kelly out. Kelly set her drink down and picked the nail polish up off the table.

"Girl, remind me to get some money from Deric tonight. My nails are beginning to look tired," Kelly said in a very calm voice as she examined her nails.

"Why don't you get your own nails done? You work and we just got paid," Cece said.

"Are you crazy? You know that the money I make goes straight into the bank. Girl, Deric has been paying all the rent and most of my bills ever since I told him that it was okay if he wanted to start looking around for a ring. He's just so happy."

"Kelly, that was about five months ago when you moved out of here."

"So what you saying, Cece? I know how long it's been and I've saved up almost five thousand dollars since I've moved."

"And what are you doing with all of your money?"

"Saving it."

"Saving it for what, Kelly?"

"For the house that I'm going to get," Kelly said with confidence. "I told Deric I had to take a pay cut at work, and he said he'd take care of me until things work out. I'm saving everything. I think he's trying to show me that he can handle things on his salary. Didn't I tell you?"

"No."

"I did too. I told you the same day I told Deric."

"You never told me that."

"I did. You just don't remember. You were getting ready to go bone Kahlil."

"Kelly, you did not have to take a pay cut. We just got our increases."

"Cece, wake up. That's just one of my lines I use on niggas. Remember back in the day it was 'I'm pregnant, I need some money for an abortion.' But nowadays niggas want to be politically correct and they tell you to have the baby. So I can't use that anymore."

"Well, I don't remember those days, Kelly, 'cause I didn't do that." Cece became quiet and still, visibly upset with Kelly. She didn't remember Kelly telling her about the lie to Deric but she didn't want to dispute it because it was possible, especially if Cece was in her got-to-have-Kahlil mood when Kelly told her, so she gave Kelly the benefit of the doubt.

"What's wrong with you?" Kelly said. "Why do you think I moved in with Deric in the first place?"

"I thought you moved in with him because you have feelings for him, Kelly. You sure are acting crazy." Cece shook her head.

Deric was the catch of a lifetime, but Kelly didn't have any solid plans to marry him yet.

"I don't know where he got an idea like marriage, because I'm going solo, and I told him that when I moved in with him."

"Well, that's not what he told me. Deric told me that you've been talking about getting married within the next six months and that you two were getting a house."

Kelly looked surprised. "Yeah, he's brought up that shit, but forget that. I haven't agreed to anything. I'm only twenty-eight, going on twenty-three, and all I'm trying to do is save the down payment for *my* house. I have to look out for self. Cece, do you actually think I could be with him for the rest of my life anyhow? Child, please."

Cece tried to leave well enough alone and just watch the television, but Kelly continued rabbling off at the mouth.

"You act like what I'm doing is wrong. Just answer me this . . . how many sisters get dogged by men and don't do a damn thing about it?"

Cece took a sip of her drink knowing that Kelly had a very weak point at best. She wasn't going to fall into Kelly's way of thinking because she didn't believe in it. She believed in commitment and giving your all in relationships.

"But that doesn't make it right. You shouldn't play Deric like that. I don't know a man that would let me do that to him, and I wouldn't want to if he would."

"That's why I'm taking his ass," Kelly said, nodding her head, trying to get Cece to understand. "Come on, Cece, don't start. You know how I feel about men . . . plus my psychic is helping out with this one."

"Your psychic," Cece shouted.

"Yes, girl, I switched from LaToya Jackson's network. Do you remember Weezy on *The Jeffersons*? Well, the Psychic Party said that she calls their line all the time. That was my girl. She had George's ass whipped. You just have to respect any psychic she calls."

"So what did they tell you?" Cece asked, but actually didn't care one bit.

"Well, I talked to them yesterday. They told me to keep on track with my aspirations and dreams. They said I should do whatever possible to make them come true, even though I may be doing someone wrong in the process, because someone is watching over me."

"So you think they're talking about Deric?" Cece asked, but really wanting to tell Kelly that the devil was the one watching over her in this instance. She didn't tell her, though, because she just wanted Kelly to shut the hell up.

"I guess they are . . . they didn't say they weren't, but I need to call them tomorrow anyway to get some other items cleared up. I need to make sure I'm moving in the right direction."

Cece quickly dropped the subject. She sat on the couch with Kelly and quietly watched the tape.

Mama's Place

Just the thought of going over to my mother's and what I was getting ready to encounter was almost enough to make me stop the car, do a U-turn, and go back home. The only saving grace was knowing that I couldn't stay long and that I would be seeing Cece shortly after.

My immediate concern was how to deal with Leandra and her know-it-all attitude that gets everyone out of whack all the time. It's just so damn hard to have a decent conversation with her because she's always on the defensive. Everyone in the family tries their best to avoid arguments with her, but this is virtually impossible because when it comes down to disagreements she's the queen. Leandra always acts like she's the victim and begins to scream like a preteenager. She'll raise her voice and try to talk over you like the only opinion that matters is hers.

There's never been a time that I can remember when she's taken someone else's advice. I think she became unwilling to take advice after she was skipped from the seventh grade to the ninth grade. She still rides high on that fact. I think they should have tested her for common sense as well as book smarts because it's evident that she's lacking in that department. That's why her life is so miserable.

First of all she doesn't have a job and deep down inside I know that it hurts her to see all of her younger siblings get up every day, go to their jobs, and be productive. I can understand her jealousy since she's been catered to all of her life and I am sure Leandra cares deeply for all of us, but I just can't comprehend some of the things she has done lately.

I remember the time Leandra convinced a guy that she had been seeing longer than her regular span of six to nine months to tell her son, Sid, that he was his long lost father, that he had decided to reconcile with Leandra and wanted to be a father for him. She had us all fooled. I thought all of my prayers had been answered, and Sid would finally begin to put things in perspective. I hoped he could begin to think about other things like where he wanted to go to college instead of worrying about his mother and trying to live his life for her. Things were going great for about six weeks. Sid and his newfound father were beginning to spend more and more time together, doing father and son things like going to sporting events, talking about females and his future. After playing daddy and starting to convince Sid that he was going to be there for him, my brother found out from a mutual friend that Leandra was sleeping around on him. He confirmed the information and immediately hung up his parental shoes. He told Sid that he was not his father and that he was just acting as though he was because Leandra had talked him into it. Sid didn't appreciate the brother's goodwill gesture and immediately began to whip the imposter's ass. I had to pull him off the brother. It took Sid almost two months to even speak to his mother again. During that time Leandra got in her Immaculate Conception mood again, claiming that she was the only person who needed to give her son direction. Then Sid got himself into trouble. He and one of his friends, who has a criminal record longer than all of the hit songs Babyface has produced, were stopped in a car with a stolen gun in it. Sid decided to take the rap for his partner. The judge sentenced Sid to spend almost his entire summer break in a youth center and suspended his eligibility to run track for the remainder of high school. I've tried my best to give Sid advice, but soon he will be eighteen and there won't be anything that anyone can tell him.

I used my key to get into the house. I didn't hear a sound as I walked through the door. Good, maybe things are squashed, I thought as I stood in the foyer. I could smell my mama's pork chops and walked down the hall and into the den where my mother, Pam, and Leandra were all watching an interview with Wesley Snipes on BET's *Screen Scene*. My mother was sitting in her favorite chair, drinking her favorite tea, and looked at me with pride when she noticed my sisters were looking up at me. Pam was smiling as though her daddy had come to rescue her. Leandra acted as though nothing was wrong. I looked at everyone trying not to show how pissed off I was because I had to come over for some simple bullshit.

"Hi baby," my mother said. "I left you a plate in the oven. Go ahead and get it."

I gave my sisters another glance and walked into the kitchen. I opened the oven and looked at the meal Mama had prepared for me. She knew I hadn't eaten any pork going on seven years so she'd made me chicken and broccoli. As I bent down to take the plate out of the oven I felt someone standing behind me and I turned around. It was my nephew Sid who looked like he was catching up to my six-foot-five frame.

"What up Uncle? If you looking for those pork chops, my brother, I just finished those up," Sid said, wiping his mouth with much delight.

"You know I don't eat pork, Sid. How are you doing?"

"Man I'm a'ight, just getting tired of hearing all this noise in here every day. You know how Moms is. I can't even read the book you gave me. She's always on my back."

I looked at him, knowing that he hadn't even tried to open the book that I had given him. "Is that right? What's the name of the book I gave you, Sid?" Sid looked at me with a blank face. "I thought so. You're still lying to me, what did I tell you about that? The name of the book is *Makes Me Wanna Holler,* and I know you have plenty of time to read it. I guarantee you'll learn something. It will give you some insight about what you went through last summer. Just like your boy, Tupac."

Sid's eyes grew wide with interest as I brought up his favorite rap star.

"What do you know about Tupac? I don't think a book can be as deep as my boy, Uncle."

"Young boy, Tupac didn't say nothin' that I could not understand. I know for a fact that he lived the things he said. That's why he could rap about police brutality, drugs, and women that he didn't trust. He went through it and experienced it. Why do you think he had to go to prison for a crime that was questionable in the first place and really never proven? You want to know why they put his black ass in jail, and more importantly, why he was murdered?" I asked, looking right into his eyes.

"Why?"

"Because he spoke the truth, something a lot of people don't like to hear over the airwaves. You can be labeled a radical and a threat when you do that. A large part of society doesn't want you to sit down and think about what's going on in your surroundings, and when you speak out against the things that should not be, you get dealt with. Just like Stokely Carmichael, Paul Robeson, Malcolm, Marcus Garvey, and Martin Luther. That's why Tupac is not among us anymore. So don't ask me what I know about the brother . . . just tell me what you know about the book I gave you."

Sid looked at me. I guess he was surprised by my knowledge of his boy and hip-hop culture. He put his plate into the dishwasher. Sid smiled. "I'm going to read it," he said with his deep voice. Then he opened the door to the basement and walked downstairs.

As I picked up my plate and walked back into the den I heard Sid start up his music. I wondered how in the hell he got a system that sounded as good as mine. I asked him about it a couple of months ago and he told me that some girl bought it for him. I didn't believe him one bit. I told him if I found out he got it illegally I was going to break it into pieces.

I walked into the den, and my mother got up out of her chair so that I could have her seat. She went into the kitchen after kissing me on the cheek.

Leandra immediately started talking.

"Ooh, Kahlil, I like that shirt. Where are you going tonight?" She walked over and started to feel the sleeve of my silk shirt.

"Watch out, Kahlil. You turn your head and she'll have your shirt off your back without you even noticing it," Pam said, looking at Leandra with disgust.

"Ain't nobody talking to you," Leandra responded.

I hadn't even gotten a chance to taste my food and they had already started in on each other. I put my plate on the table and looked at both of them, but specifically at Leandra.

"Wait a minute. Both of you are too old for this. It's the same old arguments and disagreements all the time. If you can't live here together peacefully why don't you both just leave and find your own places. Then you won't have to be around each other at all."

"I'm not going anywhere. If anybody's black ass is leaving, it's Pam's. She's got a job and she can afford to move out. Everybody knows that I'm going back to school," Leandra said in her argumentative, whining voice.

"Forget you, Leandra. You need to get your old ass a job and take care of your own business. . . . Shit, you're over thirty-five years old and haven't had a fucking job yet, you freeloading heifer."

I jumped in between them since it looked like any second they'd actually come to blows.

"Leandra and Pam," my mother shouted from the kitchen. "I mean it. If you don't stop this nonsense, both of you will have to leave first thing in the morning . . . and I don't care if you have a place to stay or not, you are going to get out of here." Both of my sisters left the room, and I sat down and tried to eat my dinner in peace. My mother came back into the den.

"Do you think they'll ever be able to get along?" she asked.

"I don't think so." I put the first forkful of food into my mouth and pointed to my plate with my fork in approval. "Mama, you know that ninety-nine percent of all the commotion that goes on over here is because of Leandra. She is just so moody and up-tight."

"I know. I keep telling her that it's not too late to get her life in order, but you know how she is. You can't give her any type of advice, she even takes encouragement as an insult. I just don't know what I'm going to do with her," my mother said with despair in her voice.

"I told you, Mama, what you should do. You should put her out, and let her make it on her own like everyone else in the world has to do. You've already carried her all of your life. I know you love her, but what more do you have to do?"

"I know, I know," she said, shaking her head, not wanting to hear the truth.

"Well if you know, why don't you do it?" I asked softly.

"Kahlil, I talked to Leandra and told her if she doesn't start doing something with her life and start contributing around here by this November she's going to have to leave . . . and I mean it."

I didn't say another word. I just kept eating my food. I didn't want to hear that shit anymore. I'd heard that same old threat and promise for at least ten years, and every time November rolled around Leandra was still doing her own thing. I left when Mama started asking me how Leandra pays to get her hair and nails done every week. I told her I didn't know. Nobody did. It was just another night at Mama's place.

The Night

Deric pulled up into the driveway of Cece's house about ten minutes early and blew his horn.

"I told Deric that he doesn't blow the horn for me. Wait until we get out there!" Kelly said.

"Now be nice, Kelly. After all, he's being nice enough to take us," Cece said, grabbing her purse and taking a last glance at her two-piece silk ensemble in the full-length mirror, noticing that her blouse was having a hard time controlling her nipples.

"Girl, Kahlil ain't going to be able to handle this sista tonight, because it's on!"

"Damn, we look good!" Kelly said, as she opened the front door and walked out of the house. They got into the Land Rover and right away Deric could tell they'd been drinking their favorite drinks by the smiles that were plastered on their faces.

"What's up, ladies? You two sure do look nice," Deric said as he tried to kiss Kelly on the cheek.

"We know we do," Kelly said without giving Cece a chance to respond. "Now take us to the Comedy Club." She pulled down the sun visor and opened the vanity mirror to look at herself. Deric laughed her comment off.

This was Cece's very first time in Deric's Land Rover and she was amazed at how nice it was. She leaned forward into the front seat. "Deric, I like your Land Rover. This is really nice. You must be doing really well on your job." Deric and his Cuba Gooding–lookalike face lit up like a three-year-old boy who just got a piece of candy. As they stopped at the light he looked back at Cece.

"Yeah, Cece, it's difficult chasing people all around town and then getting them to decide what house they want. But when you receive that commission on a sale it makes you forget about how hard it was getting it." Kelly turned to look at Deric and interrupted him.

"Excuse me, this is the weekend, okay. If you want to talk about work, do that shit Monday through Friday from nine to five. So turn your ass around and drive because the light is green." Deric turned around and looked at Kelly, this time laughing harder and louder. Then Deric got serious as he turned into a gas station.

"Oh yeah, I forgot. You don't like to talk about other people's money, you just like to spend it right?" He gave Kelly a chilling look and opened the door to get out.

"You see how he is?" Kelly said. She couldn't believe he'd spoken to her that way in front of Cece. "I told you he wasn't shit, and I don't know why he's listening to all of this dreary slow music because he ain't getting none of this tonight." Kelly hit the eject button on his CD player and quickly inserted Brownstone's CD.

"I told you he was up on you," Cece said.

Kelly looked back at Cece. "He doesn't know shit. Watch this." Kelly picked up Deric's cell phone and dialed as Deric was inside the station standing in line waiting to pay for his gas.

"Hi Lee, it's Kelly. . . . Listen I'm on the way to the Comedy Club with my girl. Why don't you come see me if you get a chance. I'll save a seat for you, okay? See you later." Kelly looked back at Cece.

"See, girl, I met this fine-ass nigga named Lee at the gym. You'll see him tonight. The brutha plays for the Lions, he's married, rich, and ready to pay me."

Cece quickly sat back in her seat in disgust. "Married and rich? No, what he's ready for is to get between your legs."

Kelly turned and looked at Cece with surprise. "Oh no you didn't. Cece, you must be crazy. How many times do I have to tell you. I don't be laying down with these fools like that. Even Deric might get to hit it only two or three times a month. How do you think I keep him coming back for more?" Cece couldn't answer because Deric had opened the door and was getting back into the Rover. Her head started to spin in disbelief when Kelly kissed him on the cheek and said, "Damn, baby, what took you so long? I missed you."

Cece went into the club and waited for Kelly, who had stayed with Deric trying to explain to him why she didn't feel like being bothered with him tonight. Even though Cece didn't like the situation she wasn't going to get into their business. She had business that she wanted to take care of herself and she combed the club looking for Kahlil. It wasn't long before Kelly came to the table looking frustrated and upset.

"Girl, men be trippin' out. I can't even go anywhere without Deric wanting to be all on my back!"

"What did you tell him?" Cece asked.

"I told him to stop acting like a little baby and be a man—you know? I'm going to get a drink. Do you want one?" Cece shook her head, and Kelly walked over to the bar.

It was about ten minutes before the opening act was due on stage so Cece kept her eyes open for Kahlil. She began to worry. It wasn't like Kahlil to be late, and she looked toward the door to see if he had come in.

"Who are you looking for?" Kelly asked Cece as she put her drink down on the table. "I don't know why you're looking around for Kahlil. He's probably out with one of those other bitches you let him see."

Cece tried her best to ignore her. She knew that Kelly thought Kahlil demanded too much respect from Cece.

"Kahlil's not with anyone else, Kelly. I talked to him earlier and we made plans to meet here tonight."

"I still don't know why you let him see that bitch for so long, Cece," Kelly said referring to Sonje. She looked coldly at Cece while she sipped her drink.

"Listen, Kelly. First of all I don't have any papers on Kahlil, and second he has not been out with Sonje for the last nine months, so get over it."

"Well, all I know is that he's not here now," Kelly said, glancing around the club as the lights dimmed for the opening act.

All through the first act Cece was so fidgety and nervous that she didn't really enjoy herself, especially when the fool on stage joked about men and what type of excuses they come up with when they have been out doing something they shouldn't. Kelly with her tipsy self started rubbing it in, laughing her ass off and looking at Cece, silently mouthing "Kahlil."

Finally the lights brightened inside the club, and Cece noticed the look Kelly had on her face, as if she saw something she didn't like. Cece followed Kelly's eyes.

"There's my boo-kee!" Cece said and stood up to wave at Kahlil. He walked over to the table and reached out to Cece. She reached up to him and they embraced as if they hadn't seen each other in years. Cece was so excited that she acted as though she was ready to leave at that very moment.

"What's up, baby?" Kahlil said, looking at Cece, surprised at how her nipples were trying to make their way out of her shirt toward him. They both sat down and Kahlil pulled Cece's chair so close to his that he might as well have sat her on his lap.

"Kelly, take a good look at my man, ain't he fine," Cece said, looking at Kahlil from head to toe.

Kahlil looked at Kelly and halfheartedly smiled. "Hi, Kelly, how are you doing?" Kelly looked at him and waved, then turned her head. Cece and Kahlil barely noticed since they were already in their own world.

Things could not have worked out any better. Cece didn't have to wait the extra twenty minutes while they took Kelly home to get next to Kahlil. Lee met Kelly at the club and promised to take her home, but before they left Cece and Kelly went into the rest room to talk.

"Are you sure you know what you are doing?" Cece asked as she touched up her lip gloss.

"Yes I do. Just do me a favor."

"What?"

"I know Deric is going to call and check on me so I need you to think of something to tell him," Kelly said, looking at Cece and already lobbying with her eyes because she knew what Cece was going to say.

"Kelly you are trippin'," Cece said looking around the rest room trying not to be overheard. "Why do you want to get me involved in this?"

"Because you are my girl, that's why."

"Girl, you ain't right."

"I never said that I was," Kelly said laughing. "How do my shorts look?"

"Shut up and let's go," Cece said.

Cece had been waiting for this moment all night. As soon as she and Kahlil walked through her front door Cece started taking off her clothes, and in seconds she was standing entirely naked.

Kahlil looked at her body as though it was his most prized treasure. "Cece, I love you and your chocolate self so much." Kahlil turned Cece around and began to kiss her well-defined back. Cece began to melt. She couldn't take the kisses on her back, and turned around to give him one of the nipples that had been calling his name all night. The telephone rang. Cece hesitated for a moment and looked at Kahlil.

"Go ahead, baby, I'm yours all night," Kahlil assured her.

Dazed, Cece looked around for the cordless but could not find it in the living room. She had to run into the kitchen to pick it up. "Hello," Cece said, trying to clear her throat.

"Cece, it's Deric. I thought you were dropping Kelly back off over here after the show?"

Cece had not wanted to lie to the brother, but at that moment she really didn't care. Her man was in the other room taking off his clothes, getting ready to give her what she wanted. Cece stomped her foot on the floor, not liking what she was about to do.

"Well, Deric, Kelly didn't leave the show with me. She ran into some people she knew and said they were going out to eat. She should be there a little later," she quickly told him.

"Did she say where they were going? Maybe I'll meet her there," Deric said.

"No, she sure didn't," Cece answered, becoming impatient.

"Okay. If she calls over there, do me a favor and tell her to call me."

"Deric, I sure will. Good-bye." Cece threw down the phone and felt bad for about five seconds, about the amount of time it took her to wiggle her horny little ass into the next room to get some from her man.

Morning After

Cece tried to focus on the glowing lights of her digital clock, but her eyes didn't want to cooperate. Instead she rolled back over as if she really didn't care what time it was. She had not even heard Kahlil when he got up to leave, but she could still smell the fragrance of his Issey Miyake cologne on the pillow. Cece took a deep breath and rolled herself into a small ball, grasping the pillow tightly. She thought about how she and Kahlil had made passionate love not once, but three times. She wanted to reassure herself that everything that happened the night before was not a dream, and that the ring he slipped on her finger while he entered her during their second go-around was real and still there.

As the big rock gleamed in front of her eyes, she was surprised by all of the passion she still felt. She'd thought it was all drained from her, but the couple of hours of sleep that she had, along with the excitement of being engaged, lit another fire between her legs. Cece reached over to her nightstand and grabbed a box of matches. She lit the candle that had burned for her and Kahlil just hours before. Cece stared at the burning flame, then stretched out in her king-size bed and thought that just once she would experience all by herself the same feelings that Kahlil had made flow through her body. Then she could fall asleep for the rest of the day and dream about the life they were going to share together.

Cece shut her eyes and began to imagine Kahlil's long, black hands touching her still slightly erect nipples and began to relax. She slowly pulled at her nipples and she felt her kitten beginning to tingle. She knew that it was just an aftershock of the earthquake that she and Kahlil had shared together, but Cece continued to run her hand past her firm stomach. She opened her legs. As she put her small, shaking finger inches from where she needed it, the telephone rang. Disappointed, Cece tried her best to shake off her desire and picked up the telephone.

"Hello."

"Cece . . . what are you doing?" Kelly said, in a very rushed manner.

"Why?" Cece said, laying her head back on the pillow.

"Because, girl . . . you ain't going to believe this."

"I'll believe you . . . I promise I will, but call me back this afternoon because I'm still sleeping."

"Girl, I can't," Kelly said, embarrassment in her voice.

"Why not?"

"Because I'm with Lee right now and I asked him to drop me off at your place . . . and guess who the hell is parked outside of your house?"

"Who?" Cece got up from bed and peeked out of her curtains. "Deric!" she screamed. "See Kelly, you've really messed up now, Ms. 'Deric ain't my man.'" Cece sat back down on the bed and put her robe around her body.

"Listen, Cece, I'm not trying to hear that right now. Lee has to be back for his morning practice in an hour. He's going to drop me off around the corner, directly behind your house, so do me a favor and open the back door for me."

"Girl, are you are crazy? What if your man sees you coming in here?" Cece asked Kelly, taking another look out of the window.

"Deric's blind. He won't see me . . . now, are you going to open the door or what, because I'm getting out of the car right now."

Cece put on her house shoes. "It doesn't look like I have a choice. Damn it, Kelly, hurry up."

Kelly came in the house, out of breath, smiling at Cece and looking like she had slept with Lee and all of his teammates.

"Girl, you can't tell me you didn't give him none last night," Cece said, looking Kelly up and down, pointing to her wrinkled shirt and out-of-place hair.

"Well, that's what I'm going to tell you and ain't nothing wrong with a little bump and grind," Kelly said as she ran into the front room of the house to see if Deric was still parked outside.

"Damn it, he's still out there." Kelly turned around and looked at Cece like she was going to tell her what to do next.

Cece looked at Kelly with an I-told-you-so grin. "So, what are you going to do now . . . *player*? You know he called here last night, looking for you."

Kelly put her hand over her mouth, because she had forgotten to call him. "He did. What did you tell him?"

"I told him that you ran into a couple of friends and you went out to eat." Kelly started smiling and picked up the telephone.

"Hello, Deric. Where are you?" Kelly said, trying to sound concerned. "I've been here at the house with my girlfriends I ran into last night from CSU, and I've been waiting on you to introduce them to you. Don't tell me you've been out all night after all the things you said to me last night."

Cece couldn't believe Kelly was using reverse psychology on Deric and that he actually began to explain to her where he'd been all night, which was looking for her. Kelly just shook her head.

"Well, I just called to see if you were all right and to let you know that we're on our way out the door to eat breakfast, then I'll probably hang out with them for a while. I'll see you later." Kelly hung up the phone and peeked out the curtains. All she could see was the back end of his Land Rover flying down the street, trying his damnedest to make it home before she left with her supposed girlfriends.

"Stupid ass," Kelly said, laughing while Cece sat down on the couch.

"Girl, I was going back to bed, but you are going to sit yourself down and tell me everything that happened last night," Cece said, hiding her ring from Kelly.

Kelly took off her shoes and sat in the chair directly across from Cece. "You are not going to believe how much fun I had last night," Kelly boasted. "Married men, especially rich married men, can get loose! First of all, after we left the Comedy Club, Lee took me for a ride in his two-seater Mercedes and, girl, I was looking so damn good. I wanted him to put the top down, along with the tinted windows, but he said he couldn't do that because too many people would notice him, plus his wife. I told him that was cool because if Deric had pulled up on us and saw me last night he would of broke down crying. Girl, it's something about a married man . . . they don't care about nothing but having a good time and being away from their wives . . . I ain't ever getting married."

Cece couldn't hold it back any longer and pushed her hand in front of Kelly's face. "Well I am!" They both began to scream, as Kelly kicked her feet into the air and covered her face with a pillow.

"Oh no, he didn't!" Kelly said.

"Oh yes, he did!" Cece shouted back to her, laughing.

Kelly grabbed Cece's hand and examined the ring. "Um, this looks like it's at least three carats. I know you ain't going to marry him right away because now it's time to get paid for real. You should make him follow that up with a funky-ass tennis bracelet to show how much he really loves a sista. Girl, I'm going to show you everything you need to do. He's going to be buying all types of shit, you just watch."

Cece pulled her hand away from Kelly. "Just finish telling me about last night."

"Well, after the club, Lee asked me if I wanted to go to a party that one of his teammates was having, and you know I was down. Maybe I'll find me another Detroit Lion and play the both of them, and Deric, too. You know how I think. So, we arrived at the party and I didn't even know where I was. I've been living in Detroit all my life and I still can't figure out where that nigga took me. I got lost up in Auburn Hills. All I know is when we got there we just walked straight up in that mother. They had people waiting in line, being searched, and Lee with his big self looked right at the rent-a-cops that were at the door. And they were like, 'Go ahead . . . because we know who you are . . . Sir!' When we got inside it was like maybe two hundred people drinking, dancing, talking, and just having a good old time. You know they all stopped and took a look at me when I walked in the door because my shorts were booming. I must have met about twenty of the players on the team. These brothers are fine and they didn't care if I was with one of their boys or not. They were looking and I was looking back."

"So how did your clothes get wrinkled up?" Cece asked pointing to Kelly's clothes just like her mother would and with a funny look on her face.

"Well, Mom, about four in the morning people were starting to disappear so Lee grabbed my hand and we went upstairs to a room. Let me tell you . . . he was trying his ass off, girl. Do you know how hard it is getting a two-hundred-and-sixty-pound linebacker out from between your legs when he's trying to stick his thing right through your shorts after he has drank four bottles of champagne his damn self?"

"So, how did you get him off you?" Cece wanted to know, sitting up closer to Kelly.

"Cece, I acted like I was all into him, right . . . like a freak or something, I had him thinking he was going to get it—then I straight told him that I couldn't feel his little-ass dick and broke that all-star ego. He got right up off me too."

"Oh no, you didn't!" Cece laughed.

"Oh yes, I did. But that ain't all. The room had a Jacuzzi in it and I took off all my clothes in front of him and got right in. You should have seen how he was looking at my body. I must have stayed in there for an hour drinking champagne."

Cece looked a little confused. "Wait a minute, didn't he try to get in there with you?"

Kelly looked at Cece with her big eyes, trying to hold back her laughter. "No . . . he sure didn't. He just sat on the side and poured me champagne . . . I guess he does have a little one and was scared to let me see it for real!" They laughed until they cried.

Kicking Game

It was Saturday morning and Sid was determined that this was the day he was going to get the telephone number of the fly young girl he'd seen three weeks in a row from his seat at the back of the bus. He'd grown tired of his girl, Keisha. She was becoming too hard for his taste. She was beginning to drink as much beer as he did and her conversation was almost identical to that of his boys. When he saw her going through his pockets, thinking he was asleep after they had sex, he knew it was time to leave her and try his hand at the fine bookworm he'd spotted on the bus. Sid had heard someone call her Rajanique, and she was a Halle Berry look-alike. She had class and poise.

Rajanique had noticed Sid's glances, but had refused to do other than what her father had taught her when it came to people she saw in public and really didn't know. "Never make eye contact with people on public transportation that you don't know, baby. If you do, you never know how the person will react and what they might try to do to you," her father constantly told her.

Rajanique did exactly that. Every time she saw Sid looking at her she would open her SAT study guide and pretend to look over some of the questions. Even though Rajanique had seen Sid on the same route many times, she didn't want to seem interested because for all she knew he was homeless and crazy or something. After all, she'd never seen him reading the paper or doing anything else constructive. He was always slouched down in the seat with that Walkman on top of his bald head, wearing jeans and a T-shirt, trying to look like he was rough or something.

Even though Rajanique knew he was fronting and thought just maybe he had untapped potential, she didn't even think about wasting her time. She knew what Sid was all about just from the way he looked at her. She was very book smart, but she was even smarter when it came to the streets. She got her street smarts from watching all four of her sisters become pregnant before getting out of high school, and she was determined not to let that happen to her. Rajanique planned to do something with her life other than have a bunch of babies. And because she refused to follow the crowd many of the neighborhood girls thought she was a bitch.

The bus stopped and Rajanique quickly picked up her backpack, to get off. Sid began to follow her.

As Sid tried his best to catch up with Rajanique, he couldn't take his eyes off her well-rounded backside. He cleared his throat and tapped her on the shoulder.

"Hey, Rajanique, how are you doing?"

She smiled, but did not look at Sid—she was surprised that Sid had followed her off the bus, and Rajanique clutched her book bag as though he was going to snatch it. Sid noticed it.

"Girl, you are as bad as all the other women I walk by, always grabbing y'all's purses like I want to steal them or something. I'm cool—I'm Sid, we see each other all the time."

"Hello, Sid," she said.

Right away Sid could tell she was not the type of female that he was used to by the way she spoke back to him and carried herself. She was more classy, with home training, and he could tell that the game he normally used when he stepped to the ladies had to be put on another level. His normal, around-the-way attitude was not going to work with her.

"So, what have you been up to?" Sid said, as Rajanique continued to walk briskly, looking straight ahead, still unsure of what he wanted.

"Oh, nothing much, just trying to enjoy the rest of my last high school summer break."

"So, you're a senior, too?" Sid asked. Rajanique smiled and nodded her head yes.

"I can't believe it's finally our last year of school. This year is going to be jam-packed with parties," Sid said, as Rajanique looked at him for the first time.

"What are you going to do when you get out?" Rajanique asked.

Sid hadn't actually thought about what he wanted to do with his life when he graduated. He looked at her like she was a teacher who had asked him a question in front of the whole class and he didn't know the answer.

"Well, I'm going to college," Rajanique said with determination and conviction.

"College?"

"That's right. As soon as I get out I'm packing my bags and leaving for college. I'm getting the hell out of this city."

"You mean you aren't staying here in Detroit?" Sid said, as though there were no other options.

"No way, I'm going to go get my college degree. There is a possibility that I'll come back after that, but I don't know yet. Are you staying here?"

Sid looked at her with another blank face. "Uh, I don't know yet."

"Well, you better make a decision, because you know how time flies and you don't want to be out of school without a plan."

They talked for another three blocks before Sid stopped. He took off his cap and scratched his head after he asked her if she would like to go out some time. Rajanique told him, "Nothing personal, but I really don't think you have what it takes."

She didn't even say it nasty or anything, which was why the word "bitch" didn't even cross his mind. I wonder what the hell she means, I don't have what it takes, Sid said to himself, totally confused. If Sid learned one thing that morning, it was that he should have kept his ass on that bus instead of letting the bright sun beat on his face for the rest of the long walk to the barbershop.

Getting Paid

Sid sat in his room in the basement thinking about the brand-new sweat suits and jewelry that his boys Difante and Rashaad were showing off to everyone in the barbershop. It reminded him of when he'd wanted a motor-cross bike and all he had to ride was an outdated three-speed with truck handlebars. Once again he was left out in the cold. He was amazed these two brothers always had enough money to fill their gas tanks, pay their car notes, buy funky gear, and even kick a couple of dollars to Sid from time to time. All this without having jobs.

Rashaad was a very hyper and talkative seventeen-year-old. He was unyielding and quick-tempered. He befriended Sid when they were just six years old. At the time Sid lived with his grandparents in the old neighborhood on the east side, and the two had become inseparable. They knew each other's families as they did their own, had fought only as true brothers fight, and would lay down their lives for the other's safety if need be.

Sid had grown envious of Rashaad in the last couple of months because he'd gotten himself a car shortly after joining the Get Paid Crew. The GPC was a two-man empire but they had the following of many (at least twenty were thought to be involved), and this was one of its greatest fronts. The self-appointed leader was Difante, a twenty-three-year-old high school dropout who had been involved in everything from armed robbery to breaking and entering since his teenage years. Difante was watching his back very carefully because if he received one more strike on his criminal record, he'd live the rest of his life in prison.

Sid had also known Difante for a long time and was well liked by Difante, especially after Sid took the fall for the stolen gun that was found in Difante's car after the cops pulled the two over cruising in Difante's brand-new two-door Lexus coupe. Sid was certain that whatever Difante and Rashaad were up to it was against the law, but he knew very little about the details of their activities. Difante and Rashaad had seen too many other brothers in their type of game get thrown under the jail for running their mouths so they were tight-lipped about what they were doing. Sid didn't think they were pushing drugs on the street because Detroit already had too many people involved in that type of activity, although Difante and Rashaad did smoke bud from time to time. The only thing Sid knew about the Get Paid Crew was their mission statement: "Doing whatever's necessary to reach lifetime goals, which don't necessarily have to be legal to obtain."

Sid sat down beside his bed on the carpeted floor and fired up incense stick after incense stick until the smell of raspberry was flowing strong throughout his room. He had moved into the room in the basement after he started to get annoyed with all of his mother's antics. Sid loved his mother very much and always tried to do what she thought was best for him, but he got fed up when she took things out on him if matters in her personal life didn't go well.

The only reason Sid stayed with his mother was because she told him she couldn't live without him. Every time he told her he wanted to go live with Kahlil or one of his cousins, she made him feel guilty about not wanting to stay with her.

"I don't believe you want to leave me after all that I've done for you," Leandra would whine. But after he changed his mind, she always told him that she'd be happy when he graduated from school, so that she could put him out. Leandra loved Sid, but she didn't have her own life together. It took Sid some time to understand this, but eventually he stopped doing what she told him if he didn't feel comfortable with her request.

Before he was too old to realize what was going on, Leandra would make him tell his grandparents that he wanted a certain item at the store. Then after they would buy it for him, Leandra would take it back and buy him something similar, but a whole lot cheaper and keep the refund for herself. Sid didn't want to take part in her schemes because of the respect he had for his grandparents. When he wouldn't help her out like that Leandra would shout at him, "You are not my little boy anymore." And Sid couldn't agree with her more. Their escalating disagreements created a large gap between Leandra and Sid. He was convinced his mother didn't understand him, and he tried many times to explain to her how he felt about events that happened in his life. For some reason, she refused to see things the way he looked at them and wouldn't listen when he needed to talk.

Like when Sid got out of jail last summer and started school again—a police car followed behind him for two weeks from the time he walked out the front door of the house until he got on school grounds. He knew they were harassing him but his mother tried to dismiss his thoughts.

"Sid, you're just imagining things because you've been locked up. You've become paranoid. Even if they are following you, it's probably because they think you're someone else. You can best believe if they wanted to stop you, they would have by now," Leandra explained.

Leandra's answer wasn't good enough for Sid. He'd seen how the officers were looking specifically at him. It was like he didn't know when they were going to just jump out of their cruiser and beat the shit out of him. When he called Kahlil and told him about it, Kahlil followed Sid to school one day, then pulled up to the police car and asked the officers if they had a problem with Sid. Kahlil got their badge numbers, reported them to Internal Affairs, and Sid hadn't seen them since. Sid was grateful for Kahlil and for all the things he'd done for him, but he'd gotten tired of running to Kahlil every time he needed something or when he had trouble in his life. That's why when he got pulled over with Difante, Sid tried to handle the situation himself, and told the policeman the gun was his without calling Kahlil first. Sid was beginning to feel like he was not Kahlil's responsibility—Kahlil has problems of his own, Sid thought.

Kahlil was great, but since he was little Sid had dreamed of how it would feel to have his real father in his life. The only knowledge Sid had of his father was the negative things that Leandra told him. Sid had asked his mother about his father so many times that it had come to the point where she would turn her back on Sid if he mentioned anything about the possibility of ever meeting his father.

"Your father isn't shit and you don't need him to help you do anything, because I can raise you myself," she would tell Sid.

Sid hated feeling like she was treating him like he was some type of prize between her and his father. She may not have needed Sid's father, but he sure as hell did. Leandra couldn't even see the messages Sid was sending her. He started getting into things that he knew he had no business getting into. He tried talking back to her and being outright disrespectful on purpose, because he hoped it might show her that he needed a father to discipline him. Sid's grades were all fucked up and Leandra knew he was having problems. Instead of talking to Sid about it and getting him help, she would try to cover for him by telling people when they asked about his grades that he was doing well in school.

Sid's grades weren't always bad. He used to get good grades when his mother would tell him how proud his father would be if he could see Sid's grades. When Sid started asking questions about him and Leandra didn't have the answers, Sid's whole demeanor changed.

Sid began to relax and get into the lyrics of his boy Tupac just like when Kahlil was home from college and Sid used to sit by Kahlil and watch him bounce to the sounds of Kashif, Melba, and Lillo. While he sat back, Sid began to compare the music of the eighties to what he listened to now. Sid thought about how, back in those days, they sang about love and the games people played. But still, everyone realized that even though games were being played, everything was going to be all right. He laughed inside as he thought about all the songs he listened to now, about being under pressure by society, making a million dollars before you're twenty-one and fearing being jacked and shot in a drive-by while getting your freak on in the front seat of a brand-new car.

Sid grabbed his large glass of Kool-Aid off the small standing dinner tray and quickly took a sip as he heard footsteps on the wooden steps to his room. He turned his head and saw his mother's legs beneath her housecoat slowly walking down each step, as if investigating the dark setting of the basement. He could tell that she had the attitude, like she knew that she was going to find something or someone down there with him that she did not agree with. She paraded herself down the stairs like she had done last week, when a girlfriend of Sid's was there. The friend had come over to play cards. Leandra had come downstairs and in front of Sid and his friend, Leandra had flipped through his sheets on the bed that was on the opposite side of the room, inspecting the sheets to see if the two had been in bed or not, embarrassing Sid and making herself look foolish.

Sid closed his eyes and pretended not to notice her. He hadn't seen Leandra all day and the way she changed from day to day, sometimes hour to hour, he really wasn't in the mood to find out if she was going to be naughty or nice toward him. Sid crossed his fingers and hoped she was going into the next section of the basement into the laundry room. Sure enough, seconds after he closed his eyes, pretending to be into his music, he felt her standing over him. Leandra knew that Sid was aware that she was standing in front of him, but Sid still didn't open his eyes. He just wanted her to go away. Leandra decided she wasn't playing Sid's game. She bent over and turned the music down.

"Ma, what are you doing," Sid said, reaching for the volume control on his system.

"What do you mean, what am I doing, Sid? What does it look like I'm doing? I want this music off and I want your complete attention, because I have to talk to you."

"About what?" Sid said defensively.

"I want to talk to you about last night."

"Last night?"

"That's what I said. I picked up the phone. I didn't know you were even on it because no one was talking. I think your little friend was holding on for you. Anyway, I listened to the filthy-ass conversation you were having with her, and I don't appreciate how you were talking to her."

Sid stood up, surprised that his mother had eavesdropped on his conversation. It was as bad as when he was thirteen and she asked him in front of the rest of the family if he had any pubic hair yet.

"Well, how am I supposed to talk to her? Did you hear what she was saying to me? What was I supposed to tell her? You're talking too grown-up right now and I have to hang up because my mama said I can't listen to things like that? You see, that's why I can't wait to get out of here. You're always in my business. What kind of sense does that make, you sitting on the other end of the phone, listening to what I'm saying? I don't know why you're so upset. I haven't said nothing that I haven't ever heard anyone say to you before."

Leandra tried to pull rank on Sid as she always did.

"You wait one minute, Sid. You have never heard any man say to me what you were saying to that silly girl last night." Sid rolled his eyes, knowing he was getting ready to hear his mother paint herself as though she were an angel and had never had sex before. She always did that. There were many nights that Sid remembered waiting up for her to come home after a date. He'd fall asleep on the couch, wake up in the morning, and see her trying to act like she'd been in the house all night long.

"Don't even try to blame it on my friends. It's this crazy music that you listen to, putting all those nasty thoughts in your mind," Leandra told Sid.

"Ma, you know this morning a fine little female told me that I didn't have what it takes to be with her. So what did she mean?" Sid asked.

Leandra stood there and began to answer his question without even thinking about what Sid had asked her. "The fast thing was probably talking about money. You know how they are always wanting you to do something for them."

Sid looked at his mother and nodded his head in agreement. "That's what I thought . . . I know how they are and that's the reason I talk to them the way I do. I got it from your old boyfriends, who used to think they were talking over my head, back in the day. But they weren't. I understood every little thing you all talked about. And I even see them in the neighborhood, when you're nowhere around and I hear them shooting game to the hunnies all the time, even females my age." It got very quiet and Leandra looked at Sid, wondering which one of her friends he was referring to. "Mama, I don't even know why you're fronting like I'm abnormal or something. . . . I've seen you date about six or seven men this year alone anyway, so it ain't about what I'm saying to the hunnies. What are you saying to all the niggas?"

Leandra quickly turned away from Sid, not wanting to talk about the subject anymore, because it was moving in her direction. She looked at the poster on his wall.

"You see Sid, this is what I'm talking about." She pointed to a poster of Lil' Kim standing as though she could take on a horse in a bathing suit. "Now you know, this picture don't need to be hanging down here, with this girl looking like that. What if your grandmother comes down here and sees this picture?" Sid started to laugh and Leandra frowned.

"What's so funny? I'm serious."

"Grandma is the one who bought it for me. She likes her because Lil' Kim reminds her of Millie Jackson back in the day."

"Well I don't like it and that's all that matters." Leandra continued to look around, inspecting Sid's room, which was very well organized for a seventeen-year-old. His bed was made, CDs were placed neatly in their rack, and all of his clothes were folded nicely in their crates against the wall. Leandra turned to Sid.

"Sid, I really think it's about time for you to get a job and start helping me out. All you do is sit around here all the time, drinking up all the Kool-Aid in the house and eating all the food. I think it's time you learn some responsibility and start paying for some things."

Sid's eyes widened. "You mean work?"

"That's exactly what I mean, Sid."

"But this is my senior year coming up."

"That's exactly why your ass is going to work, because next year this time I know you're still going to be living here. I know for a fact, ain't no college in its right mind going to let you in with those grades you got, and you're not going to be sitting up in here all day long doing nothing." Leandra turned her back and began to walk up the steps.

"You mean like you, huh?" Sid asked, then bent down to turn the volume up before she could reply. Leandra tried her best to shout over the music that Sid had turned up even louder.

"You know I'm going back to school this year, Sidney. I don't have any time right now to get a job . . . and you better watch your mouth. The Big Burger around the corner is hiring and I got you an application. I know the manager and he told me to tell you to come down and see him. When you finish down here, come on up and I'll help you fill it out. We'll use Mama's car to take you around there to meet him. I want this to be fair so we can discuss how much you will be giving me out of your check after I find out exactly how much you will be making. And change those clothes," Leandra demanded.

Leandra walked back upstairs. Sid followed her about fifteen minutes later and went straight out the back door, back to the barbershop. "Fuck that, I'm not being a slave for nobody," he mumbled.

The Back Room

"Ain't no doubt in my mind, O. J. didn't cut her. The media has your head all fucked up, brother." Sid heard a customer in the barbershop shout across the shop. He stood just inside the door, surprised to see how crowded it had become since he'd left earlier in the morning.

"Shut the door boy, and stop letting all my air-conditioning out, standing there looking like your uncle," said Blue, the owner of the barbershop.

Sid stepped in and spoke to the older customers, who always recognized him because he is the spitting image of Kahlil. He went right up to Blue's corner of the shop, where Blue was trimming the head of one of his female customers who sported the short natural look. Sid grabbed the bottle of Bay Rum that sat on the shelf behind Blue's chair, poured some into his hands, and slapped it on top of his bald head. He waited for its action. His head was still tingling from his early morning cut and the sharp straight-edge razor that Blue had used. While Sid stood there enjoying the cooling sensation, he looked around in disbelief. He could never understand why brothers and even some sisters would come into the shop so late in the afternoon and think it was not going to be packed. They were all standing against the wall, waiting for a chair to open up, just to sit in and wait their turn to see a barber. Sid could only laugh when another customer opened the door, stopped in his tracks, and looked at the crowd in amazement. Blue smiled at him, then greeted him with his usual saying: "Sit on down, brother, it won't be long." Sid knew from experience the brother was going to be there at least three hours. Blue was the owner of the seven-chair shop and, as always, it was flowing with high energy and laughter. The topic of the day was the worn-out O. J. Simpson verdict. Some of the regulars, who had gotten their haircuts early in the morning when Sid did, were still in the shop, taking up space and talking about the same old thing. The brothers were trying to sound intelligent, giving their best efforts to impress the handful of ladies in the shop as they talked their shit. They were fronting like they were the Mack, trying to sound like they were high-priced lawyers like Johnnie Cochran and Carl Douglas. Sid laughed as brothers who had dropped out of high school tried to talk intellectual and shit, fucking up the simplest type of words and phrases in a sophisticated kind of way. These brothers were quoting amendments, civil rights laws, and the Constitution all backward and shit, not only trying to sound impressive but paid.

Blue, who couldn't take it anymore, got everyone's attention by standing in the middle of his shop, with his razor raised above his head. He jokingly told all the perpetrating brothers, "All of y'all need to shut the fuck up, because I have never in my life heard as many mothafuckas mess up the word 'jurisprudence' in my life. If you want to be lawyers, I suggest you take your black asses back to school to get a law degree. . . . No, better yet, get your fuckin GEDs. Because the next person who attempts to say it and can't get it out of their mouth is going to get the fuck out . . . or I'm going to start slicing up in here!" Everyone laughed.

Sid walked toward the back of the shop. He could feel Blue's eyes watching him with approval as he headed toward the small room that Blue built years ago for storage. Sid and his partners had hung out there ever since they were young boys and had turned it into their hangout. If it had been anyone besides himself, Difante, or Rashaad walking toward the room, Blue would have stopped them. He didn't allow anyone else back in the room, except those three. Blue had been cutting their hair ever since the shag was in style. They had never had another barber and Blue knew where every bump and lump was located on each head. Blue took a liking to the three when their mothers began dropping them off on Saturdays, giving Blue the same old excuse when they came to pick the boys up hours after Blue had actually closed the shop. "I'm sorry Blue, I got tied up." Those were the words each mother would say.

He never once took it out on the boys, because he knew that it was not their fault. Instead he tried his best to do his part, giving them guidance and support. There had been times, on weekdays, when Blue had closed the shop early and sat each one of them down to tell them his philosophy on making it in the world. He told them how important communication was and that a "closed mouth gathers no food." If they didn't ask for what they wanted or tell someone, they were destined not to get anything at all. Before they all grew to be taller and much bigger than he was, Blue would make them sit out in the shop with him and listen to the stories and experiences of the older brothers who would come into the shop and talk about their lives, so that they would grow up with a wide perspective on issues.

Sid opened the door to the small room. Difante was sitting at the table with his white Fila sweat suit on and his hat turned backward, checking the number that was coming through on his beeper while Rashaad was talking on his cell phone.

"Okay, Mom, I'll pick it up for you, but it won't be until later," Rashaad said, closing up his phone. "Damn, man, at first she didn't want me to have the car. Now she's playing me like her personal butler and shit."

Sid sat down at the table and took his normal seat at the middle of the five-foot-long table. He was happy to see that his boys had bought something to eat, because he was starving.

"My brothers have come through again," Sid said, as he reached for one of the unused plastic cups and began to fill his cup to the brim with spumante, spilling a couple of drops.

"Yo, take it easy on the drink, dog. We only got three bottles. Those damn Arabs raised the price on it again. I think I'm going to have to start buying the shit out there in the suburbs where you live," Difante said, as Rashaad started to laugh. They always teased Sid about him and the family moving out of the hood. Rashaad looked into the bag that was sitting on the table in front of him and passed Sid a box of shrimp fried rice. Rashaad could feel something was bothering Sid.

"What's up Sid? Why you back down here so soon? Keisha wearing you out and you hiding or something?" Rashaad asked.

"No, man, it's my mom. She's all on my shit at the crib. She's listening to my phone calls at night and she came down today, talking about she wants me to get a job at the Big Burger around the corner so I can help her out."

"Big Burger," Difante said, putting down his box of rice and taking a quick sip from his cup, making an awful slurping sound. "Brutha, you can't make no money at no damn Big Burger. Moms be tripping me out with that type of shit, that's why I left home. They always expect us to work at those damn menial jobs, like that's what we were born to do. Man, how does your mama just come up with shit out of the blue anyway? I thought my mama was bad." Sid shook his head while throwing his arms into the air. "At first it was go to night school, then . . . no, I want you back in school during regular hours 'cause you bother me too much during the day. I don't know how you handle it."

"I know man . . . but what the hell can I do? At least if I do work I can make some chedder."

Difante shook his head. "Fuck that, Sid. How much can you make a year working at Big Burger? About nine or ten thousand. That ain't shit. The only thing that little amount of money will do is allow you to pay to get your damn uniform cleaned." Sid chuckled.

Rashaad poured what remained of the first bottle into their cups and Sid became more relaxed, biting into a vegetarian egg roll. Sid loved to sit and listen to his boys when he was in a jam. They always understood exactly what he was going through without his having to explain it to them. As they heard laughter coming from the barbershop, Rashaad pushed his meal aside, clasped his hands together, and placed them under his chin as though he was in some corporate meeting. "Peep this. My brother's father told him, the one and only time that he has ever talked to his ass, that working for the man ain't the way to go. He told him that the everyday grind does nothing for a brother but get him hooked on that damn caffeine, which sometimes is as bad as crack and shortens your life. That just goes to show you how backwards my mother is. She's always trying to tell me to join the army or get myself a job as a mail boy in some company, so I can get my foot in the door, get me some experience and work nine to five every day. To me, what she's actually saying is 'just become a slave and work your whole life away. But look on the bright side baby, you will be able to leave the plantation at night and come home.' Me, I say hell no to that. I'm not going to have to go out of my mind every damn morning, searching for that little electric plantation card they give you so the computer system can track you coming and going to work for the master. I'm going to have the key to my own shit and open me up a restaurant called the Detroit Blue Note and make me some money." They all nodded in agreement and it became quiet for a couple of seconds, as they all thought about Rashaad's plan and how sweet it would be.

"But don't be too rough on moms though," Difante said as he wiped his mouth. He was definitely a mama's boy. Even though his mother had made him very upset at times and even turned him in to the police when they came to his house looking for Difante, he always tried his best to understand his mother and to do exactly what she said because of the way he was raised. He was the only boy on his mother's side of the family and Difante really didn't know any other way, besides doing exactly what she said.

"They are only being the way they know how, bruthas," Difante explained. "Shit, can you blame them, telling their sons to just take what's given to us by The Man? I'm not saying that I agree, but don't expect them to tell us how to obtain shit, because they don't know how it is to be out here as a young black male anyway and I don't care how loud they scream and tell us that they do. They don't. You have to remember, when moms look at us, they see their little boys and shit. You know, the little punk-ass niggas who used to run to them for any and everything. You know why? Because that's their nature. Now, I don't tell many motherfuckas my business and you two are the only ones I ever discuss anything with. So if I hear this shit on the street, I'm fucking somebody up."

Sid and Rashaad looked at each other and began to laugh.

"Shut the hell up, Difante, and say what you have to say," Rashaad said.

"Maaan, women don't know nothing about raising us or telling us what to do. Why do you think they always try to get our uncles, grandfathers, boyfriends, and those big brother motherfuckas to try and talk to us? You know why? Because they don't know what the hell to say to us their damn self and hope somebody else can give us what we've been missing all our lives . . . our fathers."

Sid began to open up the second bottle of spumante, without taking his eyes off of Difante. What he was saying made a lot of sense to Sid.

"You got that right, Difante," Sid said. "Sometimes I sit around and wonder how it would be, living and being able to talk with my pops. Shit, man. I bet you he would make Mom's ass relax or some shit and tell me the real deal. I bet you half the time he would just tell her to shut up and let me do what I thought was right for a change, instead of her always putting her woman's touch on every damn thing. You don't know how much it gets on my nerves when she gets hysterical and shit and starts to whine. I'm not trying to hear that shit. I need to hear a man's voice telling me what to do, you know, maybe smack my ass with some words of wisdom or some shit. The way she talks about his ass, I have to believe he's one sturdy son of a bitch though, because nobody can piss her ass off like he can, at just the mention of him, and she ain't talked to his ass in fifteen years." The cork popped out and Sid began to fill everyone's cup.

"Shit, just look around this barbershop on any given day. How many peeps that walk in that front door know who their daddy is. Forget that, just look around at this table," Difante said. "My pop's in lockdown for life. I've never seen him and don't want to, either. Rashaad, your daddy was shot when you were three, may his black ass rest in peace. You didn't know him and you never will. And look at you, Sid. Your pops just straight took off on your ass and you don't know him either. That's why it's so hard not letting yourself get so messed up in the head, listening to our mothers and their outlook on life, as they try to fill in and tell you how to do certain things. When it actually comes down to it, we have to learn the shit on our own and it ain't nothing but a cycle." Difante pointed at Rashaad. "Rashaad, tell Sid what Mona told you the other night."

Fed Up with the Fanny

Rashaad sat up and looked at Difante like he wished he hadn't brought up his own son's mother. He became agitated, his voice lower than usual, and he kept his eyes on his plastic cup. "Man, you know me and Mona decided we were going to raise Ricky together cause you know marriage is definitely out. I mean I slipped on a one-night stand and have to pay the price and I can handle that. But all of a sudden she wants to trip. I took her some money over for my little boy and she came at me with an attitude. She told me that she'd been watching some of her girlfriends raise their kids and she's decided that she doesn't need or want any help from me or any other man with little Ricky. She said that she could take care of him by herself, just like all of her other girls are doing, and she told me that he doesn't need a man in his life," said Rashaad, reaching for the bottle.

"You see. Ain't that a bitch," Difante said. "They don't want us to be men. Everybody is getting used to not having us around and they think they can do the shit on their own. But I'm here to tell you, they are wrong. If they weren't, we wouldn't be here right now, talking about the shit. I remember when my mother tried to give me that talk and tell me how fucking should be. You know, how I should feel when I started to bust my girl's drawls back in the day. She kept telling me how emotional I was going to feel and that I was going to want to be touched all over my body for a while before anything even happened—you know, that foreplay shit. Then she said after it was over I would feel a glow that would satisfy me more than the sex. Man, she talked to me like I was a bitch or something. Like I'm going to feel a dick up in me. I think not, because you know your boy don't swing that way. It took me a while to figure it out, but I realized that she couldn't tell me how I should feel. How in the hell did she know anyway? We are two different sexes. After she finished talking to me, I didn't even know if I wanted to fuck at all, because I didn't feel no warm, glowing

73

emotions running through me and I thought something was wrong with me. The only feeling I had was that I felt like getting that hoochie the hell out of the house when we were done, so I could get some sleep. Men just don't think like that. When I fuck, all I try to do is tear that pussy up like my mind tells me to do, all I want to feel is skins! Not warm, fuzzy emotions."

Sid sat on the bus on the way home and looked out of the window at the streetlights, which looked blurry after the bottles of spumante they had finished before he left. He was buzzing and ready to go home and crash. The bus came to a stop and Sid looked up as Rajanique stepped into the bus. They looked at each other and smiled. To Sid's surprise, she didn't have any books with her and she sat down one seat in front of him.

"What's up, Nique?" She turned around and her smile made Sid think twice about even trying to start a conversation with her, remembering what his mother had told him about Rajanique's comments earlier in the day, because he was dead broke and had nothing to offer. But the spumante took over.

"Yo, where are all of your books?" Sid asked.

"The same place your Walkman is at," she said. Sid realized that she had been checking him out after all. "I don't have any books tonight, I'm coming from my father's place. We try to see each other at least once a week."

Sid halfheartedly smiled, then looked back out the window.

"What's wrong with that?" Rajanique asked.

"Oh, nothin'. It's just that me and my boys were hanging out and that's one of the things we talked about. How it would feel to have our fathers in our lives."

"You don't have a father?" Sid shook his head no, as he had done so many times before in his life when asked the same question. "Sid, I don't mean to get in your business or anything, but why not? Is he dead or something?"

"Shit, I don't know. I don't know anything about him, I've never even talked to him. Except when—" Sid stopped, like he wanted to change the subject.

"Except what?" Rajanique asked, looking at Sid with concern.

For the first time since Sid had spotted her, he wasn't lusting at her natural beauty, but talking to Rajanique as a person, something he didn't do often with females because he didn't want to be labeled "soft."

"I remember when I was real small, I may have been around two or three, and you might think I was too young to remember something like this. But this was important to me, because this was the first and only time my mother said to me, 'Here is your daddy.' I even dream about it sometimes and I remember it like it was yesterday." Rajanique nodded her head and listened, letting Sid know that she understood. "My mother gave me the phone to speak to him and I remember him saying to me, 'How's my boy?' But I don't even know where he is now."

"Well, why don't you find out?" Rajanique asked.

"I've asked my moms about him so many times and she just acts like he doesn't exist. I guess he hurt her pretty bad or something."

"Well, that ain't right." Rajanique got out of her seat and walked to the door. "Well, Sid, my stop is next. Maybe I'll see you later."

"Hold up, Nique. Why don't you give me the digits?" Sid asked.

The door of the bus opened and she looked at Sid and said, "Maybe next time."

It was almost ten-thirty when Sid finally got home. He was hoping that his mother had gone out with one of her knuckleheads or was already asleep. He walked up to the back door slowly, and looked to see if the lights were on in her room, then put his key in the lock. Suddenly the door was snatched open. And there stood Leandra, still in her housecoat, with one hand holding the door open and the other holding the Big Burger application.

"Now where in the hell have you been, Sidney? I told you to fill out this damn application so that I could take you to see about this job."

Sid walked into the house and right past his mother. He tried to open the door that led down to the basement, but Leandra blocked his path.

"Wait one damn minute, Sid."

"What, Ma?"

"I'll tell you what and I'm going to tell you when. You're going to sit yourself down right now, fill out this application, and take it down there first thing in the morning." She tried to put the application in Sid's hand, but he wouldn't take it and kept his hands down by his sides. "Take it, Sid. I'm not playing around with you," she screamed.

"I'm not playing either." Sid tried to laugh the matter off. "Mom, I am not working at Big Burger, and that's the end of the story. Why, all of a sudden, do I have to get a job?"

"Because I told you boy, my friend is the manager and he guaranteed me that he could get you a job, that's why."

"Well, why don't you take the job?" Sid asked.

"You know I'm getting ready to start school again and I can't work and go to school at the same time."

Sid looked at her like he thought she had a problem.

"But I can? You trippin'."

"Sid, you will do as I say, as long as you live here. Now take this application." Leandra tried to hand Sid the application again, but he ignored her. She moved closer to him and tried to stuff it down his shirt, but he stepped around her to open the basement door. She stepped in front of him and began to point her finger in his face.

"Boy, who do you think you're walking away from!" She lifted up her hand and swung with all of her might. Sid caught her hand, right before it landed on his face. Leandra stood in shock, not moving a muscle, realizing that for the first time in his life, Sid had stopped her from striking him.

"No, Mom, I'm not working there." Sid turned around and began to walk out the back door. He saw his grandmother out the corner of his eye, as his mother began screaming.

"Sid! You come back here right now. I'm not playing with you. I am your mother and you are going to do what I say."

"Let him be, Leandra . . . let him be," her mother said, as they watched Sid walk into the night. Sid went to the nearest phone booth and called Rashaad on his cell phone. He and Difante came to pick Sid up.

My Friend

It was seven forty-five in the evening and I was worn out from making love to Cece the night before, then coming home and sitting for almost thirteen hours in front of my computer. I was trying to project the demographics of the east side of Detroit, constructing a chart showing where the community was headed in terms of population. I researched what roles homelessness, drugs, and crime would play in our neighborhood in reference to the new welfare reform package, and I came up with one conclusion: Our community was in trouble. There was absolutely no way we were going to be able to survive peacefully without welfare and without jobs. My projections showed that if there were an abundance of jobs for brothers and sisters there would not be a problem with people finding jobs. But jobs have not been available in years, so the Coalition was going to have to step up the effort and go to even greater lengths to show the community that they would have to be the creators of their own jobs.

Normally I couldn't sit down for such a long period of time in front of the computer without getting a headache, and I was surprised that I didn't have one. I knew that if I continued looking at the computer screen it would take me a while to get my eyes back together, so I decided to take a break. I was just motivated. The night I had with Cece put energy in my bones and inspiration in my heart. I'd thought long and hard about the commitment that I made to her and after I asked her to marry me and put the ring on her finger, everything seemed final. And now the responsibilities that were before me smacked me right in the face. I was determined to make sure the transition to married life would be as smooth as possible. On the way home from her house, I kept thinking about what was ahead for us. I wasn't concerned because of any expectations Cece put on me. She said she was happy just as long as we were together, but I was worried about what I wanted to give her, which was the world. That meant I had to have everything in order to provide for her when the time came. After all the patience she had for me and all that we'd been through, I just wanted to make sure she knew she was my baby girl.

As I was driving home from Cece's I listened to the Quiet Storm and thought about how Cece had worked that little chocolate factory with her hands wrapped around my neck while we were making love. For being so small and tiny, she can certainly handle a brother. And it's funny, because if we were not into each other both mentally and spiritually, I don't think we'd react as powerfully as we do. I've never had a woman have an orgasm when I looked her in the eyes and told her to let it go, and that's exactly what Cece did. Several times. When she looked at me with those sexy eyes, like she trusted me with her entire life, it just totally blew my mind.

"Kahlil, how many kids do you want?" she asked. "Will you always protect me?" she continued. "You know I would love to be your queen," she promised me. Right then I knew I had an immense responsibility ahead of me.

I double checked, to make sure that I had saved my charts on my computer. As I turned it off, I heard a car door shut in my driveway. In a matter of seconds someone was knocking on the door and Nite was barking, announcing that he was inside the house. I slipped on my shoes, went to the door, and looked out the peephole. It was Dewayna. I grabbed Nite and made him sit and stay by the fireplace, unlocked the door, and opened the screen door to let her come inside. Dewayna took one step inside the house. When she saw Nite, she stopped, held her breath, and began to back out the door slowly.

"You got to put that thang up, Kahlil. I ain't coming in that house with that dog looking at me like I'm some kind of bone to chew on."

"Come on in. He's all right. He won't bite, he's still a puppy." I knew that would soothe her mind, although Nite was going on almost three years old. I held open the screen door. Dewayna jumped inside and grabbed me by the front of my shirt, holding on to it for dear life, as Nite began barking again.

"Dewayna, you're going to have to let me go, Nite doesn't let anybody but Cece touch me," I told her, laughing.

"Well damn it, Kahlil. Tell him I'm Cece, because I'm not letting go of your black ass!" I busted out laughing. "Drop down, Nite." He did immediately. "Now, see, you're okay."

"I don't know why you still call him a puppy, Kahlil. I'm not stupid. That dog hasn't been a puppy since he was three months old," Dewayna said, keeping an eye on Nite.

I gave Dewayna a hug and could tell instantly that my good friend was not herself even though she had a smile on her face. We'd known each other since the first grade and she couldn't hide anything from me. Dewayna was the first girl I ever had a crush on, and she never lets me forget that, either. Every time Cece and I meet her out for a drink or something, she always brings up that silliness, especially when she gets full of her favorite whiskey sours. She likes to tell Cece about all of the business ventures that I had when I was growing up and other stories about our childhood. I hate when she get going on those tales, because she can go on for hours about that embarrassing mess.

Fed Up with the Fanny

Her favorite story is about Lewis, my best friend when we were in the fourth grade. I remember that he was even darker than I was, with a bald head. He stuttered terribly, but tried to cover it up by talking fast, which sure enough didn't work. One day, we were playing basketball at recess and he stopped, took off his shoe, and began to massage his foot for some reason. I looked down at him and asked what was he doing. He made me promise that if he told me, I wouldn't tell anyone. Well, I promised him because he was my boy, and he knew my secret about having a crush on Dewayna, so he had something on me. Lewis looked around the playground with his beady eyes and made sure no one could see him, took off his sock, and showed me his foot. He had six toes. I couldn't believe that shit. Then he looked up at me and started laughing with that big-ass gap in his teeth, and wiggled that little motherfucker. I almost ran from his ass. My partner was a damn freak. That entire day in school I wanted to tell somebody. I didn't care about the promise I made. On the way home, Lewis and I were walking and I told him that he was the only person in school with six toes and we should profit from it. I told him that we could show people his six toes for a price, then go to the store with the money after school and buy bags full of candy, break the bags down and sell the candy piece by piece and make even more money. I kept after Lewis for a whole week, trying to persuade that brother to say yes to my idea. The next thing you know, we had lines and lines of people, teachers included, coming up to us at recess wanting to see his toes for a quarter each. We made a killing up until the sixth grade. Dewayna always loves to tell those types of stories and the bad thing about it is Cece likes to listen.

Dewayna lived three houses down from this very house until her junior year of high school. She had to move because during the Halloween season, on Hell Night, Dewayna's house was set on fire by a bunch of crazy fools who didn't even live in the neighborhood. She lost her two brothers and mother to smoke inhalation and she and her father moved across town, thirty minutes away from me. But we still tried our best to keep in contact. Instead of seeing each other every day, we saw each other every Friday. We still brag about the fact that, no matter what was going on during our senior year of high school, she and I talked on the phone every night. We were very close back in those days and still are. We competed against each other in school, because we were always the smartest in our classes. Our birthdays are in the same month, we were born the same year, and we like a lot of the same things.

Many people thought that we were actually an item, but we had no desire for each other. It was just like having another sister to me. We asked each other's opinions about things that were going on in our lives and on the same night, while on the phone, we helped each other decide what we were going to do after high school. We spent the entire night on the phone, trying to decide which college to go to. We had one day left for signing national letters of intent and neither of us had a clue. Dewayna had numerous athletic and academic scholarships and had narrowed her choices down to Howard, Georgetown, and Hampton, while I was undecided between Michigan State and CSU. Dewayna surprised everyone by going to Wayne State, because she wanted to stay close to her father.

"How are you doing, Dewayna? Where have you been hiding?" I asked her, as she stood looking up at me in her baggy jeans and the oversized CSU shirt that I gave her years ago.

"At the damn hospital. I worked sixty-five hours this week."

"I hope not in the emergency room?" I asked. Dewayna didn't like that department, because of all the shooting victims she would have to see.

"Yep, on the midnight shift."

"Come on back and get yourself some tea, girl." Dewayna followed me back into the kitchen.

◇

Fed Up with the Fanny

The last time I'd seen Dewayna looking this way was when I helped her through a very trying time when she was twenty-four and seeing a thirty-six-year-old man who had a wife and five kids. Dewayna was going through a lot of problems and had become sidetracked from what she wanted to do in her life. She had no self-respect or self-esteem. The man that she was seeing was a new doctor at the hospital who had taken advantage of Dewayna's confused state of mind and became very possessive of her. After they'd been intimate he thought he couldn't do without her—the problem with that was he was married and so was she.

Dewayna had been married for almost two years before she started messing around with the new doctor. I probably wouldn't have gotten as involved as I did if I hadn't been the one who introduced her to her husband, Demitrious. He was my roommate at CSU and he and Dewayna met at a party when we were home from school for Christmas break.

The doctor admitted to his wife of three years that he was having an affair after she accused him of sleeping around. Later on the doctor's wife went over to Dewayna's house, while Dewayna was at work, introduced herself to Demitrious and told him everything that was going on.

Dewayna was surprised to come home from work and see the doctor's wife on her couch, telling Demitrious about the affair. The whole situation was terrible and Dewayna came to me, asking me to talk to Demitrious for her. I did and thought they'd solved their differences because I didn't hear otherwise. Demitrious and Dewayna got through the turmoil and Dewayna had a baby boy a year later. They named the child Octavious and five years after he was born, Demitrious packed his bags and left Dewayna and Octavious without a word. She hasn't heard from him or seen him since.

I wasn't sure why Dewayna had stopped by tonight, and hoped I hadn't forgotten to pick up Octavious (my godson) for a weekend that we had planned earlier. I just grabbed the tea kettle and reached into the cabinet for two cups. Dewayna sat at the table, looking at the cup I had placed in front of her, not saying a word.

"What's wrong?" I asked her.

"Oh nothing," she responded.

"Come on, Dewayna, you're talking to me. Don't even try it."

"I just need to talk," she said.

"What's on your mind?"

"It's just Octavious," she said.

"What about him? Is he okay?"

"Yes, he's fine. There's nothing wrong with him physically or anything. But Friday, when he came home from day care, he told me he wanted to see his father on Father's Day. I guess he didn't have anyone to make a card for."

"So what did you tell him?"

"I told him that I was his father and that I was all that he was ever going to need," Dewayna said in a very low voice. "Hell, I didn't know what to say."

I took a very deep breath and got ready for a topic that had always been heated between Dewayna and I. Dewayna's situation was similar to that with Leandra and Sid. I offered Dewayna my help in finding Demitrious through the Coalition, but she didn't want Demitrious to think that she needed his help in raising Octavious so she had decided against it. It always upset me that Sid and Octavious suffered because their parents had problems they didn't want to deal with, but I tried to understand. I began to pour the hot water into our cups.

"Dewayna, look. I understand what you're going through even more than I want to. Leandra is still denying Sid the knowledge of his father. You know how she thinks, and lately Sid has been all on her case about it. He has been getting into all types of trouble and I think it's because she won't be truthful with him. It's hard for her to see that, and I just don't want the same thing to happen to Octavious."

"Well, Kahlil, what am I supposed to do? All I know is that Demitrious and I had worked things out between us and all of a sudden, one day I come home from work and his black ass is gone. He didn't even leave us a note or anything, he just took his shit and left." Dewayna's voice softened and she quickly put her head down and began blowing on her tea to cool it . . . then she looked up like she had remembered something.

"You know what, Kahlil? We were even making plans to buy another house and start a trust fund for Octavious. And you want to hear something funny?" She tried to laugh, but tears began to flow down her face.

"What is it?" I asked.

"Two days before he left, he asked me if I wanted to have another baby. Kahlil, why did he leave us? Why?"

Dewayna was crying harder. I moved closer to her and held her hand.

"I'm not blaming you, Kahlil. I know I wasn't perfect, but why did you ever introduce me to his ass?"

I felt as bad as she did. Dewayna couldn't control her tears and I continued to hold her, as I've done so many times before, until her tears subsided.

One on One

Kahlil woke up earlier than usual on Sunday morning. He had been unable to sleep after Dewayna left and Sid had called around three in the morning to ask if he could come over and lay his head down. Kahlil wanted to get down to the Coalition before breakfast was served for the Father's Day tribute, but before he left he wanted to let Sid know that he was on his way out. He looked through the door leading into the den and didn't see Sid laying on the couch where he normally slept when staying over.

"Hey, Sid, you up?" Kahlil shouted as he walked down the hallway to the kitchen. The aroma of eggs and turkey sausage greeted him. Sid was standing over the stove, turning the turkey while listening intently to the morning news coverage over the radio. He didn't notice Kahlil behind him.

"There you are. What's up, my brother?" Kahlil said, opening up the refrigerator and taking out a pitcher of cold water. Sid turned around and smiled.

"What's up, Kahlil. You want something to eat?"

"No thanks, I'm on my way down to the Coalition."

"For the Father's Day tribute?" Kahlil looked at Sid, surprised he knew anything about it.

"Yeah, we're having breakfast and from there I'm going to Bethel for church."

Sid turned around as Kahlil opened the cabinet and reached for his vitamins, opened them up, plopped them into his mouth, and washed them down.

"So you and your mother got into a disagreement I hear?"

"How did you know?" Sid asked.

"Guess?"

"Aunt Pam?"

"Yep, she called me three times before you did. If she'd gotten her way I would have been out there on the streets looking for you." Sid looked at Kahlil, glad that he had not done as Pam asked.

"I don't know why she's always in my business. It's enough that Mom listens to my phone calls at night."

"You know, Pam doesn't mean anything by it. You are her favorite and she hates to see you going through all this."

"Well, somebody needs to talk to Mom, because the only one trippin' is her. I don't even know if I want to go back over there. Just like the other day everyone was in the den watchin' television, just coolin', having a good time, and she storms out the room talkin' 'bout she can't take it any more."

"What was she talking about?

"I don't know, but she scared me when all of a sudden she just stood up, said what she had to say, and stormed out the room without a reason."

"Don't worry about it, Sid. I'll talk to your mother and try to see what's bothering her."

"I wish somebody would, because she's treating me like a stepchild—all hateful and stuff. Wanting me to work, so that she can go to school. Have you ever heard of anything like that before?" Kahlil hadn't heard the other side of the story yet so he tried to be diplomatic about the situation. He knew that even he wasn't going to believe what was getting ready to come out of his mouth.

"Well, Sid, maybe your mother really does need your help. I don't know, I haven't talked to her."

"Don't even try it, Kahlil. You know how she is. She's just trying to take advantage of me like she does everyone else."

"Don't give up so easily. She's got it hard, too, but I'm going to talk to your mother as soon as I can. Be optimistic, my brother. I'll see you later, all right?" Kahlil turned around and began to walk out of the kitchen.

"Kahlil!" Sid called out in a hurry. "Can I talk to you? One-on-one for a second?"

Kahlil looked at his watch. "Go ahead."

"What was he like?"

"What was who like?" Kahlil said, confused.

"My father." Kahlil stood silent as Sid looked at him with wondering eyes.

"Sid, I never met him."

There was silence. Kahlil was shocked that Sid brought up his father. It had been a while since he had asked Kahlil about him, even though Kahlil knew that it was eating him up from the inside out.

"Shit. Somebody has to know something about him," Sid said, as he turned the fire off on the stove, placed the hot pan in the sink, and turned on the water to cool it off.

"Sid, believe me, if I knew, I would tell you in a heartbeat. You know I don't agree with your mother, and I've told her many times that I think she's making a mistake by not telling you anything about him. That's up to her, but I can tell you this, if he's as patient as you are, then I'm sure he is a bad boy."

Sid looked at Kahlil and smiled. "You think so?"

"Yeah, man, I do. But, Sid, let me tell you something. Even though you're basically a grown man right now, don't you ever think that you can't come to me for anything you need. I know I'm not the real deal, but I'm sure that I can fill in and help out. Is that cool?"

Sid seemed to be satisfied for the moment. "I just wish I had my real father to go and talk to, like you had with Grandpa. I used to watch you two, always in the backyard doing something together, and I just wish I had my dad to talk to like that. I've always thought about how it would feel to talk to the man who made me."

"Well, Sid, like I said, I might not be him but at least give me a try if you need to, all right?"

Sid nodded his head. "All right, I'll try."

"I need some practice anyway," Kahlil said, smiling.

"What are you talking a about?" Sid said, laughing.

"Oh, you didn't hear? Cece and I are going to get married."

"You are? You mean you're finally going to marry that fine little hunnie?"

"Yep, that's right. So now she's going to be your aunt hunnie and don't you forget it."

"Yeah right," Sid said.

"Look, I have to go. But I'll be back later. Don't fuck with Nite and he won't fuck with you."

"Where is he?" Sid said, looking around.

"Out back."

Sid went over to the back door and turned the bolt. Kahlil began walking down the hallway to the front door.

"Oh, Kahlil!" Sid shouted.

"Yeah, what's up?" There was silence. "Sid, do you want something?" Kahlil asked.

"Oh nothing. It can wait. I'll talk to you later."

As Sid heard Kahlil shut the front door, he sat down at the table and closed his eyes, trying to shake the picture of the serious shit he had in his head. He wanted to tell Kahlil that he had nothing to do with what had happened last night. Difante and Rashaad had robbed a man at gunpoint in Sid's neighborhood minutes after they picked him up.

Now I know how they always have all that money, he thought. Those fools are crazy. How could Difante put that nine millimeter up to the head of that man's baby and promise to blow its head off if the man only had a two-hundred-dollar limit on his bankcard. When Difante did that shit I wanted to get out of the car and snatch that pistol out of his hand myself. Difante said he wasn't going to shoot the baby when he got back in the car. He just wanted the fool to hurry up and get the money. I just don't understand why they had to do the shit in my neighborhood. They'd always joked and laughed about coming out there and taking care of business and that's exactly what they did. Po-Po is probably stopping every brother that comes out of the house looking for who robbed that white man.

Sid wasn't worried about getting caught because he knew for a fact that the guy didn't see his black ass. He was in the backseat and didn't move a muscle. Sid was shaking as bad as the man being jacked. He should have known that they were up to no good when Rashaad circled around the bank machine three times in a row. But Sid had been too upset with his mom to even think twice about what was going on. He was just happy to be the hell out the house. But as soon as Difante and Rashaad saw that man pull up to the bank machine in his car everybody in the car knew what was going to happen next except Sid. Last night was fucked-up. He could say one thing though, those fools were professionals. They didn't waste any time at all. They stopped, got out, took his shit, and moved out.

Fed Up with the Fanny

Sid considered beeping his friends, but if Five-O had them then they'd sure as hell trace the number to Sid and come pick his ass up too. He wondered how much money they got but he quickly dismissed the thought from his head. He didn't care and decided to ask if he could stay with Kahlil for a couple of days on the downlow.

Silence

There must have been at least three hundred men with their families at the breakfast. All were being honored for being outstanding committed fathers and for taking care of their responsibilities. Three-fourths of the fathers at the breakfast had been found by the Coalition in the last year alone and we had used some very special techniques to locate fathers who were known to still be in the city.

The Coalition had the support of the businessmen and -women throughout Detroit. Donations to the Coalition provided for posters of wanted fathers that were put up in different sections of the community, exposing them to public ridicule for neglecting their children. We received funds from all types of businesses in the city who thought that what the Coalition was doing was a great credit to the city. Businesses with a high volume of customer transactions, such as supermarkets, banks, and restaurants, helped by declining checks or credit cards for payment if a customer's name appeared on our list of wanted men, which was a great help to the Coalition's If Man Be Man program.

The coordinator of the program was Police Chief Parham, who had numerous resources for locating fathers of children in the community and did not hesitate to use them. Parham was just one of the seven board members who had become affiliated with the Coalition and all were very strong and successful voices in the community. The board consisted of the chairman of the most powerful bank in the city, the minister of the largest African Episcopal Methodist Church, the chief engineer at a Big Three automobile assembly plant, a city councilman, the assistant basketball coach of the Pistons, Parham, and myself. I loved the fact that the Coalition was so organized. In fact that was what actually drew my attention to them in the first place. They always took care of business, stayed focused, and got results. I admired that.

Although I am the youngest member of the Coalition, I was being considered by all the current members as a candidate for the executive director position and I felt like I was really being primed. They were working my ass to death. They told me that they liked my drive and determination and thought I was in the perfect position to take the Coalition into the year 2000.

I was interested in the position because the work that we do is important and I'm surrounded by my brothers and sisters. It gives me the security that I have learned to love and that I could never find in corporate America. Most of the time at work there is no one at the table in business meetings that even looks like me, so I enjoy the same feeling of validation at the Coalition that my white coworkers have on a daily basis. The board specifically told me that they wanted me to use my knowledge and energy to come up with ways to reach the ever-changing urban community in our efforts to expand our already two-million-dollar facility. One of the tasks that I was assigned was finding an eighth board member who actually had the ability to bring media attention to our efforts, so that we could drum up additional support. They'd given me six months in which to deliver this new board member to the Coalition, but that was five months and three weeks ago and my first and only choice, Sonje, had turned my offer down repeatedly.

From day one I had thought of Sonje as an excellent choice, but she didn't want anything to do with community service or the Coalition for some reason. I had scheduled one last meeting with her and I was determined to convince her to help.

When I returned home, Sid was out like a light on the couch, so I reviewed the demographics of my study to check the facts before I sent copies to the other board members via modem. And after that, I wanted to take Nite on a walk.

The phone began to ring.

"Hello."

"Kahlil, it's Chief Parham. Listen, I got the information on that friend of yours and you won't believe where he is."

I had talked to Parham after the breakfast and asked him if he would get me an address on Demitrious. Dewayna decided that she wanted me to locate him and I was very interested in his whereabouts, too.

"That was fast. I didn't expect you to get it so quick, Chief."

"Well, you know how it is. We can't lose time on this type of shit, because the only people that are being hurt are the children."

"I hear you."

"I'll make this short and sweet, because the family is taking me out to eat buffet-style. He's at 3090 Chicago Avenue right off of Clairmont, across from the park."

"Shit, that's three blocks from me. I'll be damned. He's right here in the hood. Thanks, Chief, I'll talk to you later."

This filled me with energy and I became anxious to talk to my long-lost ex-roommate. I decided I better work out before I went over to pay him a visit. I needed to work off all the built-up tension I had in my body. I knew that if I didn't there might be a problem that Demitrious couldn't handle.

I grabbed one of my Minister Farrakhan tapes and went into the basement to work out on my punching bag. I enjoy listening to the Minister when I work out, because his messages and the Nation of Islam motivate me. I use them as a measuring stick for the Coalition. I really think the Nation has become a front-runner in leading the black community by encouraging us to mobilize economically, spiritually, and educationally. As I listened to the "Let Us Make Man" address in Atlanta, I artfully refined my one-two punch to the rib and chin combination. I listened intently to the Minister and quickened my pace and started to hit the bag harder when he spoke about brothers in the community not being seen by our women, families, businesses, and the entire world as competent and respectful men, but as thieves, liars, and drug addicts, explaining that we [black men] are the laughingstock of the world. I became agitated about the mind-set of many black men and I changed from my two-punch work and went to a three-punch tactic, masterfully placing my fist on the bag for at least twenty straight minutes. I swear I tried to tear that mother down. I was trying my best to work my body to its fullest, while the Minister fed my mind. I didn't even realize that the tape had stopped. I let myself become totally submerged into the message, placing my entire being and understanding into the plight of the black man, pledging to myself that I would help turn things around. I suddenly stopped when I looked down and saw Nite barking at me, bringing me back to reality.

I showered and put Nite in the back of the pickup that I bought especially to carry his big ass around. As soon as I shut the back latch, Harris yelled out my name and walked across the street. Larry Harris is a very good friend that my mother took into our house when his mother became involved in drugs. Our mothers were good friends back in the day and when his mother's habit got out of control, he stayed with my family for about three months. Harris was told to leave when my mother noticed that he, too, was coming in the house high, and he has never stopped using.

"What up, Kahlil? Where are you going?" Harris asked.

"I'm going to see an old friend of mine, who I haven't seen in a while, right next to the park on Chicago," I told him.

"Is that right? I was about to go that way myself to play some ball." Harris looked like shit. His hair was plaited up in braids, he was wearing leather sneakers that looked too big for his feet, and the jacket he had on was too big, with holes around the elbows. I'd tried to help clean this brother up, but I'd came to the same point my father had with Leandra before he passed away. You try to help people and they don't want to listen, and after a while you just have to pray for them, remove yourself from them, and trust that some day they will get the message.

"Come on, you want a ride?" Harris accepted.

On the way to the park, we talked about the old times and how we used to run the streets and be wild and free, without a responsibility in the world. Harris started talking about that's the way he still is and ain't nothing changed in his life. He made sure I was abreast of all the crew that we grew up with, who just went to jail and who just got out.

"You know, Harris, you can't live this life forever, man. You're still living the life of a teenager, brother," I tried to tell him.

Harris sat up from his slouched position and dusted off his jacket to make it look more presentable.

"Well, Kahlil, you know everybody ain't like you," he said.

"What do you mean by that?"

"You know what I mean. Everybody doesn't know what they want to do with their life. Ever since high school, you walked around like you knew exactly what you wanted to do with your life, and that shit used to get on my damn nerves."

"I don't know why, it didn't have a damn thing to do with you, Harris."

"It got on my nerves because I used to try and figure out what I wanted to do with my life. I still don't know yet . . . and I'm going on thirty-one years old, man."

"Well, brother, it's not too late. All you have to do is set a goal, get your priorities straight, and from there you can do whatever you set out to do."

"Like what, Kahlil? What the hell can I do?"

"Harris, I can't tell you what to do. . . . What do you like to do?"

"Man, I like to work on cars, that's about all. Shit, I done fixed almost everybody's car on the block cheaper than they can do at any shop, and I ain't never had a complaint."

"Well, there you go."

"What do you mean?" Harris asked.

"I mean, since you have the mechanical talent, why don't you get your certificate, go into business and open yourself up a shop."

"Kahlil, what the hell are you talking about? You know ain't nobody going to let my black ass open up a shop to fix cars," he said with firm belief. I was becoming fed up with Harris. Thank God we were at the park.

"Look, you have to believe to achieve my brother. Drop by the Coalition on Tuesday night, we have classes on how to start your own business." I didn't know why I was telling him this. He was already looking out the window at the brothers on the court. I parked directly across from the address Parham had given to me and paused for a moment as I tried to collect my bearings.

"What's up, brother? Why are you hesitating and shit? Aren't you going to get out?" Harris asked.

Lord knows I didn't want to involve Harris in this problem.

"Kahlil, what's wrong? Are you meeting some bitch out here or something and you scared? That ain't like you at all."

I opened my door and looked directly at Harris because he had just brought me back from my inner thoughts.

"Harris, when are you going to stop calling our women bitches?" I asked.

"As soon as they stop acting like that's what they are," he said, laughing. He opened the door and ran over to the court. As ignorant as that brother was I just didn't feel like wasting my time anymore. I took Nite out of the truck and let him run around, while I kept a close eye on Demitrious's place.

The sun had begun to fade along with the number of brothers on the court. Not once did I take my eyes away from the duplex that Demitrious lived in, and while I sat on the park bench, I didn't notice anyone coming or going. Soon it would be completely dark and I decided I to see if Demitrious was at home. I put Nite into the truck and walked up the cracked stone walkway, which was almost completely covered by weeds and grass. When I approached the door I thought of his face and how it would appear when our eyes met. I knocked on the door once, twice, and then a third time, as the porch light next door to the duplex came on. A young Hispanic brother, who looked to be about twenty-two years old, stuck his head out the door.

"Yeah, can I help you?" he said with a heavy New York accent. He looked as though he had a problem with me being there.

"No, thank you, my brother, I'm just looking for an old partner of mine who lives here. His name is Demitrious. You know him?"

The young brother looked at me like he was confused.

"Nope, the only brother I know that stays there is Smiley and I haven't seen him all day."

I thanked him and walked back to my pickup wondering if Parham had given me the right address. I began to drive back home, but when I looked into my rearview mirror I saw a car pull up and park on the other side of the street almost exactly in front of where I had just left. Suspicious, I stopped my truck and turned around, watching the man get out of the car. I recognized Demitrious. I pulled almost directly in front of the duplex where he was parked. Demitrious had his back turned to me, taking his grocery bags out of his trunk. I leaned over and rolled down my passenger's window.

"Demitrious, how are you doing?"

Demitrious turned around, looked at me, and immediately threw his groceries back into the trunk of his car, slammed it shut, and began to walk very quickly to the front door of the duplex.

"Wait a minute, Demitrious. Where are you going?" I said to him, then got out of the truck and began to follow him. "Demitrious, hold up a second. Can we talk?"

"We don't have anything to talk about," he said, as he looked back with his eyes wide, getting closer to his front door.

"Man, just wait up a minute," I said, trying not to shout.

Demitrious got his key out from his pocket and put it in the keyhole. I began to run after him.

"Demitrious! Demitrious!" I said as loud as I could without screaming. He opened the door, took the key out and tried his best to slam the door in my face. I stepped onto the porch right before it shut, grabbed the door with both of my hands, and was able to wedge my body in the door so it couldn't close. Now Demitrious was a good size himself, about five eleven and one hundred eighty pounds, but there was no way I was going to let him shut that door in my face.

"Hold up, man. I just want to talk to you. What's your problem?" I asked him. Demitrious didn't look me in the eye. He looked directly at the door when he spoke.

"What do you want to talk about?"

"Well, I'd rather do this inside. I want to talk to you about some things. Why do we have to do it like this?"

"Because this is how I prefer it," he said. I heard the door on the other side of the duplex open up, and the young brother that

I had talked to earlier came out with another Hispanic brother holding baseball bats.

"Yo, Smiley, what up? This fool trying to jack you or what? I saw him over here, snooping around, about ten minutes ago." They both walked closer to me.

"You didn't see shit but me knocking on the door, and I suggest you stop right there," I told them.

"Fuck you, nigga. I'll bust your big ass with this bat," the fearless neighbor said to me. The two brothers began to approach like they wanted to be saviors.

"Come, Nite!" I yelled, and all of his 155 pounds of muscle jumped out the truck, stood in front of me, and showed the young brothers his teeth.

"So what's up now, muchachos?" I asked, as they stood in awe of Nite, not moving a muscle, like they were about to piss in their pants. He was barking and growling like a wild maniac, just waiting for me to give him the word.

"Yo, Smiley, if you need us, we're in here, cuz," his neighbors said as they dropped their bats and stumbled into the house, shutting the door behind them.

"Kahlil, what do you want?" Demitrious asked.

"Look, I just came over to see how you're doing. Why are you trippin' and shit, acting like you don't even know who I am? We don't have no beef. Now are you going to let me in or what? If not, let's just go around the corner and have a drink or something."

Demitrious knew that I was not going to let go of that door. He stood behind it trying to make his mind up if he wanted to talk to me or not.

"Step back," he said. I slowly let go of the door and Demitrious came out on the porch.

"You all right?" I asked. Demitrious looked at me for the first time as I extended my hand to him.

"Yeah, I'm cool," he replied, shaking my hand.

Fed Up with the Fanny

We were both silent on the short ride over to the bar even though I wanted to jump right on him and ask why in the hell he left Dewayna and Octavious for almost a whole year. I decided to play it out because Demitrious seemed nervous and jumpy, nothing like I remembered him being, so I just waited until we were inside the bar to begin the conversation.

"So, why do they call you Smiley?"

"I don't know. It's just a name they came up with when we were out playing ball one day," he said.

"You still working with that computer firm?" I asked him.

"Nope," he said, taking a drink of his beer and looking toward the big screen, watching SportsCenter. "I'm with the state now, head of public relations. I've been there about three months."

"That's good, brother. Congrats," I said, as I half-ass toasted my glass toward him.

"It's Dewayna and Octavious, right? What's wrong with them? Is everything all right?" he asked without taking his eyes away from the screen. I was so glad that he asked.

"No. As a matter of fact they're not. They miss you. Well, Octavious misses you and he is beginning to ask Dewayna about you more and more."

"What about Dewayna?"

"Well, she's making it, but trying to raise Octavious alone is getting to her. But she's making it."

Demitrious looked at me as though he was trying to reassure himself. "I know you are there for them every time they need something, right?" he asked me.

I looked at that fool like he was crazy. "Look, Demitrious. Octavious is not my son. He's my godson and if he needs something, sure I'm there for him. But I am not his father. You are, and you should be taking care of him your damn self. Dewayna's going absolutely off of the deep end, worrying about what happened to you for the past year and trying to figure out if she's going to have to raise him all by herself the rest of her life. Why did you leave anyway?"

Demitrious paused. "Well, Kahlil, you know sometimes things aren't what they appear to be."

"What are you talking about, Demitrious?"

"I'm talking about the way Dewayna thought I was happy in that situation. I'm not blaming her. It's my own fault. I made the first mistake by telling her that everything was fine, then making plans to be with her and having more kids just to make her happy and telling her what she wanted to hear. I made too many damn promises that I didn't even want to keep myself."

"So, you just left. Just like that?"

He switched his eyes back on the screen. "Yep . . . just like that."

The damage had already been done. He had changed, and there was no point in arguing with him. Not now I thought, at least I found him. I left well enough alone.

As I was driving Demitrious home, he became quiet again and looked very agitated. He kept turning his head toward me, like he wanted to say something, but each time he would turn his head back and look out the window. When we returned to his place, there was a basketball game going on under the lights at the park and I pulled up to watch the game. At least ten minutes went by where we didn't say a word to each other. The only sounds that we could hear were the sounds on the court as we sat with the windows down and listened to the brothers call for the ball and talk shit to one another.

"So, the Coalition helps brothers who are in need?" Demitrious asked, shyly.

"What we try to do is help our people when they need it, however they need it." I began to laugh when a player missed a two-hand backward slam.

"What, you still play ball?" Demitrious asked, knowing how much I love basketball.

Fed Up with the Fanny

"From time to time, I go down to the run and shoot that we have at the Coalition and play with those brothers. I bet you three-fourths of the brothers up there could be on a NBA team." I had started to sound like the brothers on the court, talking shit, as we watched them ball.

"I played against a brother two weeks ago that could make the Pistons right now. I mean, this brother is a cross between Jim Jackson and Charles Oakley. I mean, a real man on the court." I was about to start talking about Dennis Rodman and ask Demitrious if he thought he was damaging the game. But when I looked over at Demitrious, he looked like he'd stopped breathing.

"Demitrious, you okay?" I tapped him on the shoulder and he looked right back at me like an entirely different person. I've known Demitrious for years and I had never seen him look like that before. He was scaring the hell out of me. I had to squint my eyes to reassure myself that it was still him, sitting there in the dark. The lights from the court didn't help any. Sweat was pouring down his face, his eyes were a fire-looking red, and I thought he was going to just break down crying any minute. He looked at me and wiped his eyes.

"Kahlil, I abused Octavious . . . that's why I left." Demitrious slowly turned his head away and began crying. When I realized what he said, I felt like a streak of lightning went straight through my body and tore everything up inside. I tried my best to refocus on the basketball game and forget what he said. It was not happening. I was unable to shake it out of my mind. The windows of the truck were down, but I still couldn't seem to get enough air so I opened the door, stepped out, and looked to the heavens above for guidance.

Ms. Bad Ass

It was Tuesday, two days after I'd talked with Demitrious, and I was at home instead of at work, still trying to recover from the blow that Demitrious threw my way. I called in sick again that morning, I just had to. I didn't care about those fools at work. I hadn't been sick once in my seven years there, and I thought this was a good time to take a break. Lord knows I needed it. Demitrious and I must have sat in that car until six-thirty in the morning, trying to understand why he did what he did. I guess that's what we were trying to do, but we really couldn't even talk about it. I didn't know what to ask, and Demitrious had spent so long avoiding himself and everyone else that he didn't know where to begin. All I got from him was that his father used to beat on him, and that's basically all I could understand since he wasn't talking too clear. We did come to the conclusion that he needed to get some professional help, so I suggested a counselor at the Coalition, Mr. Robinson. I knew he had assisted hundreds of individuals with similar problems and if anyone could help Demitrious figure out what was going on with himself, Robinson was the man. Demitrious was apprehensive about going to see him because he wanted everything to be confidential. I promised him it would be and he promised me that he would get help and tell Dewayna about his situation.

I wanted to break the alarm clock when it went off. I don't remember the last time I slept until two in the afternoon but I guess I needed the rest. Although I still had Demitrious on my mind, I had to get moving if I was going to persuade Sonje to join the board of the Coalition that afternoon. This was going to be difficult and I wasn't looking forward to it, but I could rest my mind later at the movies with Cece.

I showered and set the stage for my meeting with Sonje. I decided to go all out by preparing a nice salad of wilted lettuce mixed with broiled chicken and covered with creamy Italian dressing. I opened a bottle of wine and had the music of Incognito sounding awesome in the background. I left my drawstring curtains open to allow the light to shine through my dining room and I scattered some material about the Coalition on the table. I didn't want to give Sonje the wrong idea about the purpose of our meeting. I was sure that she understood it was over between us because she hadn't called me lately with any request for a booty call, but it wouldn't surprise me if she had a different agenda than talking about the Coalition. If this turned out to be the case it was just too damn bad because I was prepared to tell her that Cece would be over at seven o'clock. At six o'clock Sonje was knocking on the door.

When I opened up, I was struck for a couple of seconds by the tight-fitting red dress Sonje had on, and I tried my best not to look because she had clearly worn it to remind me of what I used to get. Her hair was pulled back and she was radiant with natural beauty. Quiet as it's kept, Sonje was forty-three and looked like she was twenty-eight—that's one of the reasons it took me so long to call it quits with her. She was as fine as she wanted to be. Her well-curved body, long legs, full lips, perfect teeth, and caramel complexion always had brothers looking at her. She even had me fooled for a while, but her attitude stank. She was an unbearable, manipulative control freak—just thinking about her foul ways was my recipe for staying the hell away from her.

The first time I met Sonje was the day I interviewed for a summer job at the local television station. Sonje was a goddess at the station because of the ratings she'd pulled in with her television show, the *Women Only Show*. As soon as I shook her hand I could tell she was the type of woman who loved to be the one in control. My first day on the job I was surprised when I was moved from the advertising department that I had been hired to work in to a special public-relations project headed by none other than Sonje. My office was next to hers and most of the time at work was spent together in her office. It soon became apparent that Sonje had more in mind than just working together. After two weeks Sonje knew everything about me but I only knew as much about her as she wanted to tell me. At the end of my first month she took me to her place to go over last-minute changes on the project, but she seduced me instead. I found myself spending not just the night, but the whole weekend with her. I thought I was something special and was on cloud nine because I was sleeping with Sonje Allen, the most popular black woman in Detroit.

Sonje was the most sexual person I had ever met in my entire life. There were times when she would meet me in Dayton for the weekend or pick me up on campus and work my body all weekend long. It was like she couldn't get enough of me, and her body is so fine there isn't a brother I know that wouldn't fall for her just like I did. Our relationship continued for the last two years I was in college, and she helped me land my first couple of large ad accounts at the Houston Corporation after I'd started working. We'd broken it off for a couple of years because her career took off, but then she came back into my life, knowing that Cece and I were seeing each other with an understanding that we could see other people just as long as we both knew about it.

Sonje walked into the house and looked around as though my covered furniture and ongoing construction were not good enough for her. I just laughed it off and escorted her back into the dining room area, where the renovation had been completed. This seemed to put her at ease and I pulled a chair out for her as she sat down.

"So, how do you like the dining room?"

Sonje looked around and smiled. "It's nice, Kahlil. It really turned out better than I thought." I took a seat at the other end of the table.

"So, why did you ask me over tonight?" Sonje asked bluntly. "There has to be a reason . . . did your little girlfriend break up with you and now you need a full-grown woman to lift your spirits?" I was happy as hell that she asked me that question so we could get any ideas about going to bed out of the way and out of her mind. I picked up the bottle of wine, showed it to her, she nodded yes, and I poured her a glass.

"No, not at all, Sonje. As a matter of fact, Cece and I are getting together later on tonight after our meeting." I stopped pouring the wine and Sonje quickly guided her glass up to her mouth.

With a nasty look on her face she asked, "So, why in the hell did you ask me over here tonight? I hope not to talk about this Coalition bullshit." Sonje pointed to the Coalition documents on the table.

"Sonje, you know that's exactly why I asked you over. I don't use the Coalition as a front for other matters."

Sonje sat back and crossed her arms like she'd already heard enough, and I just knew she was going to turn me down again. I decided she wasn't going to say no again without giving me an explanation.

"I really don't get it," I said to her. "You're the most powerful black woman in this city and you don't want to help your own people during one of our darkest hours since slavery? Can you help me understand why the hell not?" I poured myself a glass of wine. Sonje looked surprised, since I had always been mild mannered with her and always seemed to laugh it off when she told me things I didn't want to hear. But this time she knew she had a fight on her hands. I wanted an answer.

"First of all, Mr. Richardson, I don't know where you get off thinking I have to explain myself to you. Ever since you decided you wanted to date your little, limited girl exclusively, you've tried to treat me like a damn business associate who doesn't know what your naked ass looks like or how you fuck. So let me tell you something right now. You cannot treat me like a damn business associate because, in case you have forgotten, I know how you fuck . . . because, damn it . . . I'm the one who taught you. I haven't forgotten that fact and you can't either."

Sonje grabbed the bottle of wine and poured herself another glass all the way up to the rim, then took a piece of the broiled chicken out of the salad bowl and placed it in her mouth. I wasn't going to be outdone by her silliness, but I wanted to know why she didn't want to lend a helping hand.

"Come on, Sonje, it has to be bigger than that," I said sarcastically.

She stood up. "You know what? You're right . . . it's bigger than that and I just hope you can handle the truth, because let me tell you, I don't care about the brothers in the hood anymore because they have not only pissed me off, but many other sisters who day after day have been carrying them on their backs. So right now all I care about is Sonje and becoming even more powerful in my profession. And, Kahlil, my brother, that's exactly what I think your save-the-black-man ass should do too."

The wine must have been affecting her because she started to look at me like a child who needed to be scolded or one of her camera operators down at the station. I just let her talk.

"Ain't no hope for these sorry-ass Negroes . . . time has run out, Kahlil, and I can't waste my time trying to teach these confused, ignorant, and uninformed people. All they're looking for is some-one to give them something—a set-aside or welfare. I see lots of crime every day, Kahlil, and every time one of the crews from the station comes into this neighborhood to cover a story, whose sorry ass is laying in the street with a bullet in the head or coming out of the house with his hands cuffed behind his back and blaming it on the white man? Those are your brothers, Kahlil . . . the same ones who, day after day, are killing, stealing, raping, and robbing, not only embarrassing themselves, but me, too. It has gotten to the point where, when I see these sorry-ass black men do wrong, I go out of my way, just like everybody else in my business, to blow it out of proportion. And each time I hope my story will create havoc in the city, so when they are caught their nonproductive asses are thrown in jail to rot."

After her tirade Sonje got up, grabbed her bag, and placed it on her shoulder. I thought she was about to walk the hell up out of my house. I realized all of a sudden that Sonje had forgotten where she'd come from, and this pissed me off—especially with Demitrious still on my mind.

"Look, Sonje, I don't think you should forget that you are one of the beneficiaries of set-asides and affirmative action. So while you're standing there putting on your lipstick and tapping your two-hundred-dollar shoes on my carpet, like what I'm saying is bullshit, you should realize that someone helped you break into the business, or have you forgotten that? I know the brothers have done wrong in the past, but we're trying our best to turn this thing around now. If you don't like what you see, why don't you do something about it instead of tearing down what needs to be put back together again?" Then I took a deep breath and calmed down a little. "I really would appreciate if you'd help us get things back on track, Sonje. You could really be a big help."

Sonje puckered her lips and evened out her lipstick.

"Is that all?"

I just looked at her and shook my head. She turned around and left, without another word, as I listened to her quick steps echo in the hallway.

Two hours had passed since Sonje left and I was trippin' off her attitude. Cece could tell I was upset so she persuaded me to get into my garden tub to soak in a nice, hot bath for a while. As soon as I began to relax, she came into the bathroom and handed me the phone.

"Hello."

"Kahlil, it's Sonje. I'm sorry for what happened tonight. I guess I was just blowing off steam . . . you know, venting. Call me tomorrow and let me know what you want me to do for the Coalition, but I'm telling you, I'm about business and I don't want to waste my time."

I knew she had compassion somewhere in her heart, I thought.

"Okay, Sonje, I'll do that," I said, smiling into the phone.

"And, Kahlil, one more thing. Was that Cece who answered the phone?"

"Yes."

"Well, do me a favor: Tell your little girlfriend she doesn't know me."

Then all I heard was dial tone.

All I Have to Say

What? Was today classified as "Jump on Leandra's Ass Day"? Somebody needed to let me know because I didn't see it in bold print on the calendar this morning. Kahlil, Toni, Kim, Pam, Michelle, and Mama. The whole damn family was at the house. I couldn't believe they all surrounded me in the den, sat me down, and told me they were all tired of my shit. What the hell is going on, I thought. How dare they call a meeting to discuss me and the way I live my life.

Kahlil spoke first as usual to make sure everyone knew he was the man in the family since Daddy passed away. I gave my little brother his props and I listened to him. "Leandra, I'm not too much concerned with you anymore," he said. "My main concern is Sid and how you've brought him up and what he's going to do with the rest of his life. I think you know that a young black male is lucky just to have the opportunity to do anything by the time he's turned eighteen. Some of the things you've told him have been absolutely foolish and I think you're leading him in the wrong direction. Soon Sid is going to be eighteen and, God willing, he'll have a chance to do something with his life. I think it's time you tell him who his father is because he asked me just the other—" Then Pam and her young ass cut him off. "That's right, Leandra, Sid's going to turn out to be just like you, if you don't watch it. How can you make him take a job at the Big Burger, when you don't work yourself? You are a trip, a real trip, and you need to check yourself." Everybody just jumped right on in, too. They didn't even give me a chance to say a word. I wanted to tell them what was wrong with me. It would have been as good a time as any, but I swore myself to secrecy. Plus I don't want the aggravation of having to put up with them approaching me any differently than they do now. Even Michelle surprised me when I tried to open my mouth. "Just shut up and listen, Leandra. You've said too much with all of your damn empty promises. Nobody wants to say this but hell, I will. I blame you for Daddy getting sick because you put too much on his mind. And what gets me, you know he didn't appreciate you living off him like you did and you still have the audacity to walk around here running your mouth, like you're all that matters in this family. So just this once you're going to shut up and listen to us." Now she was trippin'. With my mind as burdened as it is, it was still all I could do to try not to laugh and to act like I was listening, because I thought Michelle and I were cool. I couldn't believe this was the same sister who always stood up for me—even back in our school days we faced problems together.

I didn't have any energy to deal with this. What little I did have was taken from me in the morning as I sat on the edge of my bed, shaking and trying my best to stop from shouting out loud from the feelings my medication had running through my body. I was in no mood for their shit. I wanted to scream until they all just shut up, but I didn't have enough air. I even thought about turning my back on them, but they were sitting all around me. It was just too many people for me to tell them to go to hell. The only thing I could do was take it. I don't know why everyone was so damn concerned all of a sudden. I love Sid, he's my baby and I want the best for him. When I was a child no one told me what to do, and here I am a grown woman with my own child, my own problems, and all of a sudden everybody has something to say about how I should raise him.

I had to tone everyone down, so I made sure I told them that God knew I had done my best to teach Sidney the best way I could. I knew that would get them off my back a little. In my family I've learned that when it comes to God no one wants to dispute your reasoning. If you say He knows and you have talked to Him about your problems that's good enough, and once again it worked like a charm. The decision that I made to raise Sidney on my own was my choice, something I promised myself I would do, no matter what. At least I've kept that promise. He's not that bad. I just wish I'd made him study a little harder instead of trying to finish school my damn self, but I'm smart. That's why they skipped me back in junior high school. When I first found out I was pregnant I didn't want anyone to know about it because I knew that I had really messed up, but I was having my baby, there was no doubt about that decision. I could have married the father, Waydis. He wanted to marry me as soon as he found out that I was pregnant. It was hard as hell not running off with him, but I was not going to put myself through that. He was going into the army and I can't stand that type of lifestyle—man never there and always on someone else's damn time schedule. I wasn't having it for me or Sid.

"So, Leandra, how in the hell do you get your nails and hair done almost every week?" Kim asked.

I didn't say a word but I wanted to. I really wanted to say, Ms. Thang here's the answer to your question if you must know. Waydis has been good to Sid all these years and has kept his promise by sending me money for him. Sure I've been using part of it for me but it's not like I don't need it and Sid gets what he needs. If I told them that Sid's daddy is a well-known businessman and has been sending money for him all these years, I know Sid would leave me and Mama would probably kick me out. And with all the shit I have to deal with what does it matter if I get my hair or nails done. I deserve some happiness. They have to understand that I did not ask to be given everything I ever wanted when I was growing up. Mom and Dad have always made it seem like just because I am their first born I have some mystical power that no one else has. For years I tried to live up to those standards, but I never asked for pressure like that. I even started putting more pressure on myself after I let everyone down by not graduating from college, getting pregnant, and staying with Mom and Dad all these years. I realized that I have hurt myself, but they will never hear me say it because I won't give anyone a chance to tell me I told you so. I wonder if they ever sit down and think about what it feels like to have everyone in the house wanting you to be the first to do something. Well it hurts—and I don't like the feeling so I just try not to think about it but it's no use . . . it's not going away, and I don't think it ever will. Which reminds me—I have to tell my doctor that this damn lithium is not making it. After all these years there has to be a different drug that doesn't affect my body like this. Even though I'm still not telling them, I have accepted that I have manic-depressive illness, but I don't accept that I have to take this damn medication the rest of my life. I don't like the way it's been making me feel, and I am tired of putting this shit in my system every day. I'll ask him to cut down on the dosage or switch my medication—just do something because my body can't take it. It's been almost fifteen years since I had my first horrible mood swing and with all the people in the world, it had to be with Daddy. I know I hurt him because things only got worse between us after that. He really didn't try to talk to me again after all the things I said to him and I didn't even mean one word of it. I loved him with all my heart. My condition just took over and I went berserk. For me to tell Daddy he was never a father to me and had never done anything for me broke his heart. I never got over the things I said to him, and I know for sure he didn't either. It was just one big mess. Not to mention trying to keep Waydis away from Sid. If Waydis had found out about my condition years ago, I know he would have tried to take Sid from me. That's another reason I had to keep this to myself. I'm just glad that I had Waydis sign the papers that gave me complete custody before I knew what was wrong with me. I would have been up the creek. I'm sure he regrets ever signing the document that requires him to send Sid's child support to an account. That has been the reason he doesn't know where we live. I think Seattle was the last place I told him we were living.

"Leandra, you need to move out to see how it feels to be on your own. Then you will appreciate Mama more," Kim said.

I've always wanted to move out from underneath Mama's house and have a happy family, just like I was programmed to think was going to happen, by all those stupid-ass television shows I watched growing up. You know, having two or three kids, a big house, and a white picket fence. But who in the hell wants to put up with my moody, intolerant personality—I don't even want to. I've tried for years to find me a good man that will take me as I am. Even told the last one everything about me and he left before I could finish telling him my entire situation. Sure, there are some men who play like they're interested in me, as well as my child, but that shit is a ploy. They'd charm Sid when he was too young to know better, then when they got me in the bed for three or four months, they would make up some reason why things couldn't continue to move forward. So I've come to the conclusion that none of those fools are good enough to waste time on.

Mama was the icing on the cake, though. She was trying to act like she was so mad at me she couldn't talk. If I didn't know any better I would have thought she was manic-depressive, too. I could have given her rent money and even moved out if I wanted to, but now it's just too late. Sid's money will stop coming when he's eighteen, and I'm not going anywhere now—my medication is just too expensive. Everyone else is giving her enough money already. I know Kahlil set Mama up on a savings plan and had an insurance policy on Daddy because when I went into her dresser drawer to look for money I saw the policy. With all that income she doesn't need the extra money I was going to give her. She is just putting all that money in the bank anyway. I have to give Mama credit, she really did fool the rest of them. She knows I'm not going anywhere. I'm her little girl, her first born, and always will be. I think she really wants me to stay here anyhow. After the so-called family meeting only me and Mama were left in the room.

"Mama, do you still plan on leaving me the house if anything ever happens to you?" I asked her.

She didn't answer, but I knew she planned to. When it happens, I'm kicking everybody's ass right up out of here, too. They can find someplace else to live. I thought about it long and hard. Sid is taking his ass to work at Big Burger, and he's going to learn how to take care of family. That's all I have to say.

My Girl

$$\diamondsuit$$

Cece stood by the window waiting for Kelly to pull up into the driveway so they could go to the Lions football game. She really didn't want to go, but she'd met all Kelly's other men and Kelly hadn't stopped talking about her new sugar daddy since she met him. The tickets were free and this gave Cece the chance to see for herself why Lee was so impressive. So why not go, she thought.

"Now I know what took you so long getting here," Cece said as she climbed into Deric's Land Rover. "Girl, how in the hell did you convince Deric to let you drive this to the game? You said he hasn't let it out of his sight since he got it."

"I had planned on taking my car, but when Deric started talking about his Big Brother outing today I convinced him that his bubble-gum chewing, sticky finger, big-headed little friend was not going to do anything but mess up these plush leather seats. Then I told him he should let me drive it, since I'll be driving it whenever I please when we get married."

"Kelly, why do you do that?"

"Do what?"

"You know what I'm talking about. Why do you let him believe that you two are getting married when you know good and well you have no intentions whatsoever of becoming that man's wife? I'm telling you, the best thing for you to do is tell him that you want to see other people right now, and marriage is out the question."

"Cece, I can't do that. Deric is ready to settle down and he is not hearing it. If I tell him some mess like that he will just want to drop this whole thing."

"Well, I think you need to be truthful with him. Just like me and Kahlil were with each other."

"What are you talking about?"

"I'm just saying we have been there before, and the truth is the best policy. You know Deric wants to talk to me about you, right?" Cece said.

"Yes, he told me. Did he say about what?"

"No."

"Well, do me a favor when he does. If he asks you if I'm messing around, just tell him no and mention to him that I would never do such a thing. Also say to him that I am so proud of him for going to the Million Man March—no matter what I said about it years ago." Cece looked at Kelly like she was crazy. "But if he tells you that he's planning some type of surprise for my birthday next month, tell him that he should get my gift a week before, so I can see if I like it or not. That will give me enough time to take it back if it's cheesy." Cece gave Kelly a look of amazement.

"Kelly, you're clueless. I really don't think that's right. If he asks me anything like that, I'm not going there, because that makes me as bad as you and I am not playing Deric like that."

Cece could tell this made Kelly mad but she didn't care. Deric had changed his entire life around to conform with whatever Kelly wanted. When they first met he didn't make enough money for her, even though he was bringing in pretty good money working as the sales manager at a Lexus dealership. But Kelly kept on his case and broke his spirit, no matter what type of money he made. She convinced Deric that he could do better than working as a car salesman. Then when he quit his job to find one a little more stable, what did she do? She called him a fool and didn't support his decision while he searched for something else. Deric decided to get his real estate license and worked like hell because he wanted her back. After finishing up the course work and obtaining his license he had to establish a reputation in the market before he could make any money, but Deric kept a smile on his face because of his love for Kelly.

Kelly turned up the music and tried to play Cece off.

"What's wrong with you now? Come on, Kelly, don't even act like that."

Kelly turned the music down and negotiated a left-hand turn.

"You know, Cece, ever since Kahlil put that ring on your finger, you've been acting like marriage is something sacred or something, like it's going to last forever. Girl, a lot of people get married for different reasons and many more reasons than just love. I'm no different than anybody else. Tell me this: How many people do you know who have gotten married in the last two or three years that are still married?"

"Well, there's Lisa."

"Girl, you know she left that man six months after they got married. He's seeing Tassha now."

"When did this happen?"

"Six months after they got married, girl. He'd been sleeping with Tassha for three months before he left Lisa."

"That's messed up. I didn't know that."

"Don't worry about it. She's okay. She moved in with her boss at the insurance company the very next day after she found out and couldn't be happier. Girl, we have been to more weddings in the last six or seven years than I care to remember and not one couple is still married. You want to know why?"

"Why, Kelly?" Cece said, getting annoyed with Kelly's mouth.

"Because they got married for the wrong damn reason. Love. Cece, you better recognize Tina Turner didn't make that song, 'What's Love Got to Do with It,' back in the eighties for nothing. She was a prophet."

Cece cracked her window and snickered. "Kelly, how do you know so much about marriage?"

"When I was growing up I saw marriage when it worked and when it didn't. I know firsthand how it affects people. When everything is going well, then there are no problems whatsoever. Everyone is happy and it's really a good time. You talk, have dinner together, kiss in the morning before you go to work. Call each other on the phone, three, maybe four times a day. But you can rest assured, my sister, that those times don't always last. Sooner or later all you hear is screaming, fussing, and fighting and when it quiets down, it's only because everyone is so fed up with arguing that they just shut the fuck up. Then the marriage ends in divorce."

"Kelly, all marriages don't end like that."

"You're right. Some backwards-ass people get back together after the divorce because of some stupid-ass commitment they make to God that they'll stay together forever. Then, just like it happened the very first time, every little thing is fine, but they never seem to trust each other again and the next thing you know . . . bam! They start all over with the same old shit and decide to break up again, affecting everyone who may be involved. And, child, please, don't let there be any children in the middle of the situation because then there's going to be hell to pay."

"You're talking like you have firsthand knowledge."

"I do." Cece pushed her shoulders back into the seat and thought there was something Kelly had never told her before. "Don't look at me like that," Kelly said. "You know I have never been married but I watched my mother and father go at it until they got divorced and look at them now. They're miserable by themselves, and to this day they get together for maintenance. Yuck—imagine that."

"Girl, you are silly."

"That's not all. Don't forget how, after you get into a marriage and you think everything is going to be all right for the rest of your life, all of a sudden you're left by yourself. Women are left confused and alone all the time. Then you sit around blaming yourself because your husband left you for an eighteen-year-old skinny bitch who just got out of high school."

"Well, that's not going to happen with Kahlil and me."

"How do you know?"

"Because Kahlil is a committed man and he has priorities."

Kelly began to laugh. "Yeah, that's what you think, but I'm not going to say anything. You have blinders on now—just like they put on those horses at the racetrack so they can't see what's going on around them. Some fine-ass brotha is trying to tie your ass down and you like the idea of the whole thing but you have no idea. I'm not a freak or anything."

"You could have fooled me," Cece snickered.

"No, I'm serious, Cece. Think about it. You are never, ever, going to feel the touch of another man's body again and you have to make love to the same person for the rest of your life. Imagine that shit. The thought just turns me off. That's just like watching the same episode of *Hangin' with Mr. Cooper* over and over again."

"Not for me. Kahlil and I mix it up all the time. And if I start to imagine that, you're going to have to take me by his house before we go to this game, because my baby hits it right. . . . So you let Deric think you'll marry him just for the hell of it, Kelly?"

"No, I just might. But I can tell you this. If I do, it won't just be for love. It will be for some other reason, too, just like everyone else does."

"What do you mean?"

"I'm talking about when people get married for reasons like

loneliness, money, even sex. Those are the reasons why most sisters get married these days. Not just because of any love, Cece.
What matters to people today is that their wants and needs are
met, and if you find someone that fits your needs . . . do you really
need to be in love? But I can see it matters to you so you better
make sure what Kahlil's reasons are for getting married because
don't forget it wasn't that long ago he was sleeping with Ms. Chan-
nel Two. You better think about it. . . . Is he trying to be politically
correct for the Coalition and all those other big-time organizations he is connected to? Or is it because you're so sharp and you
can have all of those multiple orgasms you always talk about when
you are with him? Girl, you better think about it—better yet you
better find out."

This time Cece turned up the music because she didn't want to
hear any more. There wasn't a doubt in her mind that Kahlil
loved her.

Look, Daddy

"All right now, Kahlil. Open the door, because it's on baby, it's on," I heard Demitrious shout through my screen door.

"My brother, didn't anyone tell you this is O's birthday and not Christmas?" I said to him as I opened the door, bent down, and picked up at least four presents Demitrious had placed on my porch for his son's birthday party.

"Man, be serious. I just want to give the little man everything he deserves. I know you can understand that," Demitrious said, as he went back out to the car to get the rest of his gifts.

Demitrious was filled with joy. Mr. Robinson, the counselor at the Coalition, told him that he was going to allow him to see his son after only three straight weeks of counseling. He discovered that Demitrious's abuse of Octavious was something that was embedded in his mind, something he only thought about doing. Demitrious was so unstable at the time that he had convinced himself that he really was an abuser. Everything his father put him through during his childhood just took over his mind and was on its way to making him believe it was the natural thing to do. After Demitrious learned that what he was going through was a reaction to his own childhood and could be controlled, Mr. Robinson told Demitrious he should not waste another minute in setting up the reunion with his son. Robinson was sure that Demitrious would be able to lead a normal life with Octavious as long as he continued to seek counseling and talk about his own abused childhood.

"Kahlil, it looks good in here," Demitrious said, as he walked around the den looking at the decorations. I'd decorated the room with red and white streamers and red balloons. The cake, punch, and cookies that Cece made were spread out perfectly on the table, waiting for the kids.

"Brother, let me thank you right off the bat for letting me throw this party over here. I thought it would be good for Octavious to have his party someplace he was familiar with instead of having it over my place. I really appreciate it," he said.

"No, brother, thank you for making the right decision, for getting involved in your son's life. I am really proud of you. Are you ready to see him?" I put the presents in the corner of the room, then turned around and saw Demitrious looking down at the birthday cake.

"Hell yes, I'm ready to see him. What do you think about my new gear?" Demitrious said. "I thought this baggy jean outfit would just blow him and his little partners away. I hope his little partners think that his old man is dope."

"Demitrious, your son and his friends don't talk like that yet." Demitrious looked at me with a question mark on his face. "Brother, if you start talking like that around them, that's exactly what they are going to think you're selling."

"Are you sure?"

"Yes, man, I'm sure. You're stressing, sit on down."

Demitrious took a seat on the couch and I took a soda out of the small refrigerator behind my bar and handed it to him.

"I haven't seen you like this in a long time."

"Kahlil, to tell you the truth I don't know if I'm ready. I hope I can handle this. I know he remembers me, but I just hope that I haven't hurt him so much that he doesn't want me back in his life. That's why all I'm going to do is let him check me out today. Then I'll ease my way back into his life, nice and slow. I'm glad that he's just turning five and he's not seventeen or eighteen, when kids have already lived their whole life without a father and think they're not any good because they have not been around."

"Exactly. Just like my nephew, Sid. You still have a chance, my brother, so don't blow it."

"Don't worry, Kahlil. We're going to be inseparable, you hear me? . . . Inseparable."

"That's what I'm talking about. Just take your time, black man," I said to him.

"That's exactly what Mr. Robinson told me. That old man really knows the mind." He paused. "You know, Kahlil, I don't know if I would have been able to do this without the help of the Coalition. At first I was skeptical when you told me about the help that was down there, but Robinson is awesome. He's really made me feel good about myself. He let me tell him about my life—really open up. He helped me realize that when I thought about harming Octavious it was only a reaction to what happened to me when I was younger."

"Demitrious, I have to admit, when you told me that you abused Octavious, I thought you had really harmed him or something. Matter of fact you almost got beat down yourself. I guess with something like that, it's the first thing that comes to mind. Shit, you told me you'd hurt him."

"You're right and I don't blame you one bit. Robinson told me the same thing, until he asked me what I did to Octavious and I said nothing. He looked at me like I was crazy. Then I told him that I had been thinking about beating him for no reason. I really thought I'd do it. I thought so hard and long about hitting him I guess it really fucked with my mind, as though I really had been

125

beating him. Robinson was so elated that he made a joke out of it, trying to act like he was upset because he had to change my file all around. But I never did anything to my son. I was just scared of myself—I didn't want to do to him the same thing my father did to me. Man, I swear I hate my father for doing that shit to me."

"Well, you're getting help now and you're doing fine. What did Robinson say about you telling Dewayna?" I asked.

"He told me that was going to be the hardest part of my rehab and recommended that I spend supervised time with Octavious for a while, to draw strength from him so I can tell her my situation. I agreed with him," Demitrious said, gulping the last bit of soda down. "I don't think it's going to be difficult to tell her though, because Dewayna and I were always able to talk about our feelings and you know what kind of shit we've been through."

I pulled two CDs off my shelf as I tried to ease his mind.

"Look, I got all of the sounds that Octavious likes and I called Dewayna and she told me it was all right to get him Brandy and Immature. His little crew is going to be partying," I said to Demitrious. The doorbell rang and we both took a deep breath before walking to the front door.

When Kahlil turned around and looked at me like we were football players about to run down through the tunnel for the beginning of the game I felt a hell of a rush. All types of emotions were running through my mind. I was about to see my son and my wife after an entire year. I had my fingers crossed and hoped I wouldn't just pass the fuck out. He opened the door and the very first person to walk into the house was Dewayna. She looked like she hadn't missed me one day and came into the house and gave Kahlil a hug. Even though we had talked on the phone many times in the last three weeks before this, she walked up to me and we just stared at each other. *Finally,* we both thought. I extended my hand to her.

"Hello, Demitrious."

"How are you doing, Dewayna?" I said to her, as she stepped back into the hallway, waiting for the others to come in. Sonje, whom Kahlil had introduced to Dewayna at the Coalition, was with her and she walked in with more gifts in her arms. Kahlil looked really surprised to see her.

"Hello, Demitrious, nice to meet you," Sonje said to me as we shook hands.

As soon as I took my eyes off Sonje, I looked at the door again and saw my little man appear from Kahlil's arms. He walked straight up to me and looked at my face. We both stood looking at each other and I could feel my eyes filling up with water. I was surprised to see how much he looked like me. I felt like I had been taken back to my childhood and placed in front of a mirror. Words wouldn't come out of my mouth.

"Hi, Daddy," he said. I bent down, shook his little hand and then gave him a hug. Kahlil noticed that I was about to break down and patted me on the shoulder.

"Okay, everybody in the den, let's party!" he said as Octavious ran into the room. I noticed Dewayna wiping tears from her eyes.

Octavious had invited about twelve of his friends and they all shouted when they saw all of the presents that I had gotten for my son. Octavious fought his way through his friends to take a better look at all of his gifts. He looked at his mother's surprised face, then at me.

"Go ahead and open your gifts, son. Happy birthday," I said to him.

During the entire party, Octavious played me like a prizefighter. Every so often he would come and ask me a question about how a certain toy or gadget worked, but he never spent too much time

around me at any given moment. I expected he would be cautious
with me, so I was very much surprised when he asked me, in front
of everyone, if I wanted to come to his team's basketball game the
next weekend. Of course, I accepted with pride. My day had been
made—Octavious wanted me in his life after all.

Dewayna also seemed to enjoy herself and I could tell she was
relieved that this day had finally come. I was totally surprised
when I noticed her looking at me with her flirtatious smile. I've always been able to make her smile, and I began to think that
maybe she missed me more than Kahlil told me she had. I didn't
come to the party with any intentions of hitting on her, but her
glances gave a brother some hope. I wondered, as I looked at Dewayna's painted on black jeans, how nice it would be to lie in her
caramel arms and hear her moan the way only she could. We had
our differences, but one thing was for sure, we made each other
crazy when we made love. I knew where to touch her and she me.
Sonje and Kahlil began talking about Coalition matters, so I followed Dewayna into the kitchen. She poured herself something
to drink, then turned to look through the kitchen window, right
over the sink at Octavious. He was playing with his new football,
periodically stopping to talk to Nite, who was caged in his dog run
in the backyard.

"Well, I see Octavious is going to take after your family. Look at
the muscle on that boy," I said.

"Yep, he is getting so big, he looks just like you. Look at him
messing with that dog. He wants a rottweiler so bad, that's all he
talks about, but I'm so scared of those dogs. Look how big Nite is,"
Dewayna said.

We stood and looked out the window, without a word, just enjoying our son together, until Dewayna turned to me.

"Demitrious . . . I feel like a thousand pounds has been lifted
from my tired back. I can't even explain how good I feel. I've
been waiting for this moment for so very long. I don't know why

God made me go through what I did this past year. But it has made me stronger and a whole lot weaker at the same time. I have to tell you face to face, Demitrious, I can't raise him alone, all by myself, anymore. You know what I mean?"

"I do, Dewayna," I said, then looked down into her eyes. "And I'm sorry that I made you go through this all by yourself, but my word is my bond. I will never leave him without a father again." And I kissed her on the cheek as we both smiled.

"Where did he go!" Dewayna looked for Octavious in the back-yard as I felt someone pull on my jeans.

"Daddy, come on outside I want to show you something," Octavious said, with a wide grin on his face.

"Excuse me, Dewayna. My son wants to show me something," I said with pride.

"Go right ahead," she said, trying to keep her eyes from watering. Octavious took my hand and we ran into the backyard and up to the fence where Nite was.

"Now, let's not get too close, Octavious," I said. He stopped and bent his little legs like he was getting ready to sit on the toilet and took his little finger and pointed underneath Nite as the dog had his backside toward us while he drank water from his bowl.

"Look, Daddy!" he said with his little voice. "Look at those nuts on Nite. Why his nuts so big, Daddy?" Octavious began to shake his head back and forth. "I don't want no dog like that now. His nuts too big."

He left me speechless.

The Dome

"Thank you ladies, you can park at the end of this row," the guard told Kelly and Cece as he took their parking pass and looked at them like he was trying to figure out which one of the players they were sleeping with.

"Girl, look at all these Mercedeses and BMWs down here. Does everyone on the team have one?" Cece asked.

"Just about. Lee said that he is signing his new contract as soon as the season was over and he's getting him another Benz. Now, don't forget what name to use if anyone asks in conversation or anything who you're here to see play. His name is Scooter, number forty-one, and if you're asked how you know him, just say you went to school with him at South Carolina State."

"Kelly, who the hell is Scooter anyway?"

"Lee's best friend on the team. He said he won't mind us using his name if someone tries to get all up in our business."

Cece pointed at Kelly. "You mean your business."

"Whatever. Let's go."

Kelly and Cece walked the short distance to the elevator, which took them up to the very top portion of the Dome. They found the suite that was reserved for family and friends of the players and stood in the door, looking at the festive blue-and-gray-colored room. The aroma of the buffet filled up the entire suite.

"Why is everybody staring at us?" Cece asked, as she made sure that nothing was hanging out of her shirt that wasn't supposed to be.

"Relax. They just want to know who we are because we're looking so good. More than likely they're wondering if the men that invited us here are the same ones they've come to see play."

Kelly loved this type of shit. She'd always gotten off on the fact that she looked good and women felt threatened by her when she entered a room. Having Cece by her side only made matters worse, because the divas were certainly working it. Kelly pointed to the table with her name on it and they walked over to take their seats.

"Look, Cece, he left me some roses! Isn't this nice? Let's see what the card says. 'Hope you have a nice time, I'll see you later.' See, girl, this is what I'm talking about. Getting pampered and paid. If he keeps this up, I just might give him some before the end of the season."

Cece shook her head and sat down. She didn't seem to be affected by the flowers—Kelly could tell by the look on her face.

"Now don't start with me, Cece. We came here to have a nice time, so let's do this."

"Yes, let's," Cece said, as she remembered how crazy Kelly had been acting all week at work. She didn't dare spoil her moment, because she wanted her to get this shit all out of her system and leave it right here in the Dome. Kelly had made herself a nuisance at work, waiting for this game. Cece had lost track of how many times she'd come up to the twelfth floor where Cece worked and plopped herself up in her office, like she was obsessed. Kelly would stay and talk twenty to thirty minutes, about everything that she and Lee had been doing, not concerned one bit about work. Cece just didn't understand why Kelly couldn't figure out the reason she hadn't received her promotion to the next job level yet.

Kelly thought they were going to promote her just because she was the only person who could troubleshoot the satellite telecommunications system in her department. If she doesn't watch it, she's going to find herself back down on the first floor, in the operator department, with a headset connected to the side of her head, answering calls and patching them through to the automated information line. That was where Kelly and Cece both started off when they decided not to return to school. Kelly hadn't taken any of Cece's advice on how to move up in corporate America. Cece had made it to manager of her own section and was in line for another promotion as soon as her boss retired. Cece constantly told Kelly that she couldn't continue to act like she was at home when she was at work. Kelly just couldn't keep her mouth shut. She didn't think they could put two and two together for some stupid reason and when she told everyone in the elevator her views on men it just blew Cece's mind. She did it unintentionally, but she should have known better. The elevator must have stopped on every floor like it was a local train or something. Kelly was so involved with the conversation that she didn't even notice that out of the twelve or so people, the only two women in the elevator at the time were her and Cece. That didn't seem to bother Kelly, but it bothered Cece because you are labeled by the company you keep at work. Kelly was Cece's best friend so she tried to deal with it, but in the company Kelly was labeled as talkative and loud. Kelly was trying to talk in her so-called Morse code, but that wasn't working very well at all. She was trying to explain to Cece that her very wealthy man called her five times at work to make sure she was still coming to see him play. That was enough for anybody to figure out she was messing around on Deric because everyone knew that, in her opinion, Deric was broke and that he didn't play a damn thing. Cece had to step in and shut her up when she started talking about how easy it was to cheat on men. She'd noticed that the man responsible for promoting Kelly to the next position was standing right in front of them along with Kelly's immediate supervisor listening to all the stupid shit she was saying. Kelly had her back to them and didn't notice them on the elevator so she just kept running her mouth when her black ass should have been at her desk working.

"What do you want to drink?" Kelly said in a tone that sounded like she dared someone to tell her she couldn't have what she wanted. "*Scooter* said they'll treat us like queens up in here and we can have whatever we want." Kelly signaled for a waiter and ordered two white zinfandels.

"I can't believe this view. This is beautiful. I can see everything going on from here. Look at those players down there. They don't look that big on television. What number is your boy?" Cece said.

Kelly moved closer to Cece. "I told you, number forty-one. Just wait until you hear his name called. I don't know who is trying to listen to us the way these hoochies are looking over here at us, and I promised Lee I would keep this on the down-low."

"You know what I can't understand?" Cece said.

"What's that?"

"I don't understand why there are so many brothers on the field and so many white women up here in the suite. If I didn't know any better I'd have thought I was at a hockey game."

"Oh, girl, you didn't know. I got to get you out more. That's what most of our black men do when they make some money. They go after the white girls, the forbidden fruit, just because they can, and these bitches up in here let them do anything they want to them as long as they get paid for it."

"Almost like you, huh?" Cece said, laughing.

"Shit, nothing like me. I, for one, ain't going for the freaky shit they pull on these white girls. Scooter told me all about it. Most of the women here are the players' wives anyway. Look at all the big-ass rocks on their fingers. Like I told you in the car, people get married for different reasons. These women want money and the brothers want to be freaked. They want to feel like they're part of a society that they could never be part of if they weren't football players. That's the trade-off. Then, after the brothers finish playing ball, these little tramps start their program all over again and the brothers get furious when they begin to give their shit up and bam! What do you have?"

"What?" Cece asked.

"That's right, my sista, another O. J. Simpson case on your ass. Let's get something to eat."

I told Kelly to go ahead and fix her plate, while I waited on the drinks and watched our things. All of a sudden my mind began to think about Kelly's situation and it was as if I was looking into a window without any sound. I began to scan the room and wonder to myself if other ladies in the suite were Lee's guest besides my girl. I hadn't realized how well-known Lee is until Kelly started bringing in all of his newspaper clippings and calling me day or night if one of his commercials was on. I guess he would be all right for Kelly if he wasn't married, but that doesn't bother Kelly or Lee. She probably likes it better this way because she doesn't have to lie to Lee constantly like she does with Deric. She doesn't have to hide the fact that all she wants from Lee is what he can buy her and all he wants from Kelly is sex. I have my doubts that Kelly isn't already giving him some, but until she tells me she has, I guess I'll just continue to believe her. I was beginning to worry though. I've known Kelly a long time, and as many crazy and stupid-ass things she had done in her life, she's never messed around with a married man while talking to another man about marriage. All of a sudden I was taken away from my thoughts.

"Is this seat taken?" A very low, husky voice said. I looked up and saw a gorgeous black man pointing to one of the four chairs that surrounded our table. Kelly was across the room taking her sweet time at the buffet table, so I shook my head no.

"Hi, my name is Scooter Thomas," he said, as he extended his hand out to me and sat down. "And your name is?"

I almost told him my name was "Confused As Hell" because when Kelly mentioned to me the name Scooter I thought his name was already odd enough. I knew that there were not two brothers in Detroit by the name of Scooter. It couldn't be our Scooter anyway, I thought because he was on the field, warming up, getting ready to play.

"Hi, my name is Cece." I extended my hand to greet him and felt him shake it with a you-are-fly-as-hell touch instead of an ordinary hello. I had to pull away from him.

"Do you come to the games often?" he asked.

"No, this is my first one." He didn't shut up like I wished he would, and Kelly was still searching at the buffet.

"So, who are you here to see play?"

I quickly pointed over to Kelly at the buffet table. "Oh, I'm just here with a friend." I looked at Kelly again, trying to get her attention. Girl get your ass back here and I mean now! My eyes were saying to her.

Kelly looked over at the table.

Now who in the hell had Cece sat down at our table already? I knew that girl wasn't ready for no damn marriage, talking all that love shit. How can you be thinking about marriage and pull a man that fine so quick, I thought to myself as I looked at her from the buffet. I mean this brother was good-looking, so I decided to take my time and circle around the buffet table one more time to give girlfriend a little more time to break the ice. I wondered who he was and looked at them very discreetly as I pretended to be all up in the potato salad. He looked like a player himself, but I knew that he wasn't because he would be down on the field. He probably had a brother or something that played and all I started thinking about was how I was going to meet his brother.

"See, that's the look, girlfriend," I heard a wavy-haired light-skinned lady say from across the buffet table, pointing at me.

"I really like your outfit and shoes. I can tell you get your clothes from New York, girl, because I just came from there and I'm telling you. I can spot New York fashion anywhere, on anybody."

"Why, thank you," I said to her with a fake-ass smile planted on my face. I knew I was looking good and didn't need anybody to tell me. "But I didn't get my outfit from New York," I told her.

She looked at me, puzzled.

"You didn't?" she said with her aggravating, whining voice.

"No. There's a store at the Renaissance Center that has a lot of the fashions that come out of New York City. They have all the latest clothes and shoes, and reasonable, too," I told her, sounding like a commercial.

"Oh, girl, you are going to have to give me the address. I'm looking for a store like that."

"I think I have a card in my purse. If you like, I'll give it to you. I'm sitting right over there." I pointed to our table and caught Cece's eye.

"I'll be sure to do that. Thank you," she said.

I usually don't tell people where I get my clothes from because I never like to see people with the same clothes on that I have. That shit really pisses me off and it's why I never, ever, ever go shopping at any of the national chain stores because when you go out you can bet your last dollar someone else has your outfit on. But she had a little style herself, so I wanted to help a sista out. I had done my good deed for the rest of the month. I took my plate back over to the table and wondered why Cece kept winking her eye at me. She probably wanted me to sit someplace else, but the hell with that. I wanted to know who this brother was at our table, because he was sho'nuff fine.

I sat my plate down and smiled. The brother smiled back and then stood up.

"Hi, I'm Scooter." I shook his hand and quickly looked at Cece.

"He got hurt in the pregame warm-up and can't play today," Cece said. She always has my back.

Before I could even get comfortable in my chair and get my mind straight from the surprise that he was Scooter, he turned to me with a big-ass grin. I quickly grabbed my drink and hoped that it would give me a buzz before I had to play this brother, but you know it didn't hit me fast enough.

"Cece tells me she's here with you."

I nodded yes as I drank.

"So which one of my teammates are you here to see play?" he asked, still smiling.

"You," I quickly said back to him. What was he going to do, I wondered. Lee told me to use his name, so I did. Scooter looked very surprised. He stared at Cece, who had a blank look on her face and raised eyebrows, then he looked at me and began to shake his finger, realizing what was going on and began to laugh.

"Oh, okay, now I know what's going on. How are you doing?"

We all began to laugh and the game started. We had to listen to his ass tell us what happened on each play of the game. Shit, he was making the whole damn game boring. I didn't care about the analysis of the game. I guess he really missed being on the field, but if I wanted to listen to that shit I would have watched it on television.

Then the lady to whom I promised the boutique address came over to our table and rescued us. I noticed her first as she walked up and stood behind Scooter, but before I could speak the entire

Dome broke out in a tremendous roar of excitement. I looked down on the field and noticed Lee had intercepted a pass. Everyone was in a frenzy. They were standing up, screaming and cheering, as he did some freaky-ass dance in the end zone.

"That's right, baby, work it!" the lady standing behind Scooter shouted and Cece and I immediately looked at each other. The lady put her hands on Scooter's shoulders and squeezed those wide things, then bent down and kissed him on the cheek.

"Did you see my baby? . . . I said, did you see my baby! That's his fourth interception this year," she shouted. Scooter smiled at her, got up and gave her a hug.

"Hi, Linda, how are you doing?" Scooter asked.

As she shook her head in exhaustion and fanned herself, I figured out who she was right away. Cece looked at me totally surprised. I thought to myself that she didn't have to worry about being tired because tonight I was going to be with her man and she could get all the rest she needed.

"I'm doing okay, Scooter. I'll be doing a whole lot better when I go to this boutique this sister was telling me about in the mall." She pointed at me. Cece was really confused now, and so was Scooter. "Look at her, she is working those clothes, isn't she sharp. What's your name? I didn't get it. I'm Linda," she said, pointing to herself, hitting her thick titties, then reaching over the table to shake my hand. I couldn't help but notice her wedding ring waving hello to me as she rested her hand on Scooter's shoulder.

"Nice to meet you. My name is Kelly and this is my friend, Cece."

"Hello," Cece said.

"Girl, you must shop at the same spot, because what you have on is sharp, too."

Cece started smiling, while Scooter looked as confused as I had been when I first met his ass.

"Here's the address to the shop, the number and everything is right on the card. Let me put my number on it, too, just in case you need someone to go shopping with. I love to shop," I told Linda.

Scooter took a drink of his vegetable juice and tried to act like he wasn't paying any attention to our conversation. I handed her the card.

"That would be great. How about all of us going together?" She looked at me and Cece and smiled. "I'll call you and we'll set something up. Who did you say you were here to see again?" Cece and I both quickly pointed to Scooter, who hadn't put down his drink yet.

"Oh, Scooter, you never quit, do you?" Linda asked.

Scooter smiled at her, playing a role that Spike would have been proud to direct.

"You know I have a thing for pretty women."

Linda smiled and rubbed Scooter's broad shoulders again. "I know you do, Scooter, I know you do."

The Lions won by twenty-one points.

Long Time Coming

What a beautiful ending to a perfect day. Octavious was fast asleep now and I stayed with him in his room laying beside him until I was sure he wouldn't wake. He was very excited to see his father at his birthday party, and I was relieved that he had a nice day. Plus I didn't have to hear him ask me anymore about rottweilers. All the way home he asked me if I'd seen his father, and if I noticed how cool he was. By the time we got home he was practically asleep.

I was tired myself from all of the excitement, and still buzzing from the mental high of seeing my son with his father, who was still looking good. I climbed into my bed and lay still for a long time with my eyes open just looking into the darkness. I felt a strong but gentle hand began to caress my breasts, as though it had not touched something so soft, so nice, in quite a while. It felt good to me—even better than I had been imagining all day. I began to tremble as both hands lightly touched my stomach, making their way down to my legs. I felt moist, tender kisses on the insides of my thighs while fingertips grazed my nipples. I hadn't been touched that way, at least by another, since Demitrious left me. It felt exactly as I remembered. I lay back and began to relax, enjoying the sensations that were running through my body. I began to shiver and shudder uncontrollably, and I became embarrassingly conscious of the wetness between my legs while my partner shopped downtown. I tried to move away from the hands that were making my body release orgasms and began to laugh because I couldn't take anymore of the awesome sensations running through my body. I sat up and wiggled my body away. Then I pulled the covers down to look at the lips that had me dancing with joy.

"I've never had that done before," I gasped.

A finger was gently placed on my lips as if to silence me. "Of course you have. Just not by a woman," Sonje said as she arose from between my legs.

I couldn't stop smiling from the embarrassment and the fact that Sonje had ended up in my bed. Even more, I couldn't believe I let Sonje touch me in the same manner as I would a man or how pleasurable it turned out to be. I looked at Sonje and I had to admit I was confused. I knew she could tell I was baffled at what had just taken place, but she seemed to be unaffected by the whole situation.

"Look, I'm going to get up and let you think about what just happened because I can see in your face that you don't know what the hell is happening right now. I've been there, too," she said. Then she slowly pulled the covers away from her body and placed one foot on the floor at a time.

Damn it, I said silently to myself, as I wanted to kick my own ass. Sonje caught me looking at her slender, tight frame and still-hard nipples.

"Maybe next time I'll teach you how to do me," she said smiling.

That was the last thought on my mind. All through our act I felt as though it was something special being done to me, for me. At least, that's what she'd been hinting to me on the phone and in our conversations since I'd met her. She never once mentioned that she was going to want me to reciprocate and I definitely wasn't planning on it. Just like a man, I thought: I'll do you then you do me.

Sonje bent down and grabbed her panties. She still seemed to be very turned on. Confidently and almost arrogantly she placed one leg on top of the bed, exposing herself to me. Unsure of what she was planning, I looked at her and sat motionless.

"Let me have your hand," Sonje demanded.

Still holding her panties in one hand she reached out to me with the other and grabbed my hand, guiding it toward her wetness. "Just follow my lead, okay?"

I didn't say a word. She took my shaking hand and molded it into what seemed like a cup, then she placed it on herself and stared deep into my shocked face. As she moved my hand up and down between her spread legs, she let go a muffled scream of pleasure, and continued to rub my hand over her hot spot until her sensations subsided.

I stared in total amazement. For the first time, I had touched another woman in the same fashion as I had touched myself for the last year. In a strange way I'd enjoyed Sonje exploding on my hand. Sonje quickly bent down and kissed me on the cheek, then disappeared into my bathroom. As I lay silent, wondering how in the hell did I let this happen and wondering if I should make sure it never happens again, Sonje came out from the bathroom, winked at me, waved good-bye, and carefully walked out without waking up Octavious.

I'm Down

◇

Sid, when you finish stacking those boxes, go out into the dining room area and mop up the floor. And hurry up, the lunchtime rush will be in here any minute, along with that fuckin' delivery truck. We don't have enough people in here today to unload the truck and take care of inside business, so you're going to have to do both jobs as best you can," Sid's manager said.

"Fuck you," Sid muttered under his breath, as he walked into the dining room area with the mop in his hand. Sid was tired. Last night he closed the place up at one in the morning and the day before Sid worked twelve hours with only one fifteen-minute break.

It had been almost two months and three measly paychecks since Sid started working at Big Burger. He'd done everything from filling up the greasy racks with French fries to cleaning the bathrooms and sweeping up used rubbers outside in the parking lot. While he was half-ass mopping the dining area, Sid glanced out the window and saw Difante and Rashaad getting out of Rashaad's smoking Lexus coupe. They were both dressed to the T as usual, and to Sid it seemed like they were on top of the world. They walked through the door, stopped, and looked around.

Rashaad went to the counter while Difante walked back into the dining area where he saw Sid trying to find a place to hide the mop in his hand.

"What's up Sid? I heard you were working up here, but I didn't believe it," Difante said, looking around for a place to sit in the empty dining area. "Come on over and check a brutha out."

Sid walked over to the table. "What up playa? What are you two doing in here? About to rob the place or what?" He reached down and greeted Difante as they both began to laugh.

"No, man, we just came by to check you out. We haven't seen you in a while and we just wanted to make sure you were all right."

"Yeah, I'm cool. I just thought I'd stay on the down-low for a while until things cool off for a minute."

"Oh, you talking about the night we showed you how we get paid? Brother, that's history. Rashaad told me that's the reason you hadn't been around. That boy knows you like a book." Rashaad walked over from the counter with a tray of food and put it down on the table next to Difante. After embracing Sid he looked him up and down.

"So, you straight or what? How you like this job, are you making out?"

"It's all right. I'm able to help Moms out, so it ain't all bad." Sid glanced out the window again at Rashaad's car. It tore him up that Rashaad had that car. He didn't even want anything that expensive. All he wanted to get was something that looked relatively nice and got him back and forth to wherever he wanted to go. Sid had only saved $175 toward his car since his mother said she needed $160 out of the $260 he brought home every two weeks. As he looked at Rashaad's car he realized he wouldn't have a car for years at the rate he was going.

"Yo man, you see my new tires on that bitch? They are hittin' aren't they?"

"Yeah, they're tight," Sid said.

"Ahh, Sid, you should hear my system. You'd think you were in the recording studio or something. Don't it get up, Difante?"

"Yeah, man, it's the bomb and, Sid, you can have the same kind of shit if you want."

"Why do you say that?"

"I say it because the Get Paid Crew needs one more member, and I've decided that you're the man I want to step with. Besides Rashaad you're the only other brother I trust in the world."

Sid looked at Difante and Rashaad. They were dead serious.

"Look, Sid. We're finally going to start the restaurant Rashaad's been talking about in the hood. We already have eighty percent of the money we need, my uncle is going to get the liquor license for us, and all we need to do is a couple more business transactions. You know the old shoe store next door to Blue's? Well, that's the spot. We're going to start the second chapter of the GPC right there, brother, and get paid."

"Second chapter? What do you mean?" Sid said.

"This shit that we are doing is getting old to us and we've been into it for too long," Difante said. "After we have the restaurant, I know hundreds of wannabes who would love to have a piece of this vibe. And we are going to use the GPC to teach others how and run this mother right out of the restaurant. We're talking Mafia-style shit, like they do in New York," Difante said, smiling.

"So, what you saying? You and Rashaad ain't going to be jacking no more?"

"That's right, baby. We are going to be businessmen and leave that shit for somebody else to do."

"Just like here, Sid," Rashaad explained. "I bet you've never seen the man that owns this place, have you?"

"H—ell no," Sid said.

"That's exactly how we're going to be—undercover, low-key, and untouchable."

Sid's manager came out of the back of the restaurant. "Sid, are you finished out there yet? Come on in the back and help out!"

"All right, in a minute," Sid yelled back to him. Difante and Rashaad looked at him waiting for an answer. "I don't know, man, I got to think about this."

"Come on, Sid, don't go getting soft on us now. Ever since you took the heat for me when we got stopped with that piece in the car, I knew you were down. We need you, man, you're family. Didn't I give you your props when I gave you that stereo equipment? I know you don't want to work here for the rest of your life mopping up this fuckin' floor." Difante took an envelope out of his pocket and gave it to Sid.

"What's this?"

"It's a third of the money we lifted off that old white dude, you remember, and a little something extra to get you some new gear. Brother, we ain't out to do one another. You were there, so you get what's coming to you," Difante said as Sid looked around before opening the envelope.

"It's probably more than you've made the whole time you've been working in here," Rashaad said.

Sid looked into the envelope. There were ten one-hundred-dollar bills staring him in the face.

"It's all about the money, Sid. So what you going to do?" asked Difante.

Sid couldn't take his eyes off the money. Rashaad was right. It was more money than he'd made working for two months. With money like this, Sid thought, he could help his mother out and get his car in no time.

"So when do you want to get started?" Sid asked.

"As soon as you let us know," Difante said.

"But we have to know if you're down right now because we have some plans to make," Rashaad told Sid. Sid looked at the money again, then at Difante and Rashaad.

"Yeah, I'm down . . . I'm down."

All Them Clothes

Kelly got out of the car, ran into the house, dropped her bags right by the front door and went straight to the toilet to pee. She'd been holding it ever since the first traffic light after she came out of the mall with Linda and couldn't even make it up the stairs to the master bath. Kelly finished her business in the downstairs bathroom and reached for the toilet paper.

"Damn it. What the hell is this?" she shouted, then pushed her feet out of her panties, stood up and flushed the toilet, realizing that she now had to go upstairs to wipe herself. "Shit, I better hurry up and take those bags upstairs before Deric gets home," she thought out loud.

Kelly didn't want Deric to come in the house and find all the bags from the mall. He had to show houses today and he said he'd be home at exactly seven-thirty, so they could go out to get something to eat. As Kelly bent down to pick up her five specialty-shop bags and three suit bags, she heard keys. The doorknob turned and Deric walked into the house. Shocked, Deric quickly shut the door and scanned the bottom portion of Kelly's body.

"Good. I'm horny, too, baby," he said laughing, as he took two steps to Kelly and put his hand on her firm ass, kissing her on the cheek. Both of them knew he was talking shit because he knew how Kelly was about the sex. She whipped him by not giving him any, and Deric knew if he continued kissing her he probably wouldn't see the na na anytime soon. Kelly told Cece that she wished Deric would show her what kind of man he was and throw her down someplace and hit it . . . until she made him quit it. But she had engraved in his mind, "Unless I say, let's do it, then don't even try it," so Deric knew better. He stepped back, happy that he just got a chance to feel her ass without her telling him to stop.

"What's up, baby?"

"Hi, Deric, I'll be ready in a minute. Hand me that bag if you don't mind."

Deric bent down, picked up the bag, and peeked in it. Kelly snatched it from him.

"Get out of my bags, nigga!" she snapped. "This is my shit that I bought with my own money, so just stay out."

Deric threw his hands in the air as though he was under arrest. "Baby, why are you trippin'? I just wanted to see what you got. You know I like how you dress."

"Well, you'll see how I look in the mornings on the way to work. Oh, yeah, I have to talk to you about that too. I'll be back downstairs in a minute, then we can go."

"All right. I'm going to look through this mail real quick," Deric said, as he looked at Kelly's sexy legs and her beautiful "back pack" as she walked up the stairs.

"Shit, I should have stopped over at Cece's like I planned and left this stuff there so I could bring it home one day at a time," Kelly mumbled as she stomped up the stairs. She actually did drive by Cece's to hide her clothes and to tell Cece about her day out shopping, but when she pulled up to the house she saw Kahlil's car in the driveway. Kelly knew they were probably over there doing the nasty or, even worse, talking about that marriage bullshit.

Fed Up with the Fanny

Kelly couldn't believe Cece didn't want to go shopping with her and Linda because Kahlil told her that he wanted to take her shopping and see his wife-to-be try on clothes for him like a model. Kelly thought to herself, I told Cece, "Don't no man like to go shopping with his lady and watch her try on any damn clothes." I swear he's got her mind. And she actually had the nerve to ask me, "Isn't that romantic?" I told her no. I told Cece to just get his credit card because Kahlil is trying his best to control her. She is never going to learn. It's not like he doesn't have any money. "He makes as much as these football players," she said, as Deric hollered up the stairs.

"What did you say?"

"Nothing, just talking to myself," Kelly hollered back to him. Kahlil is not fooling me, she thought as she went into the bathroom, wiped herself, washed her hands, and went into the bedroom to put on her tight black jeans.

Kelly was adamant that Kahlil was still sleeping with Ms. Television and she was glad that she'd seen them out together last year. She told Cece about it immediately. Kelly had been at Points, a rockin' jazz club downtown, where Straight Ahead was playing to a packed house. Kelly had plans to meet Deric there, to talk to him about paying her car insurance for the first six months of the new year.

It only took Kelly five minutes to spot Kahlil after she sat down and looked over the club. When Kelly saw Kahlil with Sonje, she walked right over to their table and hit the roof, right in the middle of a set. She must have called Kahlil every name in the book. Sonje was so embarrassed that she stormed out of the club and Kelly followed right behind her.

"Girlfriend, I suggest you get to know your roommate a little better, because she knows all about me," Sonje said to Kelly after she asked Sonje if she knew Kahlil was seeing Cece.

When Kelly got home she stormed into the house furious that Cece was letting Kahlil step out on her. Kelly took it upon herself to get into Cece's personal matters, and she was determined to persuade Cece that her man was doing nothing but taking advantage of her and treating her like a tramp. She didn't buy what Cece was telling her about their understanding at the time.

"He told me about her when we first met, so what. I'm willing to wait 'cause I'm not sure I'm ready for any commitment either," Cece explained. It took Kelly about one whole week to convince Cece that she should demand Kahlil see only her. Kelly hadn't trusted Kahlil since.

"She just needs to go ahead and get with Scooter's ass anyway," Kelly told her reflection in the mirror as she changed her shirt. All he's been doing since he met her is bug me about her. If she doesn't, I will.

Scooter became interested in Cece after he met her at the game and Kelly had been trying to convince her to go out with him, but Cece wasn't interested. Kelly had been trying to make Cece come around for years. Kelly really had it out for brothers, especially the ones with decent jobs, because the guys that she accused of raping her at CSU had all graduated and had good jobs. Kelly figured they were probably using women just like they'd used her. She'd hold that night against men forever.

Kelly vowed she'd never forget those punk frat brothers who sat in court, talking shit about how she provoked them into having sex with her. She couldn't believe the story they came up with. She knew the truth. Everyone in the room was playing strip poker after Cece left and nobody else's clothes got torn off her body, carried into another room, thrown to the floor, and stuck and poked in every hole of her body for two hours, she told the jury. The frat brothers were found not guilty, and after that Kelly had it engraved in her mind that all men think they are untouchable. She was convinced that men thought if they lay down a little money for any of the problems that a woman was having then every time they ask, they will receive. Kelly decided if these were the good men, then she sure as hell didn't want a bad one. She used to tell all of her girlfriends that if they didn't want to strike back, don't worry because she was out there doing enough damage for all the ladies who had been wronged by some simple-ass brother who thought he was God's gift because he had decent money.

That's why she laughed when she thought about how Lee looked at her like she was crazy when he asked her if a thousand dollars was enough for her to shop with. She told his two-timing ass no. Kelly needed an extra seven hundred. She had priced out everything she wanted and the shoes were expensive. What was he going to say? "I'm not going to give you any more than that"? I got that nigga where I want him now, she thought. I've only had to sleep with him a couple of times so far and if he starts some mess, I'll threaten to tell Linda since we're shopping partners now, she joked. Lee knows what type of bitch I am and I know he doesn't want to pay Linda any type of alimony because she'll take his ass to the bank. Her damn taste is as bad as mine. Kelly walked back down the steps. Deric was sitting on the couch flipping the channels with the remote.

"Okay, I'm ready to go when you are," Kelly said.

Deric turned off the television and stood up.

"Let's go, I'm starving. So what did you want to talk to me about?"

Kelly tried to remember. "Oh. I just want to let you know that starting tomorrow we have to leave half an hour earlier in the morning because they're trippin' at work. My boss is complaining that I'm never at my desk when it's time to start work."

Deric looked at Kelly. "What do you mean? I get you to work on time every morning. You've never been late."

"That's what I told them, but my boss said that sitting around talking doesn't cut it. He said that I need to be at my desk working. So, if I get there a half an hour earlier than I do now there shouldn't be a problem. I'll just sit around in the lobby and walk around the building. That way everyone will still be able to see me in my clothes. You know how they are always trippin' on my clothes, Deric," Kelly said, knowing that her request was going to be okay with him.

Deric looked at Kelly and bent down to see if she'd been drinking.

"Baby girl, wait a minute. I'm sorry, but I am not getting up a half an hour earlier than I already do, to take you to work, so that you can run your mouth and give the whole damn building a fashion show. Don't forget that I have to juggle my schedule around on a daily basis so that I can pick you up on time. I'm sorry, no can do. Maybe you should take your own car. It runs fine."

Kelly put her hands on her hips and Deric could see her winding up her neck, getting ready to let go. "Negro, I don't know what your trip is, but I ain't taking my car anywhere! Do you know how much it costs to park down there when you can just as easily get your lazy ass up and take me, then bring me back like you've been doing?"

"It's not about being lazy, Kelly. It's about you going to work, doing your job, and shutting your damn mouth. I don't know why you're talking about how much it costs to park; you can afford it. If you can't, how did you pay for all them clothes you took upstairs?"

"Oh, now you want to know where I get money to buy clothes. Listen, Deric, I had money before I met you and when I decide to leave your ass I'm going to have it then, too." Deric usually left well enough alone, because Kelly could argue all night long. But not tonight.

"I just want to know, because my bank account has been coming up short lately."

"So?" Kelly shouted.

"So, have you taken any money out this month? I just looked at my statement and it's short."

Kelly looked at Deric like he'd called her a bitch to the tenth degree or something. "And if I have? You gave me the card to use. What am I supposed to do with it? Leave it in my purse and take it out from time to time to look at it and say, 'Oh that sure was nice of my man'?"

"Kelly, you are unbelievable. I told you that the card is only to be used for emergencies. What emergencies have you had in the last month that I don't know about?"

"Deric, don't start. A couple of weeks ago, Cece wanted to go out and get some Diva perfume to wear for Kahlil, right? And I knew I was running a little low on my bottle, so I decided to use the card to get me a bottle of that, along with White Diamonds."

"Kelly, give me my card right now. This is unreal. You are trippin'. You are not going to spend my money like that and not even tell me about it." Deric held out his hand and waited for his bankcard.

"All right, that's cool, but don't you ask me for shit, Deric. If you can't trust me, then you might as well forget about ever being with me, because you are going to have to trust me before we can ever talk about getting married."

"So if I take my card from you, we're not going to get married?"

"First of all, get it right. I said, I would think about getting engaged, but if you take this card back you might as well forget about it. I need a man who's going to trust me unconditionally. So, here's your card back and stop looking at me like that."

Deric was stunned.

"What the fuck is wrong with you, Deric? And don't even think about hitting me. I'll have the police over here to pick your ass up so fast and you'll be in jail all night. And while you're there, mothafucka, I'll run this damn card up to the limit on the Home Shopping Network." Kelly tried to put the card in his hand. "Here, take it!" Kelly shouted.

"Fuck it," Deric said like his heart had been broken. "You know you're wrong, Kelly. Let's go."

Party

◇

Don't let me leave here without talking to you tonight, Sid," a young video queen look-alike said, as she looked Sid up and down with lust in her eyes.

"All right baby, I'll be here all night," Sid assured her as he stood in his new specially tailored suit, enjoying the girl's tight-fitting black dress and the other forty or so special guests down with the GPC. Sid had been to the Get Paid Crew parties before, but never as a member. He was really enjoying all of the attention. The two adjoining rooms on the top floor of the hotel had been decorated with a touch of class by four young girls who were still in high school, but didn't look a day under twenty-four. The ladies set up the party at Difante's request and it was sort of a surprise party for Sid to celebrate his membership into the crew.

Sid stood right in the middle of the twelve couples who were dancing, holding a bottle of champagne and periodically bouncing his head to the music. His eyes shifted back and forth, looking between the two rooms, at the good time everyone was having, especially his boys. Difante was on one side of the suite, playing cards, while Rashaad was in the adjoining room, enjoying the Jacuzzi with the four girls who set up the party.

Sid was playing the role of a definite playa. He was dressed in the new suit he'd bought the day before from the GPC's personal booster.

The wannabe designer goes to New York City every two weeks to buy an abundance of clothes exclusively for the Crew. It felt strange to Sid giving the booster two thousand dollars cash for all his new gear, but they were raking it in and he was sure there would be more to come in the near future. Sid was getting more comfortable with what they were doing, and he was damn sure making more money with the GPC than he could ever make at Big Burger. Since Sid had decided to get involved in the GPC they'd become more selective in the crimes they committed. They were stealing cars and having them stripped so they could make three or four times as much as the car was worth. Difante had already began peepin' out young brothers and sisters who had shown interest in working in the GPC. He was ready to appoint Sid manager of operations. Sid would be responsible for making sure that all members stayed committed to the organization by getting background checks on family members, gathering complete information about their past, and finding out if they had anyone in their families in prison. If so, they were the ones who Difante wanted a close eye on at all times. Sid was pleased with his role, but told Difante that he wasn't going to put in full-time effort until he finished high school.

Sid looked at his watch. It was ten minutes before the planned meeting with Difante and Rashaad, so he put his bottle of champagne down and began walking toward the room. He glanced at Rashaad and saw him getting out of the Jacuzzi. Neither wanted to be late. Timing meant everything in their line of business, and that was the main thing Difante always stressed. Sid stood by the bedroom door, looking at everyone, waiting for Difante and Rashaad to join him. The door to the suite opened and in walked a group of fine ladies, known as the Notorious Five.

Fed Up with the Fanny

The Notorious Five were the most fly young ladies in the neighborhood, and good friends of the GPC. Three of the five were already out of school and two were in their last year. They had a reputation in school and on the streets of not taking any mess from anybody and they backed each other up anytime anyone had a beef. These ladies were rough.

Sid watched them closely as they removed their coats. I wonder how females so fine can be so hard, he thought as he counted six ladies instead of five. He was surprised to see Rajanique hanging out with them and didn't move a muscle, hoping that she would notice him in the next couple of minutes before the meeting started. I wonder what she's doing with them. She had me completely fooled. As soon as this meeting is over, I'm going to let her know that it's on, Sid planned as Difante and Rashaad walked toward him.

Difante put his arms around both Rashaad and Sid and they walked into the room to have their meeting.

"Damn!" Difante shouted. "This is one live motherfucka dogs. I am fucked up!" He flopped his thin self down into a chair.

"Brother, hurry up, and say what you got to say, because I got a hunnie over in the Jacuzzi waiting for me and I don't want those titties to get wrinkled up before I get a chance to take care of her," Rashaad said looking at his abs in the mirror. Sid stood by the glass window of the room looking out at Rajanique.

"Yeah, Difante what's up? Because something that I have been peepin' just came in the door and I need to get to it, as soon as possible."

"Well, my brother, I'm glad you asked me that because this is all about you," Difante said.

Sid turned around and looked at Difante who was walking toward him. "What about me?"

"We talked it over last night and me and Rashaad think you're ready for the big time."

"What do you mean?" Sid asked, looking at Rashaad, then back at Difante.

"We mean it's your turn to do the next hit." Difante pulled a nine millimeter pistol out of the drawer and placed it into Sid's hand.

"You've been with us the last five hits."

"You mean the last six," Rashaad said, laughing.

"Shut your short ass up, Rashaad. You surprised him on that one, but if you want to count it, I'm down," Difante said, laughing. "But, seriously, we've talked about this and now it's your turn to do the next job that we have planned."

Sid had become comfortable watching Difante and Rashaad jump into parked cars, jump-start them, and drive to a hook up where they would get straight cash. There wasn't ever any violence, so he knew he wouldn't have a problem doing the same thing.

"So what's the next job?"

"Well, I talked to one of the boys at the chop shop in Ypsilanti and they're down with fifty thousand for a brand new Lincoln Town Car, straight cash, and I'm going to let you pull this one off."

"That's cool, I can do it. But what's the pistol for?"

"Because, my brutha, you're going to have to smoke whoever we snatch the car from."

Sid looked at Difante. "For what?"

"Because we've all done it and I feel like you need to know what it's like to be in the hot seat with something hanging over your head like we have over ours."

Sid looked at Rashaad. "Don't worry about it, Cuz. It's just for security reasons, then we'll all know something about each other. It's sort of like allegiance to the Crew."

"So after this, how many more are we going to do?"

Difante and Rashaad smiled. "This is the last one, baby. Then we're going to start remodeling the building for the restaurant and pass this bullshit on down," Difante said.

Sid stood still and just shook his head. He'd known the day would come when he'd be asked to do some of the dirty work, but he hadn't planned on shooting anyone. He looked down at the pistol and turned it over from side to side as he began to think what he was getting himself into.

"Look Sid—you know what we are doing is happening world-wide playa. All you hear nowadays is East Coast–West Coast, bruthas are just takin' what they want, when they want it, and set-ting up their territories. But when people come through Detroit, which used to be called Motown, it will be called Ourtown and when they come through here needing anythang at all—if they don't get it from us they just won't get it. And that's for sho'," Di-fante boasted.

"No doubt," Rashaad said forcefully as he began doing the Bankhead Bounce when he overheard one of his favorite songs, "Stello," being mixed with some funky new beats.

The thought of being in total control warmed Sid up inside but the feeling was not special enough for him to commit to the shit so quickly. "I got to think about this one. I don't know," Sid said, putting the pistol back in the drawer.

"What is there to think about?" Rashaad said.

"Don't front, Rashaad. What . . . you didn't have to think about it before you set it off? Or are you just that foul?" Sid said.

"Hell, yeah . . . I just set it off. You should have seen me!" Rashaad said, laughing.

"Yeah, right—Rashaad, you talk so much shit," Difante said. "Okay, that's cool, Sid, because I need to talk to the money man anyway to get some details smoothed out, so let me know when you decide. But I'm telling you, we all have done it, so you know where we stand with your decision—right?" Difante and Rashaad looked at Sid.

"Yeah, I know," Sid said.

Difante opened the door and signaled to the three young ladies who had been watching him play cards all night to come inside the room. As they walked in he placed them one beside each other, close to the bed.

"All right, since we have our business taken care of, I need my brutha's opinion on something." Rashaad and Sid stood looking at the girls, smiling.

"Look, I've already been with these two before at the same time, but she's never had a threesome before and she's never had one without her. So what should I do?"

Rashaad and Sid began laughing.

"Man you are trippin'," Sid said.

"I'm serious now, somebody help me out," Difante said as he looked them all over.

Rashaad, not wanting to waste any more time, walked over to the girls and picked the girl who had never been in a three before and the other who had never had one without her girlfriend before and began to "bounce" in front of all three while they all laughed.

"There you go, now you're set. You take these two and I'll take this one with me into the Jacuzzi. I like experience myself," Rashaad said, as he grabbed his playmate's hand.

"What about Sid?" one of the girls asked.

"Oh, I'll be all right. I have something in the next room that I need to check out."

Rajanique noticed Sid as soon as he walked into the room. He picked up another bottle of champagne and walked with confidence over to her.

"I've been wondering where you've been, I don't see you any more on the bus," Sid said.

"Oh, that was just a summer thing. Now I drive my mom's car everywhere."

"Is that right? I'm gettin' ready to get me a little somethin' myself. I didn't know you were down with the Five. How long has it been?"

"Been for what?" Rajanique asked.

"Since you've been in that clique. I've been with the GPC for a while now and we have shit rolling over here on this side."

"That's good to hear, I guess," Rajanique said.

"You're right, it's all good. So, do you think you might want to step out with a brother from time to time? It looks like we have a lot in common," Sid said, as he took a swallow of the champagne right out the bottle. Rajanique laughed and Sid smiled.

"What's so funny?" Sid asked.

"Nothing. It's just funny how people judge you by the people you roll with."

"Why do you say that?"

"Because, if I wasn't with the Notorious tonight and you saw me, let's say on the bus, you wouldn't have stepped to me like you just did."

"You think so?"

"Yes, I do."

"Well, it don't matter, baby, because we ain't on no bus."

"Sorry Sid, but it matters to me. I'm only hanging out with them because they look after me. They've been trying to get me to jump on with them, but they know I'm not because I'm going to college and they respect that shit. They just watch my back. You know how it can be, going to a private school, living in the hood with all those silly-ass, jealous bitches always trying to fight. The Notorious have stopped all that shit and take me to all of the fly-ass parties they go to. And for their help, we have an agreement."

"Oh yeah, what's that?" Sid asked, tipping his bottle.

"They told me that they will watch my back now and when I get out of school and become a lawyer, I'll represent any one of them for free. So, you still don't have what it takes. Take care," she said and walked away.

Fuck her, Sid said to himself. We'll have five or six restaurants by the time she gets out of school. I'm going to school, too, and we'll see who's making the money in five or six years, baby girl. Sid pointed to the little video look-alike queen who had stepped to him earlier. She'd been watching him all night, and as she walked over to him, he grabbed her hand and took her into his room to work her body for the rest of the night.

Step

Deric unfastened Kelly's seat belt, reached across her and opened the door. "Get out, Kelly. After all the things you've done for me, this is the least I can do for you," he said with a trembling voice.

Kelly knew damn good and well she didn't want to get out of the Rover, but grabbed her Coach bag from the floor and got out. "Fine, Deric, I don't need you. I'll have him come pick me up, you punk."

"Good. Do that. You can come by tomorrow and pick up all of your shit. I'll be there around six," Deric yelled out the window, then drove off, leaving Kelly out in the middle of nowhere.

Deric was fuming and he was glad he'd put her ass out for lying to him. During dinner they had done nothing but argue about Kelly spending his money like it was hers. When Kelly brought up the subject of trust, Deric had to bust her. He told her about the recorder that he had attached to his phone and about all the conversations she and Lee had been having. All she could do was try to turn the whole situation around and tell him he was wrong for bugging the line. Flat out busted, Deric thought as he drove home to get some rest, listening to the black women's national anthem, "Not Going to Cry," by Mary J. Blige. Deric was perplexed by the words that spilled out of Mary's mouth and began to talk to her as if she was right there next to him in the front seat.

"Damn, Mary, is it like that with you, too? I was just trying to do my best and keep Kelly from crying myself. But I just had to expose her and let her know that I've known about all the little games she's been playing on me. No one can say that I didn't try either. My only regret is that I waited so long to get rid of her. Now she has all the time in the world to be with her Detroit Lion friend. I can't believe Kelly is playing me for a married man. I mean what in the hell does she think she is going to get out of it. I know damn sure he wouldn't leave his wife for a woman who has no type of respect for a marriage. And I know damn sure I'm not going into one with her still playing games. I just can't take it anymore. I had to be real with myself. I've sat back too long, watching someone else do to mine what I wasn't even able to talk to her about. The only reason I didn't tell her ass to step when I first found out about her affair, freaky as it may seem, I started to enjoy listening to Kelly and her friend having phone sex. Mary, the look she had on her face when I told her that I knew all about her fling, is sure enough get back for me. I wanted to ask her 'How Do You Feel Now.'" Deric chuckled. "Yeah . . . that could even be a title for your next song.

"I was trying to be committed, I wanted to be caring. Damn it, I was trying to be her man! But I was going crazy dealing with all the things that she put me through. I tried my best to give her all the space she asked for, maybe that was the problem. But hell, I was trying to be up on the latest trends by giving your mate space and making sure they still retain individuality. Now I've faced the music. I was just a fool in love. I was just caught up in the fact that when I first met Kelly she just flat-out changed me. It wasn't all bad, either. I mean it might not seem like much. But I felt better about myself when we first got together. I mean when a brother has a fine lady on his arm his whole demeanor changes, my confidence was at a all-time high. She made me take chances and do better for myself. Just knowing that I had a beautiful lady changed me. But I'm sure I did the right thing. After I look back on everything, there hasn't been anything else that Kelly has ever done for me. I can't remember the last time she pulled money out of her own pocket for anything. She called herself an independent woman and claimed that she didn't need anything from anybody, but she never even wanted to pay for her own personal items.

"Each and every time I tried to do something nice for her, she did nothing but take advantage of it. I'll never forget the time I let her have her girlfriends from work come over for a little dinner party. But, Mary, she didn't even have the decency to tell me she was having male strippers in my place, and that they were charging it to my Visa. And I just let it go and let her horny-ass crew get away with leaving my place a wreck. Kelly didn't even find out that the roses she thought Lee sent to her at the football game were really from me. That's just like her ungrateful ass. If she would have thanked him for them, then she would have known he didn't send them. But it's all for the best Mary, it wasn't like we were a couple anyway. Sure, I'd see her on the way to work, but we didn't talk. We listened to the radio. She never wanted to miss the morning gossip show, to her it was more important than our relationship. When I'd pick her up, she acted as though she was too tired to even say hello. We would talk for about thirty minutes when I got back home from work if and only if one of her favorite television shows wasn't on. The entire five months that we lived together I might as well been single. Mary, they say women like to be romantic, well so do I. You know, maybe go to dinner, then a movie, then for a late night drink, and just relax. But Kelly is so much different from all that. She always wants to go out to the clubs and see the same damn people all the time. I like to get out, but I want to go to some other clubs or places, maybe in Cleveland or up in Canada for a change of pace, make a weekend out of it. All we had to do is hop in the Land Rover and go. She always said that's what she wanted to do too, but when I made plans, her favorite line was, 'Can't this weekend. Maybe in a couple of weeks.'

"Mary, it was the same thing in the bed. She thought every time I touched her or put my arm around her body, it meant that I wanted to have sex or something. No, it wasn't like that. She was always telling Cece, in my face or over the phone, while I sat on the couch that she wanted to be held, but if I just touched her when she wasn't expecting it Kelly would just go off. It was all right for her to tell me that she wanted some, but I better not talk to Ms. Kelly like that because in her mind I would be treating her like a 'ho or something. She couldn't stand that and I respected that. But come to find out that's exactly what she is, a 'ho. If I'd known what I do now about her, I would have treated her like she really deserved.

"The irony about this whole situation is that when she found out about a female friend from work who got my telephone number from the personnel office and called me, it just blew Kelly's mind. She played like I had done something wrong. Now I know why. Because it was her who was stepping out on me the whole time, and she needed an excuse to make herself feel better. I mean she started asking me questions about her. 'So who is she? Did you see your girl at work today? Who did you eat lunch with?' Kelly straightened her act up for almost two weeks when she thought I was thinking about dropping her ass. And now I have. So, go ahead and sing to me Mary, because I'm with you baby . . . I'm not crying, either."

Judgment

Sonje, what are you doing?" Dewayna asked as she put a smile on her face and looked around to see if anyone had noticed that Sonje put her arm around her chair.

"Relax, it will be fine," Sonje said, keeping her eyes on the dance floor. She began to laugh at the girls in their overly tight dresses dancing to D'Angelo's "Brown Sugar."

"It just feels odd, sitting here with your arm around me," Dewayna insisted as she combed the club again, making sure no one was paying them any special attention. Dewayna was uncomfortable sitting in the dark club called TiT'S with all the other female couples. In fact during the entire hour-and-a-half drive to the club, Dewayna told Sonje that the gay bar scene was a little bit too much for her and a hell of a lot too soon. It had been almost a month since Dewayna and Sonje started seeing one another, but Sonje was treating it as though they had openly been lovers for years.

"You want to dance?" Sonje asked.

"Um, um, no way. I'm not ready for that yet," Dewayna snapped back as Sonje smiled.

"Okay, you let me know when you're ready."

"I can tell you this . . . it won't be tonight," Dewayna said as she watched in disbelief how openly the women were acting. Dewayna was amazed and almost sick to her stomach as she watched some of the ladies kiss and grab each other all over. Dewayna didn't like it one bit the way the club was set up. The tables in the club surrounded the dance floor and a spiral staircase. She wanted to be someplace in a dark corner away from the crowd.

"Sonje, why do they keep flashing that damn light on our table?" Sonje looked at Dewayna and smiled. "That's the light of passion, baby. It's to keep order in the club."

"Order. What are you talking about?"

"Just watch where the light shines next." They watched the light. "See, it goes from table to table and gives every couple a chance to go upstairs."

"Upstairs . . . upstairs for what?"

"You know Dewayna . . . to do the nasty," Sonje said, rubbing Dewayna's back.

"What?"

"You see those couples going back and forth up that spiral staircase in the middle of the dance floor?"

"Yes."

"I've never been up there before, but I've heard that they let five couples at a time go up there and have sex if they want to. The spotlight that's shining on each table is letting each couple know that there's room upstairs and it's their turn if they want to take advantage of it. If they don't want to, the dominant in the relationship points to the DJ and they take the light off the table."

"You mean they're going to shine that damn light over here like that all night?"

"Yep, but don't worry because as soon as they do I'll wave them off us if you want me to."

"That's exactly what I want you to do, Sonje. I don't want anybody that I know to see me in here," Dewayna said, paranoid about being exposed.

"Don't worry about it. Hell, if you see someone you know, more than likely they're here for the same reason as you." Sonje had a damn answer for everything, Dewayna thought.

Sonje told Dewayna that she was her fourth lesbian lover, and that she'd met them all the same way that she'd met her. Dewayna could tell that Sonje thought she was the shit and that she could spot a potential lover in the making. Just as Sonje had done to her.

When they first met, Kahlil was talking to Sonje in the parking lot after a karate exhibition at the Coalition. Dewayna was there to pick up Octavious, whom she'd dropped off to see the show, and Kahlil introduced the two. They all stood around in the parking lot for about twenty minutes, and when Dewayna started talking about how much she'd been working and how her baby-sitter decided that she needed to cut back on the twelve hours that she watched Octavious every weekend, Sonje's bi antennas sensed that she was in need of someone to talk to because she was becoming frustrated. Unaware that Sonje was going to hit on her, Dewayna and Sonje exchanged numbers and somehow the rest is history.

Dewayna could sense Sonje growing pushy and it seemed like she'd already decided that the two were going to be an item with or without Dewayna's consent.

"Sonje, I'm very confused about what we're doing and I think I'm going to need some time to figure this out. You know technically I'm still married to Demitrious," Dewayna said several days before Sonje talked to her about coming to the club.

"Aw, you're just having first time anxieties," Sonje told Dewayna. The comment seemed hypocritical to Dewayna, especially now that Sonje was sitting in the club, looking like a totally different person. Even Dewayna hadn't recognized Sonje when she knocked on her door to pick her up for the evening. If Sonje was so confident then why was she incognito? "If someone were to find out that I am bisexual, I'm not sure how the ratings on my show would go. And I don't know how my audience or sponsors will respond," Sonje told Dewayna.

They'd had two drinks apiece and Sonje was trying her very best to get Dewayna in a better mood. She put her hand underneath the table and began to rub her French-manicured nails back and forth on Dewayna's thighs, each time coming closer to Dewayna's kitten.

"Dewayna, you sure have made me feel good this last month. You know, like I told you before, this is really special to me. If you want, we can see each other exclusively."

Dewayna, who was uncomfortable with Sonje's hand under the table, moving up and down on her thigh, wiggled away and smiled. "Sonje, you're right, this last month has been different and very interesting to say the least. But I don't know yet. It really seems too early for me to decide on something I've never been involved in before. You know that I have Octavious to think about and what he thinks about what goes on in my life means a great deal to me."

"Dewayna, Octavious is too young to realize what we are doing," Sonje said, trying to be reassuring.

"I don't know, Sonje, he's pretty observant. Let's just not make any promises. I don't know what I'm ready to do yet. I just don't know if this is even right. I'm having too many doubts."

"I understand, but we all have doubts when we first start, sweetheart." Sonje grabbed Dewayna's hand. "And I can tell you this, I'm willing to wait." She kissed Dewayna on the cheek.

One thing Dewayna really did like about Sonje, even though she was often overpowering and egotistical, was the way they understood each other. She knew what it meant to have cramps, what it felt like to be left all alone by a man, and the ultimate feeling of loneliness night after night. Sonje would cry with Dewayna when she needed to cry without asking her what was wrong. When Dewayna told her no, not tonight, Sonje didn't pounce on top of her and keep trying until she gave in. She knew about foreplay, where to touch, and how to touch it.

Sonje's views on men were another story and Dewayna didn't agree with her on that topic. The way Sonje talked about men, you would have believed she was just straight gay, instead of bisexual. She tried her best to turn Dewayna against men too by using Demitrious as an example. Every night since Demitrious left her, Dewayna had been scared to death of sleeping in her house alone because of all of the crazy fools running around the streets. Dewayna was convinced that there was nothing like a man to snuggle up to, one who was there for her and Octavious, for protection. When she confided this to Sonje, Sonje responded, "Well, our men today are nothing but broke dogs. They don't have any money, sense, or compassion. That's why I can do without if I have to." She tried her best to convince Dewayna that black men just cause too much pain to everyone.

"You want to bring Octavious down to the station tomorrow and let him see the new set for my show?" Sonje said, changing the subject. "We're entering a new ratings period and I decided I need something new so they designed a new set. How about four o'clock?"

"Tomorrow?" Dewayna asked, keeping her eyes on the dance floor. "I can't."

"Why not?" Sonje said, putting her hand on Dewayna's leg again.

"Because Demitrious wants to take Octavious to the zoo and he asked if I would tag along."

Sonje looked at Dewayna and took her hand off her thigh.

Then she put it around her chair and inched her lips so close to her ear that Dewayna could feel them touching her as she spoke.

"Listen, this is the third damn time in three weeks that you've accepted his invitation to go out. If you ask me, I think you're beginning to enjoy all of these fuckin' family outings. All he is trying to do is get you in the bed and hump on you like some old trashy piece of meat, then he's going to leave you and Octavious again."

Dewayna was not going to let Sonje treat her like she was her property and took Sonje's arm off her chair. "Sonje, you know what?"

"What?" Sonje said, daring Dewayna to speak her mind.

"I know you're strung out on the fact that you're the first woman I've ever slept with . . . and you like to tell me what to do and shit and I understand that, because you have the experience in this type of situation. But when it comes to my son's happiness and what he needs, then I'm sorry, because I'm the one who is going to make those decisions for him. So let's get one thing straight right now. Tomorrow, I'm going with him and his father to the zoo. Do you understand?" Sonje didn't say a word as the light scorched their faces. "Now, be what you want to be and wave that damn light off us," Dewayna demanded.

Dewayna walked into her living room holding her nail polish in her hand. She decided to sit down to see what was going on because Octavious was making a hell of a lot of noise. "Be careful, Octavious," Dewayna shouted as he jumped off the center of the couch and onto the floor, pretending to catch a football in his make-believe game over and over again.

"Touchdown!" he screamed. "Watch, Mommy, one more time."

Dewayna, who couldn't stand watching her angel fall to the floor, put down her fingernail polish and grabbed him by his arm.

"That's okay, baby, I've seen enough. Stand up here on the couch and look out the window for your father," she said, as she moved her things so he could get on the couch that sat directly underneath the window. Dewayna picked her fingernail polish back up and watched out of the corner of her eye as Octavious was on lookout, as though he was a cop in his biggest case.

I wonder why he gets so excited when Demitrious comes over and all cranky and withdrawn when Sonje comes over, Dewayna thought. I told Sonje that my little man notices things. Dewayna reached over, kissed Octavious on his cheek, and tried to convince herself that he didn't think his mommy was in a relationship with a woman. He smiled and fanned the smell of the nail polish away from his little nose. Dewayna looked at Octavious again and thought about asking him if he liked Sonje or not but decided against it. She thought that would give him reason to think something was not right with Dewayna spending so much time with her. She also knew that kids say whatever they think a grown-up wants to hear anyway. Dewayna promised herself that she would do anything to keep this part of her life a secret from everyone, especially Octavious.

The telephone rang and Octavious jumped off the couch and picked up the cordless. "Hello," he said, then gave the phone to his mother and jumped back onto the couch without saying another word.

"Hello?" Dewayna said.

"What's wrong with him?" Sonje asked.

Dewayna got up from the couch and walked into the bedroom. "Oh, I don't know. I think he thought you were Demitrious," she said, peeking back out into the living room to make sure he hadn't started jumping off the couch again. "Look, Sonje, I'm not in any mood to discuss last night. I am not going to classify myself gay or bisexual for your benefit. I'm just me right now. Nor will I stop going out with Demitrious when he takes Octavious out, because he needs this right now." Hearing laughter on the other end, Dewayna took the phone away from her ear and looked into it.

"Dewayna, will you stop. That conversation is over, okay? I just called to ask you a question."

"Oh," Dewayna said.

"I've thought about what you said last night, about Octavious needing to be with his father, and you're right. I was just reading a letter from a ladies group who would love to see a show on fathers being responsible toward their kids and it gave me a great idea. And guess what?" Sonje asked.

"What?"

"I've decided to do a show on that very subject. I want to feature the If Man Be Man program at the Coalition."

"Well, that's great, Sonje, I know they'll be happy to hear that."

"Thanks, girl, but I have a question to ask you."

"Go ahead," Dewayna said.

"Do you think that you and Demitrious, along with Octavious, of course, could be on the show?"

Dewayna started to laugh.

"What's so funny?"

"You want me and Octavious to be guests on your show. Well I don't know about that, Sonje, what will I say, what will I do," Dewayna said.

"Sweetheart, don't worry about a thing. It will be fine." Sonje waited for an answer. "You still there?"

"Yes I'm here. . . . Sonje, you know I'll do anything for you. But you never have men on your show. It's the *Women Only Show,* have you forgotten?

"No, hon, I've come to the conclusion that if I want to win ratings next month, I'm going to have to do what the public wants, something special, you know, raw. Do you think you can do it?"

"Well sure, I'm pretty sure I can. I just have to check my schedule at work and I can run it past Demitrious today while we're out and call you when I get back in."

"That's fine, sweetheart. Listen, one more thing," Sonje said. "I'm sorry about last night."

"Don't mention it," Dewayna said, impressed that Sonje was finally beginning to understand her situation. "Talk to you later."

Octavious began to yell and scream as Demitrious knocked on the door.

"Hello, Demitrious, how are you? We'll be ready in a second," Dewayna said as she opened the door.

Demitrious stood just inside the door and stared at Dewayna, hoping she would notice he was looking at her, and she did. She didn't take her eyes off him as she bent down and picked up O's jacket off the couch. Octavious grabbed and pulled at his mother's hand, breaking them both out of their trance. "Come on y'all, let's go."

Here, Mama

"Yes, I understand," Kahlil's mother said, quietly speaking into the phone, even though she thought everyone was out of the house. "Well, I'm just glad the government isn't messing with my money. That Gingrich is such a crazy fool. I'm not surprised, though. He and his cronies ain't never said anything for anybody who lives from paycheck to paycheck. Can you imagine how it would have been with Dole as president? They are runnin' this country into the ground. I'm just thankful to God that the crazed devils can't touch any of my money." She took a sip of her tea. "Just let me know, Justine, because I'll do whatever I can for you. Call me and let me know, you know me. I'll be right here, trying to keep the peace. Bye-bye," she said. Duty calls again, she thought.

In her frivolous forties, reaching fifty, Margaret used to think twice about loaning anything to anybody. She had just finished paying off Leandra's defaulted loans and her faith in people had been shattered. But Justine was her girl. They had been child-hood friends in North Carolina, and continued to be so even after they went to different parts of the country to get married and start families. Justine had called because she was afraid that the government would be shut down again if the budget wasn't balanced.

Fed Up with the Fanny

The last time it happened her late husband's veterans benefits were held so she'd called Margaret to see if she could ask for help if the shutdown took place again. Margaret was more than happy to help out because she knew if she ever needed anyone Justine would be there for her. They were from the old school and when friends need help, a true friend is always there.

"Mar-gar-ee," Sid said with concern, coming from the basement, smiling because he knew his grandmother liked to hear him say her name. He was the only person in the family that called her that.

She quickly turned around. "Boy, I didn't know you were here. You scared me."

"I was downstairs and woke up when I heard you talking to Ms. Justine. Is she all right?"

Margaret looked at him surprised. "How do you know anything is wrong?" she said.

"Because I was listening to what you were saying to her, you know, keeping my ear to the ground."

Sid told his grandmother the God forsaken truth, the straight-up down-low, this time and every time. Sid had never forgotten the time his Mar-gar-ee got tired of him running around the house begging for someone to tie his shoe even after he told her that he knew how to tie it himself. She spanked him for lying to her then sat him down in the middle of the kitchen floor and made him learn how to tie his shoe. For the first fifteen minutes, he'd thought she just wanted him to stay home with her because she loved having her only grandson around. She hadn't had a little boy around since Kahlil and she spoiled him to death. But when he found himself still sitting on the floor half an hour later, he realized that she meant business. He missed the entire first day of second grade but learned a valuable lesson. Sid had decided she wasn't one to mess with it and hadn't tried her since.

"You better stop listening to my calls," Margaret said, as Sid reached into his pocket with confidence and slid a neatly folded money roll on the table.

"How much does she need? I can help her out," Sid said as he opened the refrigerator and took out the ice water.

Margaret looked at the money and grabbed her cup of tea. "Boy, pick your money back up. She's going to be all right. Everything is already taken care of," she added, surprised by Sid's generosity.

"You sure? Because I have a little money saved up and I can help her out if need be."

"That's all right baby," she said, picking up the money and handing it back to Sid. "It must be fifteen hundred dollars here. That job must be good to you."

Sid didn't say anything. He just drank the ice water out of his glass, then sat down at the table and plucked his fingers on the roll of money.

"What's wrong, Sid?

Sid looked down at the money, then at her face.

"Mar-gar-ee, why does the government think it's okay if they stop everybody's way of life when they shut the government down? How can they do something like that?"

"Well, baby, you have to realize the government is a machine and lots of the time the decisions that are made are made without feeling. Remember, it's the same government that enslaved my grandfather and grandmother. They can be real nasty folk."

"So what's the difference between the government taking something that is rightfully someone else's and a criminal who does the same?" Sid asked, earning a concerned look from his grandmother.

"There is no difference. They're both wrong—except the criminal is the one who's going to be hurt by the situation because he has no power."

"Well, I don't like being told what to do all the time and expected to do it, no questions asked. It seems like everybody else is going buck wild and getting whatever they want by just taking it— just like the government. It seems like my father did the same thing when it comes to me. He just took my mother, made me, and forgot all about me. That's why I don't care who the hell he is anymore, but no matter how I try to forget, he's still on my mind. One day I'll be able to put him out of my head. So as far as I'm concerned he ain't shit." Sid covered his mouth, realizing what he said, and looked at his grandmother. "I'm sorry, Mar-gar-ee."

"That's all right, baby, you're just fed up. All I can tell you is that you better get used to evil people and evil ways because that's how the world is." Margaret saw rebellion on Sid's face.

"Sid, I hope you're not doing anything crazy. Life is not always fair and you know they don't play with young black males. They'll put your butt in jail so fast your head will spin and then they'll throw away the key. Grandson, don't let yourself be pulled down by what's going on around you. You hear me?" Sid nodded his head yes and looked at his grandmother and began to think about how she'd put up with all the commotion from her family and this crazy world for so long.

"Mar-gar-ee, I'm okay. I just have a lot on my mind. You know when I graduate, I'm thinking about taking business courses at City College." He smiled, trying to ease his thoughts about the decision he had to make concerning doing the carjacking. Sid knew that his time was rapidly approaching to give his partners an answer.

"That's good, baby. Have you told your mother yet?"

"Naw, not yet. I'm going to wait until I actually start classes because she always tells me that I can't get into college anywhere with my grades. I don't even think she believes I'll get out of high school."

"Sidney, now, don't you go letting your mother put negative thoughts in your head. You're a very smart young man and you can be anything you want to be. All you have to do is put forth your best effort. You know, you remind me so much of your grandfather. Believe it or not, he didn't know what he wanted to do when he got out of high school either, but he took his time and made the right decision from a whole lot of other bad ones he could have made. And I know you probably have a hundred more choices to choose from than he did and it ain't easy, but I trust you will make the right choices, too."

Sid looked at his grandmother, smiled, and took the last gulp of his water, then began sucking on the ice cube he put in his mouth.

"Thanks, but I still want you to take this money. It's the least I can do. I've never been able to help out around here," Sid said. "Now that I can help, at least let me." Sid grabbed her hand. "Here, go ahead. Take it and give it to Ms. Justine. I'm not going to take it back anyway, so you might as well keep it."

Margaret thought about telling him to take his money back, but she could tell he really meant it.

"Okay, baby, I'll take it. You are something else, a true Richardson."

Sid bent down and kissed her on the cheek. "See you later. I'm going down to the neighborhood for a while," he said, and opened the back door.

"Sidney," Margaret's soft voice called out. Sid turned around. "Be careful out there, baby." Sid nodded his head and walked out the door.

Leandra came home to an empty house. A note from Margaret was sitting on the kitchen counter, to let everyone know she'd gone to the grocery store. Good, Leandra thought. It will give me a little time to sit down and think about this bullshit Paula told me about Sid and the GPC.

Fed Up with the Fanny

Leandra was at the beauty shop when her friend Paula, who knew anything and everything that went on in the neighborhood, began talking to her as they sat with towels on their heads waiting for a dryer to open up.

"Leandra, I hope I can tell you this in confidence, because I like you and your son," she'd said. "Word on the street is that he's running with the GPC. They're raking it in and are about to open up a restaurant right next to Blue's. I hear they're carjacking, selling the cars to chop shops, and keeping the profit for the front money to open it up. Now, girl, I'm not telling you this so you'll go and beat Sid across the head. I'm telling you because I know you, and if mine was acting up, I'd expect you to tell me what was going on."

Leandra sat down at the kitchen table and tried to put things in perspective but all of a sudden she felt agitated and confused. She knew right away she was about to have a mood swing. Her doctor told her to immediately take her lithium when she began to feel this way and to lay down and relax. But she didn't want to take the medication. It only helped for a little while, then it would make her sick. Leandra took her medication out of her purse and opened up the bottle, then slammed the bottle on the table. "I'm not taking this shit!" she shouted. She felt like her head was about to split and began to mumble.

How stupid could Sid be, letting his name float around in the neighborhood in association with a gang? she thought. Well, everybody knows that he's hung around with Difante and Rashaad since they were small. It's probably just gossip. Sid knows better than to get involved with their activities. If he is running with them maybe I should just let Sid be, like Rashaad's mother is doing. Hell, I know Teresa knows what Rashaad is doing. If it was serious she would have called me by now. I think it would be great for those young boys to start their own restaurant. At least they have goals. I'd love to tell people when they ask me how Sid is doing that he's the part-owner of a restaurant. I have to admit, that thousand dollars he gave me sure lasted longer than that measly one hundred sixty dollars he was getting from that damn Big Burger. How do they expect kids to make it off that? Shoot, I can pay for school, pay Mama some rent, get the family off my back, and put some away for a rainy day, all at the same time.

If he was hurting somebody it would be a different story. But if all he is doing is taking cars and stripping them, well, I guess he can't get too much time for that if he gets caught. It's not like he's into anything different from any other kids these days and like they say, what I don't know won't hurt me.

Right to Know

It was four o'clock on Saturday afternoon when I pulled into the parking lot of the Coalition. I looked around and didn't recognize any of the cars there. Good, I thought, as I maneuvered my Mark VIII between two very old, outdated cars, trying to camouflage my license plates that had SONJE1 plastered on them.

As I suspected, the only people in the business section of the Coalition were the cleaning crew. I was relieved, because I could take care of my business quickly, without any distractions. The business section of the Coalition was quiet and almost scary. I could smell the heavy scent of pine and noticed that the floors had just been mopped. As I walked down the hallway, I looked at all of the name plates on the doors and thought about how easy it was to get the master key from the guard. A lady's charm works all the time.

I found the office I wanted, placed the key into the lock and in seconds let myself in. The room was dark so I walked over to the window and twirled the shades open so that enough light could enter, but not so wide that someone could see in from the outside. I stopped and looked at the couch, wondering if that was where he told the counselor all of his secrets. I'd seen him leaving this very office, not once, but at least four times since I'd been here and I wanted to know why they were spending so much time together. There were three file cabinets in the office, but I chose the right one on the first try. Finding the file that I needed was easy and I placed it into the zipper portion of my briefcase and locked the door.

I was going to take the file home to read it but I was just too anxious to see what was inside. I decided to go into my own office, read it completely, then put it back. I put the master key in my own office door and as I opened it, I was startled by a hand on my shoulder.

"Hey Sonje." Damn it. It was Kahlil. "I didn't know you were coming in today. What brings you in here?"

"Oh . . . hi, Kahlil. I just came in for a while to work on an idea that I have for the show. I thought about going to the station, but if I showed up there I wouldn't get anything done. So I thought I'd hang out here for a couple of hours. Come on in," I told him as I sighed. I wanted to tell him to get lost. We stepped into my office and I placed my briefcase on the desk. "I didn't see your car in the parking lot when I arrived. Are you just now getting here?" I wanted to find out if he saw me coming out of the office down the hall. Kahlil grabbed the towel that was hanging down from his shoulder and wiped the sweat from his forehead.

"I left the car at home and jogged up here to play some ball with a few of the boys. So tell me. What are you working on?"

"Well, Kahlil, I'm about to give you and the board members exactly what you want."

"And what might that be, Sonje?"

"I thought about it last night and I'm going to do a show on the black men in the community. I'd like to feature the If Man Be Man program. And guess who I've already asked to be guests on the show?"

"Who?" Kahlil asked.

"Demitrious, Dewayna, and Octavious. I'll let Police Chief Parham pick the rest as he sees fit. But I just have to have them. I saw how they were when Demitrious wasn't around, and the difference is like night and day now that he's back in their lives."

Kahlil smiled like I hadn't seen since I showed him how I masturbate.

"I think it's an excellent idea, Sonje. This will give brothers nationwide insight into what we have accomplished here and hopefully it will make a difference in other communities."

"The show, more than likely, won't be until next month, during sweeps. Hopefully we'll be able to get a crew down here soon to tape some of the activities. We may even be able to set up a live shot and show the facilities during the show," I told him.

"Sonje, let me be the first to thank you. This is exactly what we need. You go, girl!" he said.

I laughed along with Kahlil's happy-go-lucky ass, and watched his eyes as they shifted to my desk. The cover of the file that I had just taken was sitting plain as day in the side pocket of my briefcase.

"What's this?" he asked, picking up the book titled *Afreketa* that sat right beside my briefcase. I took my briefcase off of my desk, trying to play like I couldn't see what he was talking about, relieved that he meant the book instead of the file.

"Oh yeah, I've read about this book in the *Quarterly Black Review.* This is a book written by African-American lesbians about creative expression." There was silence for a few seconds and Kahlil acted as though he didn't even want to ask me the next question. He looked at me, then at the book twice, before he decided to open up his mouth.

"This is some deep shit, Sonje." He chuckled. "What makes you want to read it? You thinking about going that way?" Then he began to laugh because he thought he knew everything about me.

Kahlil just knew I could never be bisexual. I had never told

Kahlil about any of my female lovers, even the one or two I had while we were seeing each other. I looked directly at him and decided to have a little fun. "Oh that. I just got that back from a friend. But how do you know I'm not that way already? Just think about it. Have I ever told you that I was or not?" I said to him, smiling. He looked at me, not knowing if he should take me seriously or not. His eyes widened.

"Well, are you? . . . At least I have the right to know. I mean, all those years we were together. Oh, hell, yes, that's something I should definitely know the answer to." Kahlil got up from the chair across from my desk. I didn't change my expression one bit and looked right into his worried eyes.

"I'm sorry, Kahlil. That's something that only me and the other person . . . excuse me . . . woman should know. If you remember, we're not together anymore and you're now engaged to what's her name. So, as Salt-N-Pepa say, it's none of your business."

Kahlil looked at me like it was the first time we'd met and I looked right back at him, smiling from ear to ear over my joke.

"What's wrong, Kahlil, are you wondering if I had a lady friend when I was with you . . . if she was better than you or not? You didn't think all those nights you were with Cece that I was sitting at home waiting on you, did you? What was good for you was sure enough good for me."

"Look, Sonje, I don't think this is very funny. With all the shit going around these days, you could have infected me with some stupid shit. I was one hundred percent up front with you about Cece. Thank God I always used a jimmy with you." Kahlil began to walk out my office.

"Yes, you did, Kahlil . . . every time but once," I reminded him. Kahlil stopped and turned around. "You remember when we were outside in my backyard?" I could see his eyes becoming red. "Yeah, you remember, don't you? And it was . . . soooo . . . goooood." He stared at me for a moment, then left the office without saying anything at all. I knew I didn't have anything, but I couldn't pass up the thrill of teasing Kahlil. In my eyes, after the way he treated me, calling off our relationship and wanting to settle down to get married, he definitely deserved it and much more.

I pulled the file out of my briefcase, sat back and stared at it for a couple of minutes, to ensure that Kahlil took his scared ass home to examine his dick, before looking through it. While waiting I thought about the plan that had been going through my head and ran my finger across the name on the file. I thought about who this would affect but when I thought about my career and how it was going to benefit me, all of a sudden I didn't care about anyone else. This had the potential to put me in the ranks with Ricki Lake, Sally Jessy Raphael, hell, Oprah, too. I imagined how much more powerful I would become. Not only would I make more money, but I would gain more control over my talk show instead of letting my fucking producers tell me which markets are good enough for my show and which ones are not. I didn't want to hear it anymore. I wanted complete control. Most important I wanted my name to be a household word. After I decided the coast was clear, I pulled out the paperwork from the file and read it thoroughly.

Flockin'

It was Sunday afternoon. Demitrious had been so busy that he hadn't been able to catch up with Kahlil for a week. He knew that Kahlil was on his way to Philadelphia to attend a summit of community organizations and wanted to stop by to see him before he left. Kahlil was packing his bags preparing to go while talking on the phone with a brother from Philadelphia who wanted to get information on the Coalition in hopes of starting the same type of program in Philadelphia.

"Sure, brother," Kahlil said as Demitrious picked up a magazine while he waited for Kahlil. "I'll bring you that, too, and anything else I think will help you to get it off the ground. See you there." Kahlil hung up the phone and turned to Demitrious. "Well I guess it's on. The meeting is all set and it's time to get down to business. Things are starting to look up now. Cece and I are engaged, the Coalition is taking off, you got your son back. God is so good," Kahlil said.

"Yeah, things are looking up, brother, and I am really glad that you and Cece have finally decided to tie the knot. She is one down-to-earth sister," Demitrious said.

"Thanks."

"But you know who's looking good?" Demitrious asked as he sat back on Kahlil's couch and put his hands behind his head.

"Who's that?" Kahlil said as he sat down across from Demitrious and began to put some polish on his leather shoes.

"Dewayna."

Kahlil looked at him and smiled. "I knew you were going to say that. I saw her checking you out at O's birthday party."

"That's what I'm saying, brother. And I was checking her out, too."

"Well, tell the truth, and shame the devil!" Kahlil said. He could see Demitrious was anxious to talk about Dewayna.

"Two weeks ago . . . right . . . she went to the zoo with me and Octavious and she was looking so damn good. I mean the entire package. I'm not just talking about her body, because that has always been there, but her smile and her whole damn attitude is just starting to bring back memories and turn a brother on."

"Well, why don't you try to get things back together? Don't forget you two are still married."

"Man, I have. At least I've started to. But your girl Sonje is always over at the house or calling on the phone for her and I just can't seem to break any ground with her."

"What do you mean she is always over at the house?"

"I mean, every time I go over there, she's there or has just left. Even my boy mentioned it to me. We were at the zoo and Dewayna went into the rest room and he asked me. 'Daddy, why can't I watch TV in mommy's room no more when Sonje comes over?"

There was silence.

"I'll be damned. You won't believe this shit. I ran into Sonje at the Coalition, and we were talking about an idea for the show and when we finished talking, I noticed a book called *Afreketa* on her desk. I asked her about it and she said, she'd just gotten it back from a friend. The book is about—"

Demitrious interrupted. "I know, about lesbians written by lesbian writers. Kahlil, I saw the same book over at Dewayna's and she tried to hide it from me, but I looked at the back cover before she could take it away. Do you think they're getting together?"

"Brother, I don't even want to entertain that question."

"Well, from all the articles I've been reading, and from what I see on the streets, it seems like more and more women are doing that type of thing now. I don't know if it's right or wrong. I guess when you're let down by so many brothers, myself included, you probably grow tired of having your mind fucked with. I really don't know if I can blame them." Demitrious turned the page of the magazine. "You know how we can do them sometimes, and there's always the possibility that she was born with that type of gene and it's just now coming out."

"Demitrious," Kahlil said in disbelief, "I'm sorry, but I think you're being a little soft about the situation, my brother."

"Why do you say that?"

"Do you actually believe that?" Demitrious didn't answer. "Well, I don't. Women are supposed to be with men and vice versa. How can you buy into that gene rhetoric? What does a homosexual or bisexual gene look like, anyway? Who in the hell was looking in the microscope when they discovered what it looked like? I just want to know who's coming up and sending out all of these analogies that everyone seems to believe and doesn't challenge. I am not being insensitive here either, but I really don't understand all these people, talking about they were born gay. They only say that so they can have an excuse for their activities."

"You really don't think that can happen?" Demitrious asked.

"Man, get real. You can't tell me that when two people of the same sex lay down with each other, I don't care how young or old, that they don't know and feel that it's an unnatural act. If it's not unnatural, why do people stay in the closet all their lives or try their best to keep it a secret from everyone else?"

Demitrious looked at Kahlil and shook his head. "You have a point there."

"Like I said, brother, I ain't bashing but I have yet to be convinced," Kahlil said.

"But what I try to do is just go with the flow, because it seems as though so many people are into that type of thing nowadays. So I just leave well enough alone," Demitrious explained.

"I hear you, but I can't help but be concerned. I think it's wrong. But what really kills me is when our women accept gay men with open arms and just flock to them, as though they're really women. I mean, you see them downtown, eating lunch together, looking at men together. I wish our women would just stop that nonsense and straight-up tell these men to be what God intended them to be—*men*."

Demitrious smiled. "Kahlil, are you sure you're not still upset because that gay guy that works downtown found out where you worked and was leaving messages at your job and all over your car, signing them Dawn, and you thought he was some fine-ass woman," Demitrious asked, laughing.

"Fuck you, Demitrious." Kahlil began to laugh. "Yeah, I told him if he ever called my job again I'd kick his ass, too, didn't I?"

Demitrious looked at Kahlil sarcastically. "I guess you did. At least, that's what you told everybody."

"You know damn well that's what I told him. But seriously, if you're a man then be a man, and if you're a woman then be a woman. I'm talking about in the mind, body, and soul. I'm just glad I'm not a teenager having to grow up in this society because everyone's sexual connotation is so screwed up. You have your straights, gays, and now the bisexuals are mobilizing. I even read an article where a reporter asked a confused so-called bisexual black man if his newborn baby was a boy or a girl . . . and you want to know what he said?"

"What?"

"Ask the baby. Ain't that a bitch. Putting pressure on a baby who has just come out of the womb to decide if it's a boy or girl! People are sick. They are misrepresenting Scripture and trying their best to give themselves a reason for having valid existence. Case in point," Kahlil said pointing to Demitrious with his shoe. "If in fact women don't need a man and they are truly gay, why do they buy sex toys to use on each other. You don't even have to answer because I'll answer it for you. They use them because when they are together they are missing something that they just don't have to give."

Demitrious shook his head, speechless.

"To top it off, they always blame it on God for being the way they are! Why don't they ever blame it on the devil?" Kahlil asked.

"Well, brother, there's not much we can do about it because it's the way of the world," Demitrious said, set in his way of thinking.

"Well, my brother, let me tell you something that I think you already know. 'Greater is he that is in me than he who is in the world.' So my advice to you is, you better start thinking about the world your son is living in, if Sonje and Dewayna are over in that house, being in the way of the world. Demitrious, boys need guidance, support, and tough love. And I believe the only place they can get that is from us. Look what happened to Mrs. Betty Shabazz—her own flesh and blood is now charged with setting her on fire. Now what kind of sense does that make? Brother, these young boys think they are invincible and are not growing up with the proper direction, and I look at it like this. If we can give them a solid foundation and understanding about what they are going to be faced with, then damn it, we should." Kahlil hit a chord. There was no way in hell Demitrious wanted his son to grow up in that type of environment.

"Kahlil, you know what? You're right. Octavious is involved and I'm going to have to see what's going on with these two. I didn't even think about it like that. I've already let my boy down once and if I stand around while this is happening, then it's just like I'm doing it again. You know I can't let him down anymore."

"Speaking of letting down, have you decided what you're going to do about Sonje's show? You know this is the Coalition's chance, brother."

"Kahlil, I haven't made up my mind yet. I just don't think I can sit up in front of the cameras like I'm some kind of hero or something. I'm just doing what I should be doing and that's taking care of my son."

"Demitrious, you are a hero and that's what we want to get across to all the other brothers in the community. We want to show black men doing right and what's necessary for the betterment of the community and their families, instead of being shown as the top crime story on the six o'clock news all the time. We finally get to have our day. Plus, when I talked to Sonje, she guaranteed everything would be great. Brother, you can't pass this up."

"I guess you're right, I owe you one anyway," Demitrious said.

Might as Well

I was pissed off, cold, lost, and I couldn't get anybody to come pick me up. I couldn't believe Deric made me get out in the middle of the street and left me in the middle of nowhere at two in the morning. I just knew he was going to circle around the corner and feel bad for putting me out, like he does when he tries not to talk to me for days, then breaks down. But that was not the case. I watched his sorry ass disappear into the night. I was all alone and by myself, at least seven miles away from home, and in the middle of the hood.

Lee didn't help the situation either. After finally remembering my calling card number, I phoned and told him what had happened and asked him to pick me up. He started explaining how he couldn't, because they had a team breakfast at five in the morning and he couldn't get away from Linda. That son of a bitch. "You won't see any of this again," I screamed at him. To top it off, after I told him that Deric had found out about us, he hinted that he thought we had better slow down, because he didn't want any problems with Deric. So there I was, without a quarter for a cab to my name.

Fed Up with the Fanny

I wanted to call Cece, but her car was all messed up and I didn't want to hear her I told-ya-so mouth, so I stood for a second to think about what I was going to do. The only thing that I had on my body was my short leather jacket that barely reached my waist, tight black jeans, and my brand-new Dolce & Gabbana shoes that were made for styling, not fuckin' hiking. I didn't expect to be exposed to that cold ass air. I was beginning to shake and my fingers were beginning to go numb. I knew that Kahlil lived about six blocks from where I was and decided to walk over to his house and ask him to take me home.

I was stepping as quickly as I possibly could and I prayed that Kahlil would have enough forgiveness in his heart to take me to get my car without holding the things that I'd said to him in front of Sonje at Points against me. We had never discussed it before but I knew through Cece that he didn't appreciate what I did. I tried my best to hurry past the abandoned buildings that now served as shelters for homeless people. I threw my I'm-the-shit attitude away seconds after I realized that Deric wasn't coming back to get me. I knew that if I stumbled across the wrong person in this neighborhood I was going to be in big trouble.

I walked past a Church's Chicken restaurant. It was closed, but there were four cars in the parking lot and a group of men hanging out talking. I tried my best to walk past them without being noticed. I jumped and damn near screamed when a car stopped right in front of me on the corner. I stopped and held my breath, then noticed a hooker clutching her purse tightly as she got out of her trick's car, quickly shutting the door before the car sped off. The hooker acted like it was just another day at the office. She looked at me with a tart expression on her face and spit out whatever she had in her mouth. With disgust, she turned to me as I tried to walk around her with my head down. "Girl, these tricks are getting younger and younger every day. How did you make out tonight?" she asked me. I looked at that ho and quickened up my pace to get away from her nasty ass. My night was not supposed to end like this.

I'd planned on letting Deric buy my dinner while I comforted and soothed him with my good looks and promises, so that he would get over the fact that I'd been using his bankcard without his knowledge. I was even going to promise to give him some. But not that night. I'd planned to tell him that the drink I had was too strong and gave me a headache. But definitely, absolutely, tomorrow, which wouldn't have come either. He would have just been happy that I owed him something.

My shoes were beginning to hurt my feet. As I got closer to Kahlil's house, I remembered what Cece told me about Kahlil letting his big-ass dog sleep outside on the porch sometimes. I hoped and prayed that was not the case. I knew I was only about three blocks from his house. For the second time, I noticed an older model car with a broken headlight drive past me. I didn't dare turn around and see where it was going. As I turned off the well-lit street into the residential area, I realized the car was now behind me. The driver turned off its one good light and was following me down the narrow one-way street. It was completely dark and there was no light coming from the houses on the street.

I was getting scared and I could feel my body begin to shake. I hadn't felt that way since the judge read the verdict when I was raped. I started to wonder if I should take off my shoes and run like hell.

"Yo, baby, you need a ride?" a voice said, as the car coasted beside me. "Me and my boys will take you anywhere you want to go . . . with yo' fine ass."

I could tell there were at least four guys in the car—the same number that raped me. I could hear laughter coming from the car and the sounds of beer bottles being thrown out of the window on the other side. I tried to ignore them in hopes that they would just drive away and leave me alone.

"You know, I hate a bitch to walk past me when I ask a question. Um . . . um . . . um, look at the ass on that mothafucka . . . damn she looks good," I heard a voice say from the back of the car. I was one second from bending down and snatching off my shoes as they continued to comment about my ass.

"Baby, I'm goin' to ask you again. Where are you headed?"

I could feel my stomach beginning to tremble and I was beginning to lose my breath. I was already walking as fast as I could. Without looking into the car I said, "Over to a friend's."

"What's your friend's name?" a voice shouted.

"Kahlil!" I shouted back. Immediately, the one headlight on the car came back on.

"Well, why didn't you say that in the first place, black woman?" the driver of the car asked. "We'll give you an escort, 'cause niggas out here are ignorant." The others in the car agreed with him.

"Tommy, apologize to the lady for calling her a bitch," the driver said, and Tommy did.

When I heard him apologize to me, I didn't know what the hell was going on. As soon as I mentioned Kahlil's name their whole demeanor changed like he was some type of celebrity or something. They not only knew exactly where Kahlil lived, but guided me in the right direction when I almost turned down the wrong street. I didn't hear any more mean or nasty things come out of their mouths about me or my behind as they followed me. They were talking about Kahlil as though they admired him and knew they better respect me.

We arrived at Kahlil's and as I walked up to the porch, my escort got out of the car and for some strange reason stood behind the car on the far side of the street. I knocked on the door.

"Watch out for that rott now, sister. If that thing gets a hold of you, cancel Christmas," one of my escorts said. No wonder their punk asses were behind the car, I thought to myself. I held my breath. I could hear them talking about how damn big the dog was. I am scared to death of dogs and I jumped back from the door when I heard the animal begin to bark.

When I heard Nite barking and the knocking on my door I just knew it was Ms. Doris, my neighbor down the street, wanting me to do something for her. It was always something. She continually asked me to do things for her at all times of the night and I did them because her family didn't care anything about her and she was going on ninety years old. She would usually scream "Kahlil . . . Kahlil," as loud as she could but this time it was quiet. I looked down from my bedroom window and saw a familiar car but I was unable to tell who it was. I opened the window and yelled down, still half asleep.

"Yeah, who is it?" My eyes focused on some brothers who were standing in the street.

"Yo Kahlil, it's Harris. I escorted a lady friend of yours over here. She's down here on your porch." He pointed over to my porch and Kelly, of all people, stepped off it and looked up to my window.

"Kahlil, it's me, Kelly. Can you let me in? I'm stranded." She was rubbing her hands together and shivering. I grabbed my robe and went downstairs. I had to calm Nite down before I opened the door. He was going crazy from all the activity outside. I opened the door and there was Kelly, looking cold and tired.

I looked at Kelly and just shook my head. "Come on in." I waved to Harris and the brothers who had jumped in the car when I opened the door. They blew the horn and drove away. As I locked my door Nite moved in on Kelly and began to sniff her. He seemed like he enjoyed her perfume and I was too tired to tell him to stop.

"What happened? Your car break down or something?" I asked.

"No, me and Deric got into an argument and his sorry ass kicked me out of the car."

I wasn't surprised. I could tell she noticed I was looking at her like, "so what do you want me to do?"

"Kahlil, I know it's late, but can you take me to get my car? I wouldn't have bothered you, but it's just too far away for me to walk," Kelly said.

"Kelly, I would, but at five forty-five in the morning my plane is leaving for Philly, and I have to get some rest." She looked back at me like, "so what."

"Why don't you do this, just sleep here on the couch and in a couple of hours I'll take you anywhere you want to go." I reached up into the hall closet and gave her a blanket. Then I began to walk back up the stairs.

"Okay, that will work, but, Kahlil, what about this damn dog?" Kelly asked, looking agitated.

I looked back downstairs at Nite and he was slobbin' down Kelly's shoes.

"Oh, don't worry. He likes you," I said and went upstairs to sleep.

I was speechless. I walked over to the couch and pulled that cover over my head. I couldn't even look that big-ass dog in the face with his big head. He wouldn't stop licking my shoes, so I just took them off. He took one of my shoes into the back with him and left me alone.

I only slept for about an hour or so. I was thinking about how I was played, not only by Deric, but Lee as well. It had been a long time since I'd been abandoned, rejected, and stunned by two men on the same night. As a matter of fact it was the first time. I lay on that couch as quietly as I possibly could for about two more hours. I knew it was almost time for Kahlil to take me to get my car from Deric's.

Nature was calling me and I couldn't hold it any longer. I peeked over the couch and saw Nite laying in the hallway leading to the kitchen, sleeping with my shoe under his enormous paw, holding it like it was his. I quietly got off of the couch and tiptoed upstairs. As I walked down the hall to the bathroom, I heard Kahlil in the shower and I just stood there at the door and started thinking.

Wouldn't it be nice, since I'm already having a fucked-up time, to throw another skeleton bone in my closet, seduce my girl's man and find out if everything she ever told me about him was true; just be nasty because everyone was treating me that way. I remembered it had been a long time since I had slept with a man that I couldn't tell a soul about. I did let a guy that Cece had a crush on before Kahlil eat me out in the dorm at homecoming, but that was years ago. Cece never figured out why he stopped coming around. He probably thought I told her. I didn't, though. Being sneaky and knowing what a girlfriend's man had in his pants always turned me on. The temptation got the best of me. I enjoyed the feeling it was giving me, and I didn't want to control it. Cece was always bragging about Kahlil and I wanted to find out for myself what the hype was all about. I mean, really . . . could Kahlil be that devoted to my girl and pass up all that I have to offer? Uh-uh . . . I don't think so.

In a matter of seconds I had my clothes off and was standing naked outside the bathroom door. I opened the door hoping to have a chance to surprise Kahlil and get into the shower with him, but the water stopped as soon as I opened the door. There he was, standing outside of the shower, completely naked, dripping wet, looking like a black king. Before he could say one word, and without any hesitation, I had my arms around Kahlil's waist, moaning lightly while I scanned my eyes over his entire body. I was surprised that Kahlil's body actually looked better than Lee's and Lee was paid to keep his in shape. When I looked up at Kahlil's face he looked like he was being jacked or something. I reached up and put my arms around his neck and placed my head on his big, black chest. I felt him flinch and I bent my legs to get down on my knees. Kahlil pushed me away from him, almost knocking me on my naked ass.

"What in the hell is wrong with you!" he said, reaching for his robe. "I don't know if you're still buzzing from whatever you had to drink last night, but I'm here to tell you it's not that type of party up in here!"

Kahlil tied his robe together and looked down at me. I regained my balance and stood in front of him with a smile on my face, hands at my sides, giving him a perfect view of my perfect body, which no man has ever turned down before. "Kahlil, I just thought I'd come in and, you know. . . . This may sound funny, but I've heard so much about you and I've never been with one of Cece's men before. The whole thing is just turning me on. I just want to see if what she says about you is true. It's all right, we can keep this between us . . . come on, just do me like you do Cece and Sonje."

I walked toward him to get closer, and reached out to him. He looked at me, then pushed me to the side, as I stood directly in front of the bathroom door trying to block his path.

"You better get ready or you will find your ass stranded again," he said and stormed out the door.

"Kahlil, why are you driving so fast?" I asked, as he kept his eyes on the road, while an early edition of the Rush Limbaugh show played on the radio. I think that made him drive even faster.

"I told you, Kelly, I have to get to the airport."

I just sat there wondering if he was going to drop me off and run to the phone to call Cece as soon as he got to the airport to tell her what had happened. You know how some men are always wanting to tell their women when someone has hit on them to show their commitment, loyalty, and sex appeal. I didn't know if I should bring up the situation with Kahlil or wait for him to say something. As quiet and cold as he was acting, I sure as hell wasn't going to wait long for him to say anything because in the next ten minutes I was going to be in Deric's driveway starting up my car.

"So, what happens now?" I asked.

"I don't know what you mean," Kahlil said back to me.

"You know what I mean. Are you going to tell Cece and ruin our friendship over some stupid shit that just happened out of the blue? Or are we going to forget about this little misunderstanding?"

"Misunderstanding?" Kahlil said. "You are a trip. How are you going to play Cece?"

At least he was talking to me—now was my chance.

"Well, Kahlil, I just want to explain to you why I walked in on you like that. Like I told you earlier, Cece is always telling me things about you that I've wondered about ever since you two have been seeing each other. I guess all of her stories kind of aroused me and got the best of me. I just wanted to see for myself if the things she said about you were true. I'm not saying I was right, but I'm telling you the truth."

He acted like he didn't even hear what I was saying to him. I knew I had to be more persuasive because I just had to make him understand.

"Look, Kahlil. I'm sorry. I wasn't thinking straight. For the first time in a long time, I don't have anyone and I guess I wanted to feel needed and wanted. Do you know how it feels to be put out in the middle of town at night all by yourself? I was scared, cold, and upset. My head wasn't clear. I'm sure you can understand." I wondered if I struck a chord because he turned and looked at me for a brief second.

"Kelly, you don't have to explain anything to me. I've known what you were about ever since I met you. You haven't changed and I don't think you ever will. You've never done anything for anybody except Kelly and I'll tell you just like I told Cece: I wish you would change your ways or get out of Cece's life because it's apparent that you don't care anything about her."

Now Kahlil was trippin'. I know he didn't think I was going to let him talk to me like that.

"Wait a minute," I said to him. "What I did and how I feel about Cece are two different subjects. What I did this morning was about me. Cece had nothing to do with it. She is my girl and I love her. You just happened to be available and her man at the same time. To be honest with you, all I wanted to do is get Deric back for putting me out in the street. You know how it is."

"No, I don't. If you're with a person and you aren't being truthful to them then you deserve to be left. I don't know why you play that brother the way you do anyway."

Oh no, he wasn't talking about me after all the shit he's done to my girl, I thought.

"Don't even try it. You act like you've never been in this type of situation before. Don't forget about your on-the-air lover," I said with spite.

Kahlil stopped the car, turned down the radio, and looked at me. "No, don't you forget. Everyone involved knew the truth and was completely fine with it, until you brought your ass into the situation. But I'm okay because Cece and I are making things happen, and soon you won't be able to control her like you do."

He put the car back into drive and sped off. Kahlil is nothing like Deric. He wasn't even going to let me lay any guilt trip down on him, so I just shut up. We pulled into Deric's driveway.

"Look—if you're worried that I'm going to tell Cece about this morning then you don't need to be," Kahlil said. "I don't think she'd be able to handle it. Plus your pathetic ass needs all the friends you can get. As a matter of fact, just forget that you ever came over." Kahlil put the car in park and took his foot off the brake. Then he looked deep into my eyes. "But let me tell you something. Don't you ever try that again or I will expose your ass and not only will you be without a man, you'll be without the only person that considers you her best friend."

I opened the car door and got out without another word.

Dinner

◇

I was excited by the turnout in Philly and by the very fruitful meeting that I attended with other community leaders around the country. I couldn't wait to get back to the Coalition and put some of the ideas we discussed on paper for the board. It felt good to know that I wasn't the only brother in the country taking it hard on the corporate level and trying to do what was needed in the community. Seeing all of the lawyers, doctors, accountants, vice presidents, and CEOs of other companies only fueled my determination to keep up the struggle.

Cece and I had made plans for a late dinner when I got back. While I waited for her in the restaurant, I ordered wine, grilled chicken, and penne pasta for myself, and for my baby, I ordered her favorite chicken Florentine. When she arrived she was looking good, as usual.

"Baby, just give me your hand, you are so fine," I said.

"Thank you. Did you have a nice time?" she said, smiling.

"Yes, it was nice." I watched her eyes as she picked up her wine-glass. The reflection turned me on and she knew it.

"Guess what, baby?" Cece said, as if she had good news. "Kelly asked if she could move back in with me."

My good mood disappeared with the quickness.

"What did you tell her?"

"You know I said yes. That's my girl, but she was acting strange."

"How do you mean?"

"I don't know. She was real quiet. She and Deric got into it again. She said that they were finished, but I think she realizes already that she really likes him more than she thought she did."

"I doubt that," I said. I was about to blow off the handle and tell Cece that her girl wasn't worth her time. It took everything I had to keep cool.

"Why do you say that, Kahlil?" Cece asked.

"Oh, nothing, baby." I looked around the restaurant and tried to clear my head. "So what did you decide? Are you going to let her stay or what?"

Cece nodded. "I just hope it doesn't interfere with our time," she said.

"Come on, baby, you know better than that. By the way, have you thought about what you want to do with that place when we get married?" Cece shook her head no.

"Well, I was thinking about going ahead and paying it off and renting it out. If that's what you want to do."

"That's fine with me. It really never crossed my mind. Yeah, let's do that. You know Deric is a realtor—maybe he can find some people who might want to rent it from us. Kelly might even want to rent it."

I took a deep breath and looked at Cece, then turned my head.

"What's wrong, Boo?"

"Nothing, baby." I tried to hold it back, but I really had to say something about Kelly. "I just wish you'd surround yourself with more positive people."

"What do you mean?" Cece said, taking a bite of her French bread.

"I'm saying that you're doing well on your job. Things are moving in a positive direction, and I really think you should encircle yourself with friends who are a little bit more positive than Kelly."

Cece put down her bread and took a sip of her wine. "I knew you were going to bring this up sooner or later, Kahlil."

I didn't know what she was talking about.

"Why do you want me to do that? Is it because I'm going to have to act a certain way or be around certain type of people when we get married? Like the wives of all your professional and community activist friends? If you can remember, Kahlil—Kelly is the one who helped me get my job in the first place. She didn't have to do that."

"No, Cece, that's not it at all," I said, then held her small hand again. "It's just that, sometimes, people outgrow others, and I think you're much too special to be troubled with Kelly's silliness."

Cece looked at me and sort of laughed as if what I was saying was unbelievable. "You know what? Kelly told me something weeks ago, but I didn't even mention it because I knew you weren't like that."

"So what did she say?"

"When she and I were talking about marriage she told me that I better find out why you really wanted to marry me." Cece took her hand away from mine.

"Baby, what are you talking about? I want to marry you because I love you."

"Are you sure? Sometimes people get married for different reasons besides love and I just want to make sure you didn't ask me to marry you because you're in need of a wife to make you look stable to your colleagues." Cece was talking to me like she had been brainwashed.

"Colleagues? Cece, you know I don't give a damn about what those fools at work think about me, and the Coalition likes me just the way I am. I thought you knew I wanted to start my own business anyhow. What has gotten into you?" I asked.

"Nothing, and don't start thinking that I've let Kelly fill my head up with things either because that's exactly how you look. I've been analyzing things since we've been engaged and it seems like you have been taking me for granted because you have me now."

"Cece, what are you talking about?"

"You've broken off things that we had planned to do together because of business and I don't want that to be something that happens all the time when we get married. And as far as surrounding myself with so-called positive people, Kahlil, I've never gone out with those stuffy, cutthroat hussies at work, and I never will. They act like they're positive, but I know they aren't. All they care about is money."

I had to interrupt her.

"That's all Kelly thinks about, right or wrong?"

"Yes, to a certain extent, but Kelly likes to have fun, go out, and act crazy. I haven't met any professional women who want to go out and have a good time. The ones I know only want to go out to ladies night once every blue moon and watch the brothers strip because they're too busy to find a man to do it for them. I don't want any part of that. I am happy with being Kelly's friend and she needs me."

"Cece, you have it all wrong. I don't want you to stop seeing Kelly. I just wish you would go out with other people, too. People who are more positive, who know themselves, and who are not playing childish games anymore."

"What do you mean, childish games, Kahlil?"

I wanted to tell her. I swear I did, but I didn't. She loved Kelly too much and it would crush her. I didn't think she'd believe me if I told her anyway. Kelly was her girl and there was nothing I could do about it, so I just left well enough alone. Besides, our food was getting cold.

For Ol' Times' Sake

Demitrious stared at the very porch he'd sat on each and every time after he and Dewayna made love in the summer months when they were first married. He paused one last time before knocking. He'd been back to the house many times since getting back into his son's life, but this time was monumental. It was the first time he and Dewayna had a chance to be alone.

"Oh hi, Demitrious. I thought I heard you knocking," Dewayna said as she stepped back and opened the door wider so he could walk in. Demitrious sat down looking over the room he'd shared with Dewayna.

"What's wrong?" Dewayna asked when she noticed he was looking at the floor.

"Nothing . . . nothing at all." Demitrious shook the thoughts out of his mind. "So, are you enjoying your time away from Octavious?"

Dewayna smiled and sat down next to Demitrious.

"You know I am. I think it was great for the girls at work to come up with this idea."

"So, every weekend the kids stay over at someone else's house?" Demitrious asked.

"That's right . . . I went over to Sandy's to see how six little kids look, running all over the house, because next weekend it's my turn to watch them and they'll be all here," Dewayna said, laughing. "I'm thinking about sectioning off the back room, turning on the TV, and renting some movies and letting them go at it all weekend long. Don't you think that would be fun?"

"Oh yeah, they can have their own little party. Need any help? If so, I'm here for you," Demitrious said with hope.

"Thanks, but Sonje has already volunteered and I accepted," Dewayna said in what seemed like a blushing kind of way to Demitrious.

"You know, she's real good people," Demitrious said, trying to feel the situation out.

"Um, hmm. . . . She sure is," Dewayna confirmed.

Dewayna and Demitrious were quiet. Demitrious had originally intended to ask her about Sonje, but on the way over he decided not to. For one reason, he didn't know how she would react and it was definitely too early to be getting her upset with him after he'd been gone for so long.

"You know, since I was the one who asked to come over, I'm going to start this off." Dewayna sat back and prepared herself for what Demitrious was about to say.

"I wanted to come over tonight just to let you know that I really have enjoyed the couple of times that we've all gone out together. I'm especially grateful that we've been able to stay friends and I hope that we can continue to see one another. To be serious with you, I've been thinking about what we should be doing and where we would have been if I'd never left in the first place."

Dewayna smiled and started to say something.

"Hold on, let me finish, because I didn't even think I'd be able to say that, and I'm on a roll. I haven't told you this in such a long time, but I really think you're looking good. Not that I expected you not to look good, but you're looking as good as the day that I first met you and I'm just happy that you're still my wife."

Dewayna was surprised.

"Technically, baby."

"I understand, Demitrious," Dewayna said, smiling.

"I don't know how many times I've thought about you and Octavious while I was gone. I know that I hurt both of you like hell. But I want you to know there wasn't a minute I didn't think about my wife and my son. I know it was hard on you, but it was very difficult on me, too. I fought and wrestled with myself about picking up the phone to just hear your voice and my son playing in the background. But I was afraid and I kept away each time. . . . I've decided that I want to tell you why I left in the first place and maybe this will clear up some things you don't understand."

"Demitrious, you don't know how happy that would make me. I always wondered why." Dewayna sat there waiting for him to continue.

"Dewayna," Demitrious said, laughing, "I'm going to tell you, but I want this to be special because I've been told that what I did was a very smart thing to do. I feel good about it, so I want to treat it as something special."

"What are you talking about, Demitrious?"

"You remember the vacation I promised you in Manhattan where I was going to let you shop until you drop, wine and dine you, and show you the city? Well, that's what I'd like to do and the plans have already been made. I've been so sneaky about it. I've made sure that you're off for the weekend and Octavious will be staying with Gayla according to the schedule you gave me of who he stays with each week. So, all you have to do is say you will go."

Dewayna was speechless. She thought about Sonje right away. Did she really want to run off with her husband? How could she run off with her husband after they'd been separated over a year?

A romantic weekend at that. I can't, she thought. I better not. It wouldn't be right. Maybe Sonje would feel like I did when Demitrious first left me. But it's only a weekend and I'm having second thoughts about Sonje anyway. There's no way I'm going to take her to Daddy and say, "meet my new lover." And I'm sure Octavious is already fed up with me spending so much time with her.

All of a sudden, her thoughts disappeared. Demitrious had grabbed her and planted his lips right against hers.

"That's another reason I came over," he said. Dewayna grabbed him back. In seconds they were all over the couch.

That's right, girl. This is what you've been missing, and there's nothing else like it, a voice told Dewayna.

On My Way

"**M**r. Thomas, are you sure you won't be needing limousine reservations during your stay?" the stewardess asked.

"No, thank you Denise, I believe the rental car will be fine. It will give me a chance to relax and drive back and forth to Canada myself."

"That's fine, Sir. I've confirmed your hotel reservations and you're all set. Is there anything else that I can do for you? If not, we'll be landing in about thirty minutes." Denise took Waydis's coffee cup and smiled as she tried to keep her balance when the plane shook violently, making its way through the storm.

His eyes moved directly to the envelope that sat before him. He'd already read the contents thoroughly at least three times since he boarded the plane and was pleased, to say the least. He was scheduled for a very important business merger in Winsor, Canada, but as he boarded the plane for his meeting his private investigator had surprised him by jumping out of his car on the runway and telling him that he had good news. The news was so encouraging that Waydis decided that he would stop in Detroit on his way to Winsor for a very overdue visit. He picked up the envelope and read it again.

"To: Mr. Waydis Thomas, Vice President of WorldLine Airlines."
He looked out into the terrible storm outside his window. You
think it's storming now, he thought. When Ms. Leandra sees me,
she's going to piss her proverbial pants. He slammed the shade
shut on the window next to his seat as the plane started to de-
scend.

Waydis Thomas, Sid's father, was overjoyed that he had finally
found out the whereabouts of his son. At the same time, he was
mad as hell that it had taken him so long. Waydis and Leandra
met at Tennessee State after he'd finished running for 135 yards
in a football game against Hampton University at homecoming.
All through the game he heard a tiny voice calling from right behind the bench. When he finally turned around to see who it was,
he was elated to see that it was the smartest lady in his accounting
class. After the game Leandra walked up to Waydis to congratu-
late him on his stellar performance and he asked her to a party.
From that night on, they were like rabbits in heat until the end of
winter quarter, when Leandra left unexpectedly and without a
word. Waydis was upset, and he tried to find out what happened
from her friends, but no one knew anything. Leandra had just disappeared.

Waydis was stunned and his life changed dramatically the day a
teammate came to his room right before practice to tell him he
had a phone call. It was Leandra. She'd called to tell him that he
was the father of their baby who was to be born in a matter of
weeks. From that very day, he wanted to take responsibility for his
child. Waydis walked into the coach's office, quit the team, then
marched across campus and signed up for R.O.T.C.

Waydis and Leandra kept in touch during his last two years of
school. Waydis found a job at the local grocery store and worked
forty hours a week while still maintaining a full load of classes. Leandra was too embarrassed by her condition to go home and have
the baby in Detroit, so she moved to Chicago with family, which

was where Waydis thought she was from all along. They talked on the phone almost every night and Waydis even convinced Leandra to marry him and go overseas with him so that they could be a family for Sid.

Exactly one week before Waydis was to be shipped off to Germany, Leandra called him and told him that she'd decided she would raise Sid on her own. She never gave him a reason why she felt that way. Waydis didn't agree, but tried to put himself in her position. He tried to understand that Germany may have been too much of a change for her. Leandra promised Waydis that he would be a part of Sid's life. That's why he agreed to have his child support taken right out of his check and sent to a bank account in Chicago. Leandra never told him she moved to Detroit with Sid.

Waydis spent ten years of his life in the army, so that he could take care of his son to the best of his ability. He hated that atmosphere. During his service he was stationed in France, Lebanon, Texas, and Ft. Bragg, North Carolina. The army was no place for a black man, particularly Waydis. He was too outspoken and wasn't allowed to express his views like he wanted to. Most of the time he was the only black officer in his company, so he was held to a higher standard than the others. He despised that shit. Still, he made it to the rank of major and got out when his obligation was over. During a trip to his hometown of Philadelphia, at a stopover in New York City, Waydis met a terrific man who thought he would be a great leader and would fit perfectly into his company. They exchanged numbers, and Waydis was called shortly after and flown to Boston, where he was offered a job at WorldLine Airlines as the Vice President of Communications. Ever since, he had been making a six-figure salary. He was married shortly thereafter and had two sons, but his marriage ended in divorce after his wife became tired of hearing about his long-lost son.

As the FASTEN SEAT BELT sign came on Waydis thought about how Leandra prevented him from being a part of his son's life for all of these years. This was not the way it was supposed to turn out. He'd missed the best years of Sid's life. The only thing he had to prepare for, he thought, was Sid asking him questions about where he'd been all of his life, and what the hell did he want after all this time. Waydis couldn't understand how anyone could keep her son from his natural father all of his life and still be able to look in the mirror every morning. Waydis tried to figure out what he was going to say to Leandra once he saw her again. He knew they would be choice words and he didn't give a damn how she was going to take them.

I'm Out

I was sitting at my desk, cleaning up the mess I'd made during the four-hour meeting with the eastern regions' largest manufacturer of household goods. I am telling you, Kahlil Richardson was at his best today if I do say so myself. Those suckers were intent on getting a cheaper deal, but after two hours of going back and forth they knew they weren't going to get a better deal. I wore them down and they decided to let me take their company to the next level. I signed them to the largest contract the Houston Corporation had ever seen. I was just about to sign off on the memos when my boss, Mr. Gales, called me to say that he was on his way in. "Well, he better hurry his ass up," I thought to myself as I looked at my watch. He knew how I felt about staying late.

Gales walked into my office five minutes later. He looked as if his day had been worse than mine. His gray hair was out of place and he kept trying to put it back as he had it that morning. Then when he saw that his shirt was out of his pants he looked at me as if to say "the hell with it." He sat down, grabbed his lower lip, and sighed like he knew he was going to have trouble saying anything to me.

"So, you wanted to see me?" I asked.

"Kahlil, hell, I've tussled with this all day and I've come to the conclusion that there's just no way to sugarcoat it, so I'll just come straight out with it. I'm selling the business," he said. Then he took his eyes off me.

"What are you talking about, Don? We're making more money than ever before. We're not in any trouble."

"Yeah, I know, Kahlil, but I'm getting old and Nachi offered me a hell of a deal. More than seven times what the company is actually worth on paper, plus stocks, and I just can't turn it down."

"Nachi. Don, that's the competition. Have you gone crazy?"

"No, Kahlil, after they offered me that money I was ready to call them our brothers," he said smiling. "They're taking over the Houston Corporation as is."

"You mean they're just going to buy you out and leave everything in place?"

"Exactly, except one thing . . ."

"What's that?" I asked.

"Without you," he said so quickly that I barely heard him.

"What did you say?"

"Kahlil, the deal is contingent on my letting you go. You know how the foreigners are. If they're going to work with anyone in America, they prefer them to be white." Don got out of his chair. He knew that I was about to turn the place out.

"You mean to tell me, if you fire a nigga, you can ride off into the sunset and live carefree the rest of your life?"

Don smiled. "And my kids, too, and probably their children's children," he said. "Kahlil, this is not a race thing. I'd fire my mama if I had to and my wife right along with her for this type of money."

"Well, Don, I think that's bullshit . . . and I know it's against the law."

"Kahlil, don't worry. I told them that you're not the type of person to fuck around with. And they have made it very nice for you, too." Don reached into his shirt pocket and took out a piece of paper.

"Look Kahlil, here are the particulars. They offered to buy you out at top dollar plus triple anything that you have in the company's savings plan with a commitment to pay all taxes on every cent of it, whenever you withdraw it."

I snatched the paper out of his hand and looked at their numbers. When I saw all the zeros, I didn't have to think about what I wanted to do, not one bit. I'm out, I said to myself. Don must have read the expression on my face as I kept my eyes on the numbers.

"You see, I told you. One point eight million. Plus they will triple your savings. That's over four million dollars," he said, rubbing his hands together. I placed the paper on my desk and looked at it.

"So, when do you need an answer?" I asked.

"They're not going to present me with a contract for another month, but I'll need your answer in two weeks. Look at it this way, Kahlil, you'll be able to do the things that you've always dreamed of doing," he said, then walked out.

That's mighty white of you, I thought.

Straight Set Up

Cece ate her Mickey Dee's French fries one by one, enjoying every bit of her favorite snack food. She'd been sitting, waiting patiently, going on twenty minutes for Kelly in the food court at the mall. She began to laugh and looked back at the sisters who sat behind her. They were talking about how much they missed the music of Steve Arrington, Eric Gable, Keith Washington, and Christopher Williams. They all laughed when Cece moved her head in unison when one of the sisters started singing Steve Arrington's "Sugar Mama Baby." Cece stood up. She figured Kelly was running late from her hair appointment so she took off her jacket and draped it over her chair.

"Now, aren't you a sight for sore eyes," she heard a voice say. It was Scooter. Surprised, Cece looked up at him while Scooter smiled.

"Aren't you going to ask me to sit down while you eat your fries?" he said, laughing.

"Sure, Scooter, have a seat."

"Now, what is a fine sister like you doing in the mall all by herself? When I first noticed you sitting here from across the way, I said to myself . . . she is too fine to be in here all alone. As I got closer I saw how elegant you were, and I promised myself I'd say hi when I walked by. Then I realized it was you. How are you do-ing?" he said as he put down his things.

"I'm doing fine. I'm supposed to meet Kelly here so we can do some shopping, but she hasn't gotten here yet," Cece said as she picked up another fry with her fingers, trying her best to protect her freshly done nails.

Scooter just sat and stared at Cece trying to figure out what to say next. Cece noticed his shopping bags and jokingly pointed to the bags with another fry.

"So, what did you get me?"

Scooter smiled. "I'm glad you asked me that." He reached into his oversized shopping bag and pulled out a bag from the Coach store. "Here, this is for you. I heard that you might like it," he said. Then he held it out for Cece to take.

Cece began to laugh. She thought he was joking. But as she continued to laugh, she realized that he was serious. Her eyes were full of surprise.

"Please, Cece, don't ask me any questions. Just open it for me . . . please," he said.

Cece took a deep breath, in a surprised, frustrated kind of way and she took the shopping bag and opened it up. It was the Bar-clay tote bag that she had told Kelly she wanted.

"Scooter, how did you know this is what I wanted?"

"A little bird told me." He began laughing and pushed his chair up closer to the table as though he thought he was in there.

"Now, this bird's name wouldn't be Kelly, would it?"

Scooter's face gave him away instantly. "Cece, I just thought I'd do something nice for you. I've been asking Kelly about you ever since we met."

"I know, Scooter, she told me. But didn't she tell you I'm en-gaged?" Scooter's eyes dropped for a quick moment and then he raised his eyes.

"Yes, to be honest, she did. But she also said that she didn't know if things were still serious and that you might be interested if I showed some interest. You can never have enough friends, you know?"

Cece glanced at him, embarrassed that Kelly had told him that her relationship with Kahlil was not going well. Their disagreement about Kelly could never tear them apart because Cece had known how Kahlil felt about Kelly for years. She looked at the bag and touched its soft leather, then put it back in the shopping bag and gave it back to Scooter. He looked at her, confused.

"I really appreciate this, Scooter. I really do. But I can't take this from you. I'm engaged right now and I don't feel right accepting gifts like this."

Scooter looked at Cece like what she was saying was totally the opposite of what he expected. Cece took a sip of her water, put her napkins on the tray, and began to pick up her things to leave.

"Now, don't you two look nice sitting here together," Kelly said as she stood over the table, trying to act surprised. "Who would have imagined you two ever running into each other," she said sarcastically. "So, how are you doing, Scooter? Long time no see."

Scooter and Cece both looked at her like she had royally fucked up.

"What's wrong with you two?" she said defensively, looking at each of them. Scooter was obviously embarrassed and not accustomed to rejection. He got up from the table and motioned to the gift he bought.

"Cece, you go ahead and keep it, okay? Let it be my wedding present to you." He looked at Kelly, shook his head, pulled in his bottom lip, picked up his things and was ghost into the crowd. Kelly quickly pulled off her coat and sat down.

"Now, Cece, what did you say to him? What . . . you don't like the bag? I thought you said you wanted it in red? Shoot, if you don't like it, let's go down there right now and exchange it for something else." Kelly reached into the bag. "He left the receipt, didn't he?" She looked through the bag, nodded her head when she found the receipt, and then took one of Cece's fries. "Girl, after you finish those I'm going to have to take you to the gym and work your ass out," she said bluntly.

Cece was flattered that Scooter liked her, but she was upset that Kelly led him on as though she was fair game. "Kelly, what is your problem?" Cece said, as Kelly pulled her head up out of the small Coach bag pamphlet. "Why did you set me up like that? You know that Kahlil and I are engaged. Why can't you respect that?"

"All I was trying to do is help you out and give you something to do, Cece. Relax."

"Kelly, I don't need anything to do. I have plenty to do and I don't appreciate you telling somebody lies about my relationship either. I know my man has been busy and I support his reasons because he's doing something that he believes in and I respect that."

"You just don't seem happy to me," Kelly snapped back.

"Well, I've seen firsthand how you've been behaving and how you spend your time, and believe me . . . I'm not lonely, you are. You have too many men in your life to be happy," Cece said.

Kelly didn't want to hear it. "So, are you going to keep the bag?" she asked Cece.

Cece started to get hot. "No, Kelly. I don't want it. You keep it, because I don't need it." Cece stood up from the table. "Come on, let's go shopping."

Kelly tried to hand Cece the bag. "Cece, go ahead and keep it because he bought me one, too," she said, smiling. "You don't think I'd hook him up with you for free, do you?" Cece didn't respond. "Well, come on, let's take it back and get the money for it," Kelly said.

Cece sat back down. "Kelly, sit down for a minute. What is wrong with you? Don't you care about anything anymore? Why have you become so damn doggish? You're really beginning to worry me."

Kelly sat down and turned her head in the opposite direction without answering Cece. She began to shake her leg in anger as if she was really getting ready to give her girl some choice words but was trying to hold it back.

"Cece, I do what I do because it's either take from these niggas or be played by them." There was a pause. Kelly didn't want to— but she did anyway. "Just like you are being played," she said. Kelly looked at Cece as though she wanted to cry, but Cece didn't understand what Kelly was saying to her.

"Played, what do you mean played? Kelly, what are you talking about?" Cece said, shaking her head.

Kelly turned her face toward Cece and tears were forming in her mad eyes. Pain was coming from somewhere that even Kelly couldn't comprehend.

"I'm talking about Kahlil," Kelly said with anger.

Cece looked at Kelly with her eyes squinted as though her soul had been cut deeply.

"Kelly . . . what about Kahlil?" Cece said. Kelly noticed Cece inhale and hold her breath, trying to prepare herself for the worst. Kelly tried to touch Cece's hand and as Cece saw her reaching for her hand, she opened her hand up to her. Kelly came inches from her hand, but pulled her hand back and placed it on the table instead. Cece looked at her strangely.

"Cece, you have to believe me. I didn't tell you as soon as this happened because he begged me not to say anything to you. I wanted you to be happy, but you are my girl and he has your head all messed up and I can't stand it."

"Damn it, Kelly. Tell me what you're talking about," Cece said, as she tried to suck back all the air she just let out of her lungs. She had seen the same look on Kelly's face when she told her about Sonje. "What? You saw him with Sonje again?" Cece said.

Kelly paused. She didn't know if she could be so foul and hurt Cece like she knew she would, but Kelly saw this was her chance to get Kahlil back for turning her down and an opportunity for Cece to finally understand her views on men. "No, Cece, this time it was *me*."

"What!"

Kelly was on a roll, so she continued. "Yes. Remember the night I told you Deric put me out of his Land Rover and I called Lee to pick me up?" Cece nodded yes. "Well, I lied. Lee refused to come pick me up because he had a team meeting the next morning. I walked over to Kahlil's house and asked him to take me over to Deric's to pick up my car. It was about two in the morning and he told me that he would, but it would have to be on his way to the airport because he had an early morning flight. He told me that I could sleep on the couch and I did. When I woke up a few hours later and went to the bathroom, Kahlil came out into the hall butt naked and tried to take me into his room." Cece looked like she was about to pass out. "He was saying all types of shit about how much he wanted me and that you told him so many nasty things about me that he wanted to sleep with me before he was married to see if they were all true."

Cece began wiping the tears from her eyes and Kelly handed her some napkins.

"I told you, girl, men ain't shit. Cece, don't you let him tell you otherwise, either. I'm telling you I saw his whole fucking body. I'm talking from the scratches you put on his shoulders all the way down to that mole on his thigh. I am not lying to you. He'll probably deny the whole thing, but don't let him mess with your head, girl."

Cece and Kelly sat at the table for another hour. When Kelly thought that Cece would be okay she went down to the Coach shop and got a refund for the extra bag. When she got back to the table, Cece had already left. She had heard enough.

Family

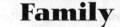

Kahlil was sitting in his family room listening to Miles Davis, thinking about the proposition from Nachi. It was Saturday so he had the weekend to just sit at home and think things over. As soon as Kahlil wandered off deep into thought his doorbell rang; Nite went berserk and he lost his train of thought. Kahlil opened the door—of all people it was Harris.

"What's up, Harris?" Kahlil said through the screen door.

"'Sup Kahlil," Harris replied, looking around to see if anyone noticed him on Kahlil's porch.

"Man, what's wrong with you?"

"Kahlil, you know I don't normally stop by here. I need to talk to you . . . but I be damned if it's going to be out here on your front porch. I don't want nobody to see me."

Kahlil opened the door to let Harris in. Harris paused, lifting up his index finger as if to remember.

"Dog?"

"In the back room," Kahlil said, then he stepped back just enough to where Harris could step into the house. "So what's so important?"

"Man, I need to talk to you about Sid."

226

"I'm listening."

"Yesterday, right, I overheard some brothers talking about the GPC and some of the shit they have been doing." Harris paused.

"And? . . . Harris, are you high?" Kahlil asked.

"Yeah, just a little," Harris said, paranoid.

"How are you going to be just a little high, man? You need to leave that shit alone. Go ahead, I'm listening."

"You didn't hear this from me, but I overheard brothers talking about the GPC and Sid's name came up."

"Sid?"

"That's right . . . they were talking about those two fools—Difante and Rashaad. I heard them say that Sid joined ranks with them and they are in the streets trying to be gangsters."

"Are you sure?"

"Yeah man, I'm sure. I might have been high but I know what I heard. You know my sources are genuine and there is no way I would come over here spreading no damn rumors. Especially about your peeps." Kahlil nodded his head in agreement. "I just thought you should know. I mean, it's like we family, right?" Kahlil didn't say anything. "Right, Kahlil?"

"Yeah, we family, Harris." Kahlil extended his hand and Harris smiled like Kahlil's words meant the world to him, then turned around to walk out the door.

"Stop smoking that shit, Harris," Kahlil said.

"I'm tryin' man . . . I'm tryin'."

"Well try to get yourself some help," Kahlil said and shut the door.

Kahlil was out the door and cruising the neighborhood in no time after he called over to his mother's house and no one answered. His mind had changed from Nachi to Sidney all in a matter of minutes. He was fuming because he and Sid always discussed the danger of gangs and Sid seemed to have a strong understanding of the issue. Kahlil drove by Blue's and saw Harris talking to a group of brothers on the street. Kahlil looked at Harris. Harris's eyes directed him across the street to the barbershop. Kahlil parked the car and went into the shop. Sid was sitting in Blue's chair with a hot steaming towel on his head. His eyes were closed as Blue was sharpening his razor, preparing to shave Sid's head.

"Hey Kahlil—what's happening?" Blue said, and Sid opened his eyes.

"What's going on Blue, you all right?" Blue nodded yes and Kahlil tapped Sidney on his leg. "I need to talk to you."

Sid looked surprised to see Kahlil. He knew by the look on Kahlil's face that he'd better get up and see what he wanted, so he followed Kahlil out to the car. Kahlil got in and Sid stood outside with his hands on top of the car.

"What are you doing?" Kahlil asked Sid.

"Kahlil, can't you see I am getting ready to get my head shaved? I have been waiting too long as it is."

"Now I know you trippin'. Sid, get your ass in here now." Sid got in and slammed the door, and Kahlil didn't waste any time.

"I hear you running around trying to be a gangsta with the GPC."

Sid wasn't surprised that Kahlil found out. He knew he would eventually, and he'd thought about what he might say to Kahlil if he ever approached him about being in the GPC. Now was the time to find out, he thought. Sid knew that this decision was his and his alone. All of his life someone else had made his decisions for him and this time was going to be different. Sid looked at Kahlil sternly.

"Yeah, I'm down with the GPC . . . so what?"

"So what? What do you mean so what? If you don't know then I'll tell you. I don't think you know what the hell you are doing, Sid."

"Kahlil, I know what I'm doing. I've known these brothers for years—they are my family now."

"Family, huh? . . . You mean like always there for you no matter what. Always willing to listen even if they don't have the time. Like showing love in every type of situation?"

"Exactly," Sid said with hardness. Like he really understood where Kahlil was coming from.

"WELL WHAT THE HELL AM I, SID!" Kahlil said at the top of his voice, as he pounded his hand on the steering wheel.

Sid had never seen Kahlil when he let his emotions go, but it was too late to turn back now. "You just don't understand, Kahlil, that's all. Things ain't the same when you were growin' up."

"What is it that I don't understand, Sid? Man, this gang shit ain't no joke. Once you are in it . . . you in it for life and nothin' . . . I mean nothin' . . . good comes out of the thug life. I know you haven't had the best of life so far. I mean I couldn't even imagine growing up in these times that you are living in." Sid looked over to Kahlil as Kahlil looked out the windshield trying his best to say something to change Sid's mind. "But brother let me tell you . . . this lifestyle don't pay. Look at all the want-to-be gangsters who thought they'd made it. They all are dying. First Tupac then Biggie . . . who's next . . . you?" Kahlil asked, not wanting to think about what just came out of his mouth. "All I'm saying is you're a man now, and you make your own decisions, but you better think about this one. If I were you . . . Ain't no way I would get involved in this shit." As soon as Kahlil shut his mouth he saw Difante and Rashaad walking into the barbershop. Both Sid and Kahlil had their eyes on them.

"Well . . . there goes your family," Kahlil said, looking over to Sid.

"Yeah . . . Guess I better jet." Sid paused, looked at Kahlil, opened the door, and walked back into the shop.

Kahlil just sat in his car and thought if this were a scene in a movie they would have just faded to black.

True Love?

Maybe he had forgotten just who I was. I had been so patient and supportive of Kahlil that there is no way he was going to play me—Cece—like that. And I'm here to tell you, I was madder than Whitney, y'all. I didn't wait but a second to go over to see Kahlil after I went home, cried, and took myself a hot shower. The initial pain I'd felt had subsided and I knew I was going to blow my top as soon as I walked in his door and saw his doggish face. When I pulled into his driveway I had been so tangled up about what must have been on his mind to approach Kelly like he did and disrespect me, that I didn't even remember driving over to his house or stopping at any red lights or anything. I would still be sitting out in the car, thinking about how he must have looked going after Kelly, trying to stick his thing in her, if he hadn't called me on my cell phone when he saw my car in his driveway.

He opened the door for me and smiled, then tried to kiss me on the cheek. I just let him do it, instead of jumping up and smacking him on his simple face. I walked straight upstairs to give his ass an idea of why I wanted to talk to him. I could tell that something was funny when he stopped on the top step and sat down. I began to feel queasy and dizzy as the pain crept back into my body and mixed with the madness. I didn't want to just jump on Kahlil because I've always tried to believe him and give him his due. But when he hesitated before turning to me after I asked him why he didn't tell me Kelly had come over to the house, I knew something was wrong.

He just sat there surprised, like he couldn't believe that she said something to me after she promised she wouldn't. That's my girl and we have a bond that he could only wish he had with a friend. I looked at him as he started to laugh and tried to pull his coolness routine on me. He muttered about how much he could not believe me as he tried to figure out what next to say to me. I'd already planned to stand tall and firm and not let Kahlil turn this thing around, just like Kelly said. When he got off the step, called me baby girl, then grabbed my hand to go back downstairs, I SWEAR I almost fell into his arms, but I sat down right in the hallway, refusing to go with him, my arms crossed, waiting for what he had to say.

Kahlil didn't even try to address what Kelly had told me. He tried to lay some type of guilt trip on me. He said he couldn't believe I came over to his house and accused him of trying to get with Kelly. When he said he had other things on his mind. I knew he must have done it because Kahlil has never been lost for words. The only thing he said was that he had thought the power Kelly had over me was gone, but now he knew different. Kahlil told me that this had been my all-time greatest mistake with him and that he didn't appreciate me taking Kelly's side . . . period. He couldn't believe I didn't trust him. After all he'd never lied to me—not even about Sonje. He looked at me with so much anger. I had never seen him that way, and I didn't like it one bit. Hell, I was the one being played.

When he stopped talking to me I just went crazy and I told him, "I thought you liked how I made you feel in bed, Kahlil. Answer me." He scared me half to death when he picked me up from the floor by my arms. I thought he had snapped, but I didn't care. He carried me down the steps, holding me at eye level. I knew he was putting me out, so I hollered, "What is your reason for wanting to marry me, nigga!" He just sat me on the porch outside, turned around, and shut the door.

He doesn't have to have a reason now because as far as I'm concerned, it's over.

Shame of It All

I have never in my life seen Cece act like that. I am fed up with her letting Kelly take her mind and fill it up with bullshit. I thought she was over it, I really did. And I'm not going to accept it. Fuck it. Let her keep the ring. She and Kelly can sit around and compare gifts like we used to do with our basketball cards as kids.

I don't even know how this happened. I was sitting down, thinking about the proposal Gales had given me and how Sid is ruining his damn life, and I don't know anyone who can think about two things at once. So I looked out the window to clear my head and there she was. Sitting in the driveway. The way she looked, I thought someone had died, but after she told me what was wrong, I didn't even want to talk about it. I told Cece the only things on my mind were Sid and my job. My thoughts were running deep.

I was thinking that if I took the money then it would seem like I was selling out all of the things that I believe in and have fought for with the Coalition. How the hell could I continue to tell brothers in the compound to continue holding on through the discrimination they face and stand tall. Yeah they offered me the money. But over four million dollars not to work with a black man? Those motherfuckas have problems. I've been helping people with discrimination for years and when it happens to me it still hurts like hell. It makes you realize how much further we have to go, and I wonder if things are getting worse instead of better for the black man in this country. At the same time Sid's situation was pounding away in my head as I tried to figure out how he got mixed up with those fools. I know the Big Burger job wasn't paying him any money, and these young brothers don't know anything at all about delayed gratification or working for what they get. As I drove away from the barbershop my instincts told me to go back and snatch Sid away from those fools and beat that want-to-be-gangsta-this-is-my-family-macho-ass attitude out of him, but he would only go back later. Damn, what a situation to have on my mind at a time like this.

Cece didn't even ask me if anything was wrong or wonder why I sat so quiet while she screamed. She just lost it. Her mind was made up that I'd tried to sleep with Kelly's foul ass. I don't understand why she couldn't open her mind and put two and two together. Yes, Kelly came over, but not only was I preparing to go to Philadelphia for a meeting, but more importantly I love Cece. The power Kelly has over Cece's mind is boggling. It's more than just a woman's bond. It's downright disgusting, and Cece should stop holding herself hostage, feeling like she was the reason Kelly got raped. I always remind her when she brings it up that it wasn't her fault. Most people don't even believe what the doctor tells them the first time, but Cece treats Kelly's words like the gospel. No questions asked.

At least I found out how much Cece trusts me before it was too late. This could have happened after we were married, and that would have been a trip. Even though I love her, she made up her mind for both of us. Maybe I should have just let her sit in the car.

Do You Mind?

It was late Friday morning. Dewayna didn't have to be at work until midnight and Sonje not until six in the evening to rehearse her national debut of the *Women Only Show*. Dewayna lay still, listening to the water falling on Sonje in the shower. When the water stopped, Sonje grabbed her towel, stepped out of the shower, and walked through the wide-open French double doors into the bedroom.

"Aren't you going to comment about how good my body looks?" she asked as she tried to dry her back. Sonje loved the bashful compliments Dewayna had started to give her.

"Oh shoot, give me a hand, baby."

Dewayna raised up from her pillow and took the towel from Sonje, without saying a word.

"What's wrong, Dewayna?"

"Oh, nothing . . . Just thinking."

"Let me guess. You like what you're doing, but you're confused about who you're doing it with. If I was a man there wouldn't be a problem, right?"

"Well, yeah . . . kinda sorta. You know what I mean?" Dewayna moved her hands toward Sonje's breasts. "Turn around, so I can dry these off." She tried not to sound odd.

"Baby, I know exactly what you mean. I went through the same thing when I started having relationships with women."

"So, what did you do?"

"Well, I was scared to death someone might find out about me and the lady who took my virginity. I was more scared then than I am now, and I have a hell of a lot more to lose."

"See, that's what I mean, Sonje. I've always felt if I can't tell someone what I'm doing then what I'm doing must be wrong. I mean I enjoy spending time together, but this is way more than I ever imagined. Just so much more than I have ever experienced in my life and I can't say this is right."

"No, baby, it's not like that at all. It's just that you've lived your life a certain way and now that you're deviating from that behavior you're confused. You don't understand the feelings you have for me." Sonje reached over to her nightstand, picked up the lotion, and gave it to Dewayna. "Look, I've noticed that you have become a little more relaxed about what we're doing, Dewayna. When we make love, it used to be that your hands never touched my body. Then you slowly began to touch me and now I feel your hands giving me pleasure, just like you're doing now with the lotion. This relationship is nothing like any you've ever been in before, that's why I enjoy it. We can sit down and talk. Just the other day I was thinking about how we have a big sister, little sister thing going here."

"But, Sonje, that's not all. . . . I'm confused about two things. The first one is how much longer can we really . . . I mean really continue to do this?"

"What do you mean?"

"I want to know how much longer we can be together. I mean we hide out over here at your place and I know that you are in no position to have your private life divulged to everyone. Don't get me wrong, Sonje, the things we have done together have been an experience, but I think we should think about what we are really doing. I'm just so confused right now and I don't want to hurt you. Do you understand?"

"I understand . . . So what's your second question?"

Dewayna paused. "Well you know I'm still married to Demitrious, and he wants to try to work things out between us, so that we can provide a solid foundation for Octavious. He's asked me to go to New York with him, so we can sit down and talk, have a heart to heart and find out what we're going to do." Dewayna stopped putting the lotion on Sonje's back because she knew Sonje was going to become upset.

"Baby, you know what?" Sonje asked.

"What's that?"

"I really think that's a good idea. I mean, you are still married. I've never been married before, but I'm sure that's some deep shit. And that's another reason I'll never get married. It's just too damn complicated."

Dewayna was surprised and didn't know what to say. "So, you're not upset?"

"Why should I be? I told you, Dewayna, this relationship is unlike any you've ever had in your life, and I'm determined to make you realize that one way or another."

"See, that's what I like about you. You just understand," Dewayna confessed.

"I sure do. Just remember the promise we made to each other. You do remember, don't you?"

"Yes, I re-mem-ber," Dewayna said as she began to pay attention to Sonje's nipples. "We promised that we would never hurt one another, nor would we give anybody what we've been giving each other." She giggled.

"That's right, baby . . . That's right," Sonje said as they went back between the sheets.

Creepin'

It was going on three weeks and both Kelly and I were trying to be strong. We made a pact not to talk to Kahlil or Deric, but it was hard. We had a lot of time, Kelly more so than I, to reflect on our relationships. Maybe too much time. We decided that we wouldn't make the same mistake as other women and run back to our supposed men for the sake of having a man. We were comrades in the struggle and we used each other as support. Kelly continued to play Lee's game and take any and everything that he was willing to give. She talked constantly about the good times that she and Lee were having, and I have to admit her stories were beginning to get the best of me.

It was the third straight weekend that I had nothing to do. I'd gotten tired of doing my nails, reading books and Kelly's damn *Black Romance* magazines to pass the time. I sat down on the couch in my nightgown and picked up the remote. The loneliness that I had so desperately tried to fight off crept up on me. I couldn't take it any longer. Not that I wanted to go and jump in bed with any man, but I missed someone telling me nice things and making me feel special. Kahlil did that all the time and I missed it dearly. I wished I could just satisfy that need. Even a knucklehead telling me nice things might get me through my anxiety. I looked in my phone book and there was not one man I could call. I had let Kahlil handle all of my business for years and now I was hurting.

Kelly came downstairs in her provocative, tight-fitting black dress and stood her ass right in front of the television.

"If you're not jealous, then you don't have a conscience sista, because I'm working this and you might as well say so."

"Girl, that is fly! Where are you going tonight?"

"To another party," she boasted. I looked at Kelly and waited for her to ask me out, but she didn't.

"I know you're going to ask me to tagalong tonight, aren't you?" I was not staying in by myself another night.

"No, Cece, I'm not. Every time I do, you act like you can't go out and have a good time, so I'm just going to stop asking you."

"Well, Kelly, there's nothing wrong with wanting to be by yourself for a while, is there?"

"No, there isn't, but when you're by yourself and feel pitiful, then there's something wrong with that."

"Oh, so you mean that you don't feel bad about not being with Deric anymore?" I asked her.

"I didn't say that. As a matter of fact, I do miss him . . . but hey, life goes on." Kelly turned the television to BET and began shaking her ass to the music.

Kelly was right, just think about it. Kahlil had not called me or anything. I guess he was out there doing whatever he had to do in order to maintain, so I decided that I was going to do the same. I got up off the couch.

"Girl, I'm going with you. I'm tired of sitting around here by myself, watching this TV."

"What? I can't believe this. It's about time."

"Don't even try it, Kelly. What's this party all about and who is having it?"

Kelly looked at me.

"Sure you're right Cece, don't even trip. You know Scooter is having this party. I told you about it weeks ago and you just blew me off, but now you want to go. You are sly, my sista."

I didn't remember Kelly telling me anything about Scooter having a party. Maybe she did and I was so embarrassed and upset about Kahlil that I didn't register what she had said. It was turning out to be the night that I had needed. I knew that I could get Scooter to tell me what I wanted to hear, even if I had to tell him what to say.

"So, has he asked about me lately?"

"Who?" Kelly said, still trying to perfect her little grind move. "Hey . . . Hey!" She cried out as she danced to the music, trying to be funny.

"Scooter."

"Yes, he's asked about you and he's asked me to tell you hello, through Lee, every damn time I see Lee."

"Why haven't you been telling me?"

"Because, girl, you already told the man that you didn't want to have anything to do with him, even though I was trying my best to keep you on the right path. I had a feeling that you were going to get back with Kahlil sooner or later, so I just left it alone."

"Well, he won't have to ask about me tonight because this sista is going to be all up in there with my red on," I said, smiling.

"Oh, no! . . . Not the red make-sure-you-tell-me-I'm-worthy diva dress!" Kelly screamed over the music.

"That's right. I'm going to show the flava tonight."

Kelly began to look at me like she was surprised.

"Cece, what is wrong with you?"

"What do you mean?"

"You're acting like you're trying your best to get over Kahlil and things."

"I am. I can't say that I have yet because that would be a lie. I've spent my last seven years with Kahlil and, of course, it's going to take me awhile to get over him. To tell you the truth, I picked up the phone today and called his number twice, but when I heard his voice I hung up the phone. I know he knew it was me because he has Caller I.D., but I don't care. I know I need to be strong and keep that chapter of my life closed. So tonight, when we go out, I'll begin another chapter and see what happens."

Hearing the loud music and seeing the smiles of everyone in the party did wonders for me and it was what I wanted out of the entire night. Everyone in the clubhouse seemed nice, and this party seemed as if it was going to go down as one of the best in my memory. People were dressed so nice and carried themselves like they had a purpose in life. I didn't know a soul there except Kelly, but I really had a good feeling about the atmosphere. Most of the people there were die-hard Lions fans and were talking with the players, treating them like they were gods or something.

I walked around with Kelly, who worked the entire clubhouse magnificently, like she was running for some type of political office or something. She introduced me to everyone that she knew, including most of the football team. It tripped me out because the majority of the people asked her about Lee as though he weren't even married. No one there looked at her like what she was doing was wrong or mentioned his wife. They just accepted her like everything was normal, and treated Kelly like she was very well liked.

Kelly was right, these brothers were fine and I worked them all, just for the fun of it. I don't know how many times one of them called me Dark and Lovely, and I was eating it up. Just before or after Kelly would introduce me to one of the brothers, she would tell me as much history about them as she knew. I'm talking about height, weight, salary, marital status, illegitimate kids, and even sexual preference. She knew everything about all of them.

I knew this was Scooter's party, but after being there almost an entire hour I hadn't seen him. I have to be honest, I was sort of looking forward to seeing him. I wanted everything that I'd set out to get that night and conversation was at the top of my list. I'd walked around the clubhouse and spent time on all three floors. I danced some and watched a card game, then was surprised when I saw Scooter as I came out of the ladies room. He did a double-take when he saw me, and, unlike the time when Kelly set us up at the mall, this time his smile was for real. I was stunned when he reached out and pulled me to his chest, giving me a very tight hug.

"Cece. I didn't know you were coming tonight. If I did, I would have been waiting for you at the door." He was already doing a good job at telling me what I wanted to hear.

"I didn't know I was coming either. It was just a spur-of-the-moment thing," I said, looking up at him in his crewneck shirt.

"Well, I'm glad that you could make it. Can I have a dance?" Before I could answer, Scooter grabbed my hand and we must have danced for thirty straight minutes.

"You sure do dance nice, Scooter."

"Thanks, Cece. You look good out there yourself. But you always look good." All right now, the brother was on a roll, as he stood smiling at me. "Let's go down to the first floor. It's a little bit more quiet down there. They should be playing some jazz. If not, I'll tell them to. After all, this is my party . . . right?"

"Right, Scooter," I said back to him.

Scooter found us a nice, cozy little table and made sure I was comfortable, then he left for two minutes. He came back with a bottle of champagne, opened it, poured me a glass, then sat down and began looking at me like I was some type of unbelievable creature.

"Why are you looking at me like that?" I asked him, blushing and trying to laugh it off.

"I'm just amazed at how fine you are. I mean, I knew you were nice looking, but Cece, you are the most beautiful woman I've ever known." Scooter picked up his glass and held it up. "Here's to you."

I raised my glass and he gently placed his glass against the side of mine. I melted as he looked at me and we drank from our glasses. Damn, I thought, Kahlil wasn't the only romantic man in the world. Scooter put his glass down.

"So what's up? Did you and ol' boy decide not to get married after all?" He looked away and smirked.

"Yes, how did you know?"

Scooter looked at me like all of his prayers had been answered.

"Be serious."

"I am."

He leaned over to me. "So what happened?"

I hadn't planned to talk about it, but I felt it was time. I had only been talking to Kelly about the situation for weeks, so I decided to spill my guts and get a man's point of view.

"Well, something very personal happened that I didn't agree with and I decided that the engagement wasn't going to work out."

He put his hand on top of mine. "Well, I'm glad . . . I mean, sorry to hear that," he said jokingly. "Cece, I tell it like I see it and you probably heard this already, but whoever let you go was a damn fool."

No, I hadn't heard that yet and it actually made me feel better. Scooter and I must have talked for two hours. To my surprise he was not as shallow as I had originally thought. I was impressed that he could talk about my past relationship and see my point of view, as well as just listen intently without passing judgment.

"Cece, let me apologize for how I approached you in the mall. I mean, that wasn't even me. I'm sorry."

"You don't have to explain."

"Yes, I do. Not blaming Kelly, but she had almost assured me that's what you wanted. She was positive that you would see me again. I mean, Lee's my boy and she's your girl and I thought just maybe you two were exactly alike. But I was definitely wrong and it was my fault."

"Yes . . . Kelly is my girl, but we really have different opinions about how to get a man."

"Good. I think I'm going to like your way better," he said.

I finally noticed most of the people had already left and I told Scooter it was time for me to go. He helped me find Kelly, who was upstairs in one of the bedrooms with Lee. She opened the door without letting me see her face and gave me the keys. I could tell she was butt naked up in there. Scooter walked with me to the car and, in no time, I found myself in the front seat of Kelly's car, embraced in a passionate kiss. I was embarrassed when Kelly began tapping on the window screaming, "You go, girl!" as Lee stood by and laughed.

When we pulled out of the driveway Scooter and Lee stood there and waved good-bye. I just sat quietly because I knew Kelly was about to start some mess.

"You don't have to tell me. You want to hear my Xscape CD, don't you? Those girls sound so good when you want some. I've been there too," Kelly said as she looked for the CD.

"I don't have the slightest idea what you're talking about."

"So, are you going to get with him or what, Cece?"

"It never crossed my mind, Kelly."

"Oh, so, now you want to play stupid. . . . Girl, I ain't crazy. I saw you two in my front seat about to set it off." She began to laugh.

"Kelly, we were just kissing . . . that's all . . . kissing."

"Can he kiss? Look, you don't have to even answer that one because I was standing outside for five minutes, and you didn't seem to mind how he was wrapping those lips around yours. It must have been good to you."

I can't lie, y'all, it was.

"Gurrrl, you better wake yourself up and tell me about you and Lee tonight. We're halfway home," I said to Kelly as she struggled to stay awake, apparently tired from what she and Lee had done. "Oh nothing . . . but the same old thing. You know, talk about what I wanted from him then fucking," she said in her worn-out and weary voice. She yawned. "He thinks that he owns the na na now, Cece. Every time I see his ass, all he wants to do is get me in the bed. I've never been in a relationship like this before. I've always called the shots."

I stared at the road to make sure she didn't drift, and began to realize that I'd never heard Kelly sound so defeated. It was not like her not to be in control.

"So, are you slippin' now or is Lee just turning you out? I can't believe you're letting him have you whenever he wants. It wasn't like that in the beginning."

Kelly hesitated for a moment, thinking before she opened her mouth. It seemed like she couldn't understand herself. "Girl, this Negro is just too powerful. I thought I could handle him, just like the others. I've always wanted someone who could give me whatever I wanted. But now that I finally have him, I've realized that there's nothing that he won't give me, as long as I keep giving it to him. Sometimes I don't even have to ask for any money. He just gives me some, because he knows eventually he's going to have me whenever he wants. It's like he's running a tab on the pussy. It makes me wonder when he and his wife have sex together because, Cece, we never do it just once."

"Don't you feel like a prostitute, Kelly?"

"No, I sure don't. It's not even like that. We just agreed on some things and have an understanding that is deeper than I thought it was going to be. But I have to admit, I really do miss Deric."

"What!"

"Yes, I miss him. When I look back on it, he was the best thing that could have happened to me. He doesn't have as much money as Lee, but all in all, I can really say that he's the better man. I've been thinking about it, too, Cece, and I need you to do me a favor."

"And what's that?"

"Will you talk to him for me?"

I took my eyes off the road and looked at Kelly. "What did you say?"

"I said that I miss Deric and I want you to talk to him for me."

"Kelly, have you lost your mind? After he found out about you and Lee? You want me to talk to him about getting back together with you? Um . . . um . . . ain't no way."

"Please, Cece, I'd do it for you," Kelly whined.

"Absolutely not, Kelly," I said back to her and we went back and forth the rest of the way home.

Surprise

When Danielle buzzed me and told me that Waydis Thomas of WorldLine Airlines was in the office to see me, I double-checked my calendar and quickly scanned through my cards to see if I'd forgotten an appointment. I knew for a fact that I wasn't pitching an ad campaign because I'd already closed out all of my accounts. I wasn't going to generate any more money for the corporation. I was just waiting for my final week to end, so I could walk out the door. I had accepted the offer from Nachi.

I didn't find any reminders, but I happily told Danielle to send him in. I thought to myself if it's advertising expertise he's looking for, I'm going to recommend him to an all-black firm. I stared intently at his face as he stood outside my door. He looked like someone I knew and I thought I had seen him somewhere before, but I couldn't for the life of me figure it out. I could tell right away that the brother had money because of the tailored suit he had on and the way he carried himself. It looked like he was somewhere in his upper thirties, maybe forty.

"So, Mr. Thomas, how can I help you?" I said to him as we shook hands.

"I'm here on a personal matter and I desperately need your

help," he said in a very educated and distinguished way. "I understand you're very active in the Urban Coalition, and I've had great difficulties locating my son. It's been going on fifteen years since I've had any verbal contact with his mother. I'd like you to assist me with this endeavor."

"Well, Mr. Thomas."

"Please, Waydis," he insisted as we took our seats.

"Waydis, I usually don't discuss Coalition matters at my place of employment. I really do prefer to keep them separate. But if you would come down to the Coalition on Friday, I'll be there from three to six in the afternoon. I'd be more than happy to take some information from you then and—"

"You don't understand. I'll only be in this area for the next couple of weeks. I'm traveling back and forth to Canada on business. That's why I came directly to you. I was hoping that I could give you some information today, so you could get started right away. I'm willing to make a donation, or even pay you for your troubles." He reached into his jacket to pull out his checkbook. Watching him as he spoke to me, I finally remembered why I knew who Waydis was.

"Wait a minute. Waydis Thomas, V.P. of WorldLine Airlines? And *Black Enterprise*'s businessman of the year, two years in a row." He nodded his head yes. "Brother, I'm sorry it took me awhile to match the face with the name. Sure, I'll be happy to assist you in any way that I can. I've read all about you and I would consider this an honor." I took out my pad. "First of all, I'm going to have to take some background information from you and then I'll turn this over to my people and we'll see what we can come up with. Now, are you sure that your son is in the Detroit area?"

"Yes, I am," he said bluntly.

"Okay . . . what is your son's name?"

Waydis paused, forcing me to look up from my notepad. When my eyes met with his, he said, "Well, his real name is Sidney

Thomas," with force and conviction. I smiled at the coincidence and put my pen down.

"You know my sis . . ."

"Yes, your sister Leandra has a son named Sidney. I'm his father," he said, rocking his head back and forth.

I would rather have taken a punch square on the chin from Mike Tyson the first day he got out of jail than hear that. Waydis definitely dazed me. I was punch-drunk. I immediately got up from my chair and felt all the years of worry and concern for my nephew, especially lately, begin to surface and make its way out of my body. I walked over to my open office door and started to slam the door as hard as I could but instead held it firmly, took a deep breath, and shut it softly. I knew I would have broken the glass windows that surrounded the office. I stood with my back to Waydis, with my head down, and tried as best as I could to collect myself. I'd always wanted to meet the good-for-nothing bastard who left my sister stranded alone with Sid. Kicking his ass crossed my mind. I walked back to my desk, but this time I stood in front of it, about two feet away from Waydis. I pushed my telephone and nameplate to the side and sat on the edge, squeezing the front portions of it firmly, trying my utmost to break a piece off, wishing it was his neck instead.

"You son of a bitch," I said to him, as I tried to keep calm, wishing we were outside. He didn't react, almost like he expected it. "I have prayed to God that someday I would meet your sorry ass, so that I could jump square in your ass." I became more enraged when he crossed his legs, revealing his snakeskin shoes.

"I am very sympathetic to how you must feel, Kahlil," he said with dignity. His voice grabbed my attention. "And I trust that, after we finish talking here, the one and only ass that you will want to pounce upon is Leandra's."

I sat and listened to what he had to say.

Messenger

Apprehensive is the only word to explain how I was feeling as I waited for Deric in his office. Kelly had begged and pleaded for me to talk to him for her. "Cece, please . . . Cece, please . . . Cece, please," is all Kelly kept asking me, day and night. I wouldn't have thought about approaching him, if she hadn't promised me that if things worked out she would be one hundred percent committed to Deric and call things off with Lee. I wanted her to leave that married man alone, so I'd called Deric earlier in the week to make plans to come to see him. Deric had seemed very happy to hear my voice.

Deric came into the realtor's office a little late after showing property to clients, and as usual he had a smile on his face. I tried my best to smile back at him to hide my nervousness. I felt like getting out of my chair and running out the door. I hated to get involved in the personal business of others, best friend or not. I couldn't fool him. He knew right away that I had come to talk about Kelly.

"She sent you here, didn't she?"

"Why do you ask?" I said, for lack of anything else to say.

"Because, Cece, it's written all over your face. I know how Kelly can be sometimes. She keeps asking you to do things for her until you get tired of her mouth and then you just break down and do them so you won't have to hear her voice anymore." His words were solid. For the first time someone other than Kahlil told me Kelly had too much over me. I couldn't lie to the brother. He was on to something.

"Yes, Deric, she did ask me to come here and see you, but I can truly tell you that she does miss you."

Deric began to smile. "That's nice to hear. But it doesn't mean anything. I'm just happy to hear it because since I've been away from Kelly, I've come to the conclusion that neither she nor any other woman is worth being played like I was."

"Why do you say that, Deric?"

"Because I'm fed up with the games you have to play these days. To tell you the truth I was thinking about getting in touch with Kelly right after we broke things off, but I've never reconciled with a woman who's cheated on me. And she has done it three or four times. I treated Kelly too good for that, don't you think, Cece?"

"Well, Deric . . . I always thought you were very nice to Kelly and I told her that all the time. And this is no excuse, but my opinion of the matter is that you really have to think about everything Kelly has been through in her life. Try to put things in perspective. I even have to do it sometimes."

"Cece, I tried that. She never once let me forget that she'd been raped and I understood that. Look, Cece. I didn't rape Kelly and you didn't rape her. But we always seem to have to bow down to her because of some incident which was years ago. All I tried to do was be there for her. She took advantage of that, and that was wrong."

"I understand, Deric."

"So what has she been doing lately?" he asked.

"Not too much of anything . . . just recently she's been talking about how much she misses you."

"Let me tell you. I miss Kelly too and I want to talk to her so bad. But I just can't be played like a fool. I just can't do it."

Deric continued telling me about how lonely he had been. I listened to Deric very intently and decided that Kelly really was a fool for treating him the way she did. He really loved her. When I left I thought just maybe he would give my girl one more chance.

When I got back home there was a brand-new Mercedes in my driveway, and I thought that Lee had come over to see Kelly while I was gone. I walked into the house and was surprised to see Scooter, of all people, standing in the living room.

"Surprise. Look what the wind blew in," Kelly said. Scooter smiled and walked toward me. I was surprised because I hadn't made any plans with Scooter when I talked with him the night before.

"What are you doing here?" I asked.

"I just came by to show you my new car and see if you wanted to go for a ride to get something to eat?"

I was feeling a little hungry, but I hadn't been out on a date since Kahlil and I stopped seeing each other. I knew if I went with Scooter, it would absolutely be over with Kahlil.

"Come on, I know you're hungry . . . I know I am," Scooter said, as Kelly smiled, motioning her arms as if to say go ahead.

"Okay, why not," I decided. It was so strange, walking out to get in his car as I had done for seven years with Kahlil. I was embarrassed because Kelly stood in the door with her eyes on me, as a mother would do to a daughter. Scooter laughed like crazy at Kelly while he opened the door for me. I heard Kelly slam the front door as soon as I sat down in the car. I looked up and noticed Kahlil pulling up into the driveway. It seemed like everything stood still for minutes while everyone thought about what they were going to do next. Scooter stood silent, trying to figure out who had pulled up behind him in the driveway. I could see Kahlil's eyes through his windshield of his car and he just stared at me. His eyes made me want to speak to him.

"Give me one second, Scooter . . . okay?" I walked over to Kahlil's car and he rolled down the window.

"Hi, Kahlil. I didn't know you were coming over."

He glanced over at Scooter, who was still waiting for me with his door open. "I just came from my mother's. I thought I'd stop by to see if you wanted to get something to eat over at Steve's Restaurant, so we could talk."

I looked at Kahlil and then at Scooter, not knowing what to say.

"You don't have to say anything. I understand," Kahlil said, and his window began to close.

"I'll call you, okay," I said, touching the window of the car. He didn't respond. He just backed out of the driveway and pulled off. I stood there and watched him drive away as Kelly reappeared at the door.

My Brother

Waydis and I agreed to have a couple of drinks when I got off work. In the two hours that we talked in my office we realized we had many of the same concerns, and that my sister Leandra had really messed things up. Although the surprise was hard to digest, I was happy that Waydis wanted to be part of Sid's life, and I told Waydis he couldn't have come at a better time because Sid certainly needed something to shake up his life for the better. We decided to meet at Points where we could settle our only disagreement thus far. We had yet to agree on who was the best bass player in the country. Stanley Clarke, Marcus Miller, or, my favorite, Foley. The three were playing at Points in a showdown and were going to be accompanied by guitarist Kevin Turner, funkyass drum-playing Troy Jones, and, on the keys, the silky smooth Ed Clay.

When we walked in that joint my brothers had the entire place rocking and everyone was listening as the music flowed through their bodies. Foley was on stage making his bass talk to the crowd as Jones, Turner, and Clay had caught the fever in the background. Their instruments sounded like magic and the crowd begged for more when Foley ended his set.

"You're right, that boy is bad. I knew he was special when he played with Miles but damn he has elevated—he definitely has skills," Waydis said over the crowd of cheers.

"What did I tell you? He's got the total package," I said as Waydis signaled for a waitress.

"Kahlil, let me tell you. I didn't mean to make your day full of drama, but I decided that you were the best person to talk to instead of showing up on the front porch and talking to Leandra."

"You're right about that, Waydis. I don't know how Sid would have reacted. I mean, after all the negative things that Leandra has said about you to all of us all these years. More than likely it would have been a very ugly sight."

"Man, I just don't understand these women nowadays. No disrespect to your family."

"No, go ahead. Believe me, I understand."

"It's just that, how could Leandra hide from me all these years? What has it solved? Nothing positive has come out of it. All these years just wasted away and now I have to live with the possibility that Sidney might not even want anything to do with me."

"No, I doubt that. He asked me what you were like on Father's Day, and I think with time he'll be able to get through this."

"You have any kids yet?" Waydis asked.

"Not yet. In fact, I was engaged to be married, but my better half decided that she wanted to be more committed to her girlfriend than she wanted to be to me, so its not going to happen now." Our waitress came up to the table with a coy look on her face and quickly looked back at a table of three women.

"Good evening, gentlemen. Before I take your order, I'm to tell you that the group of women on the platform have informed me that if you two would like to buy them drinks tonight, they would happily accept them."

Waydis and I looked behind the waitress at the three very attractive women, who all looked like they could buy themselves drinks.

They were obviously thinking that they were so absolutely fine that we would jump at the chance. One of the ladies was talking on her cell phone and the other two were having a conversation, trying to act as though they weren't aware of what was going on.

"Uh . . . Tamarra, I think I'll pass." We both looked at Waydis.

"And I'll have a cognac. What about you, Kahlil?"

"I'll have the same." The waitress smiled and went to the bar to get our drinks.

"Can you believe that?" Waydis said.

"Brother, that's what I'm talking about these days with women. Buy them a drink! And they wonder why they walk around holding their breath all day, waiting to exhale," I told him, shaking my head.

"It's the nature of the beast, brother," Waydis testified. "Women these days don't understand what it means to be patient. When we sat down here, I saw them sitting up there and, to tell you the truth, I thought about sending drinks over, but they blew it big time. They rush everything. It's like, if they don't get things when they want them, then there's something wrong with you." Waydis just went off. "When they reach thirty, it's like a light goes off in their heads and they just have to have kids. They just have to have a husband. They just have to have a house. They just have to become more responsible, and feel bad about all of the wrong things that they have ever done in their lives and to others. I'll tell you what they just *ought* to have."

"Shame the devil, and tell the truth," I told him.

"They just *ought* to have some patience and a little self-respect," he said, glancing at the ladies again. "Buy them a drink." He laughed.

"My brother, it sounds like you're fed up with the fanny," I said, laughing.

"Kahlil, I am. No matter what you say or do, women love to be caught up in some type of commotion. If they don't have anything to go to the beauty shop and complain about, then they're not happy. They want to be married, but don't want to respect those who are, and sleep around with four or five married men. But when it happens to them when they get married, the man is no damn good and they forget about all the mess they pulled in their own lives."

I was in total agreement. His words got me started. "I hear you. I was in a church and the preacher got off into the hierarchy of a household. I'm only talking about in a biblical sense, brother, and he mentioned that women need to respect it. It's God first, husband second, then the wife. Don't you know that I could hear the grunting and see the attitudes on some of the ladies' faces that I sat around. Now I can understand if brothers are not doing the right thing but sisters have to put the load on the brothers from the outset and let them know they are supposed to take charge, by God's law."

"When I settle down again, she's definitely going to have to be a spiritual woman, who loves God and believes in commitment. If not, then I'll just be by myself," Waydis said.

Tamarra came back with our drinks and sat them on the table. "I see why you didn't buy them hoochies any damn drinks." We looked over at their table and they were gone. "They spent one hundred and ten dollars up in here, and had the nerve to leave me a twelve cent tip! And I tried my best to make sure they had a nice time. You see, those type of women give us all a bad rap, with their fake asses." She stomped away, clearly upset at the ladies.

"See, they even have their own sisters tired of their shit," Waydis said. "Kahlil, let me tell you something. It's probably best that you didn't get married. Before I got married, I enjoyed the hell out of my baby, but once we got married, it took her exactly four months and she changed on me something terrible. I'm telling you everything changed. From the sex to her personality, the difference was like night and day. But she still expected me to do the same things to her that I was doing before we got married. Gifts, movies, romantic evenings out. When she started that shit, I knew I had made a mistake. It's like they forget what attracted you to them, and will swear to God that they were never that way. Then after you realize that they've changed and mention it to them, they try to turn the shit around and convince you that you have growing up to do. I'm tired of it." Waydis took his cognac straight down. "But I got two great kids out the deal, two sons. One is ten, the other six. That's a major reason I want to see Sid, to let him know that he has two little brothers that know all about him and want to meet him."

"So, how do you want to approach this?" I asked, as Marcus Miller was going buck wild on his bass.

"Well, like I said, I'm going to be in this area about two weeks. I'm driving up to Canada for negotiations on a new deal and I hope it won't take that long. But I don't want to introduce myself to Sid, then leave him again. I want to be around in case he wants to have a meal and just talk a while."

"I understand."

"So, what I'm thinking about doing is finishing up business up there, then driving back down here to finally meet my son."

"Do you want me to alert him?" I asked. Waydis gave my question some thought.

"No . . . I think it would be better if we did this together. I don't want him to have time to sit down and wonder why I haven't been in his life, then not want to see me at all."

After dinner we both left Tamarra a hundred dollars each.

Let the Chips Fall

I had made plans to go over to Scooter's for dinner. Kelly promised to tag along with me because I wasn't going to give him a chance to try anything. We'd gotten close, but I wasn't near ready to give him any parts. We'd been to the movies, out to eat, and we even went to the Anita Baker concert. I was beginning to consider him a good friend.

"Cece, I'm not going with you tonight," Kelly said as she sat at the kitchen table, eating her breakfast. "Deric and I are going out and I think I'm staying over again tonight."

"Kelly, what is your problem? I told you I don't want to be alone with Scooter in his place yet. I mean I am glad you are seeing Deric again, but you promised me that you would come along."

"Well, Cece, these last two months with Deric have been all of that. Girl, he's been working it, however I give it to him and we've been having a good time." She put a large helping of food into her mouth. I looked at the clock on the wall. It was six-thirty in the morning. Kelly was supposed to be working out. She'd always worked out from six to eight in the morning on weekends, even if she stayed out all night for one of her Friday-night escapades.

I glanced over at Kelly's plate as I poured myself some grapefruit juice, and even though it was still a relatively small plate of food, it was way more than what she normally ate. I sat down at the table and thumbed through the morning paper. I thought about how strange Kelly had been acting. She'd become much more quiet and reserved, like something was laying heavy on her mind. Her daily routine was changing. She was going to bed earlier during the week; she even had fallen asleep during *New York Undercover*, which was her favorite television show. Come to think of it, her workouts had become a little less strenuous. She wouldn't work out as long, but still did something twice a day during the week. Scooter even mentioned to me one night, while we were sitting on the couch, that Kelly was acting differently. I put down the morning paper and I knew I was reaching.

"Girl, are you pregnant?" She looked at me like I had some nerve and I did.

"Damn Cece . . . ain't you a trip. If you must know, yes I am."

"What did you say?"

"I said, yes . . . I'm going on seven weeks now."

I grabbed my grapefruit juice and tried to wash the surprise down. I knew something was bothering her, but not a little one. I was thinking more on the lines of something like she'd fallen in love with Lee after getting back with Deric or, even worse, she found out that Deric was gay. But not pregnant. I think I would have been ready for anything else. I couldn't even imagine Kelly, of all people, pregnant.

"Kelly, why didn't you tell me? I've been walking around here worrying about you like crazy. How long have you known?"

"Since I missed my period last month. Then I took a test."

So many questions ran through my mind that I wanted to ask Kelly, but I knew how she was. She didn't want anyone to worry about her. She's the type of person who would tell you things when she was ready to talk about them. I just sat there, looking at her and hoped she'd want to talk.

"Oh . . . so I guess, you want to know who the father is?" she asked me with an attitude.

"Not unless you want to tell me."

"That's bullshit, Cece. You want to know and I can see now that if I don't tell you I'll have to put up with your Snoop Doggy Dogg investigative looks all day long. I know how you are. I've known you too long."

"Well, why don't you tell me what's going on with you. If not, I'll just sit here until you do." She told me everything and I was, to say the least, flabbergasted. I sat and listened to her, and I was very displeased with what was coming out of her mouth. Not because she was pregnant, but because of her master plan. This plan sounded too scandalous even for Kelly to come up with. What really surprised me was that she talked about the plan like she'd gone over it in her head time and time again, calculating and making sure that nothing could or would go wrong. I told Kelly she was wrong and that she was making a very big mistake. In the long run, her plan was going to hurt her as well as the baby.

I couldn't understand why she was going to tell Lee that he was the father of the baby when she was almost positive that it was De-ric's. We went round and round for hours, debating her so-called Special K plan. She was so sure she was going to be taken care of and it made me sick to think she would stoop so low. I thought about all of the people she would be hurting: the baby, Deric, Lee and his wife. Damn it. I promised Deric that she was through with Lee. How was I ever going to look at him again after he'd taken her back? Kelly kept saying she was just like most other women who would rather have a wealthy man taking care of her child than one who had to hustle and sell houses to buy diapers. I tried to explain to her that her intention to tell Lee would be fine, if he was the father. Then he would be expected to provide, but she was sure that he wasn't and she couldn't overlook that fact. I told her that Deric should be told the truth and she should let the chips fall where they may. Let him provide as best he could. After all, he loved her. She wasn't even going there.

I called Scooter and told him I couldn't make it to our dinner date because something came up. If I was in Kelly's situation I would have wanted my best friend with me. Scooter became upset when I told him I couldn't make it, and I couldn't understand why he felt that way. I didn't have any allegiance to him. We were just friends. His attitude of, you don't turn me down, I'm a pro ball player, was real ugly and I didn't care for it.

Times like these I missed Kahlil the most.

Payback

Seven weeks had passed since Cece talked to Deric about us getting back together. I was sure about how long it had been, because I'd been seeing him again for six weeks, exactly one week after she talked to him. More important, I was four weeks late with my period, starting one week after I had slept with him every day of the week, several times a day. I'm almost certain that the baby is his even though I did sleep with Lee once . . . okay twice, during my transitional period of getting back with Deric. I just wish I hadn't slept with all these fools around the same time. Then I'd know for sure.

I was sure that everyone was pulling out when the time came. Another reason I suspect Deric is that he's the one who was going without any lovin'. Each and every time we lay down he went buck wild up inside me like he was trying to prove a point. Something told me that I was laying on my back too much and way too often. In Lee's case, you might as well say my hands and knees, because he was starting to get freaky. I can't believe I let everything get out of control, but I have to make this whole situation benefit me.

I weighed the benefits of having the baby and naming Deric as the father. After all, Deric loves me, but what can I say? The list was just not long enough. I'm sure with his belief in family values and God that things would be okay. But I just cannot lay my future with those odds. So I decided to play the mint card. That's right, the government card that has all those dead presidents in the middle of those bills. I have no other choice; everything canceled out. I checked and double checked. Deric probably would be a great father, but Lee could take care of the baby and me for a long time.

I know that Lee will probably want to keep pregnancy a secret, so I'm going to tell him to get his lawyers to prepare a contract with a statement that I will never divulge to anyone that he is the father of my child as long as he makes it worth my while. I don't think he's going to have a problem with that because if Linda finds out, he'll be in double trouble. I knew that befriending her was going to be helpful.

My whole life is getting ready to change. I'm planning to quit my job as soon as I start showing because the only thing I've ever wanted to do while I was pregnant is work out and try my best to keep myself in shape.

All hell was breaking loose. Deric and Lee both knew about Kelly being pregnant, but her plan had one major hitch in it. She couldn't tell Deric that the baby wasn't his after she sat him down and broke the news to him. He was so excited that he told her right off the bat that he wanted a baby girl. He jumped to the conclusion that the baby was his and took full responsibility with pride. Kelly told me he didn't even have a second thought about taking care of her and the baby. He called most of his relatives to let them know that they were having an addition to the family even though Kelly told him that she wasn't going to move in with him just yet nor did she have any plans to get married. He was so full of joy that he said that didn't matter to him because they would work it out.

Kelly thought she really had no choice but to stay with Deric. But still she was going through with her plan to tell Lee that the baby was his. She wanted to get as much from him as she possibly could and Kelly decided Deric didn't have to know anything about it.

Lee started to act really ignorant when Kelly called him to set up a meeting so they could discuss how much he would give her and the baby. Lee would not return her phone calls or answer her pages. Kelly even went to see him at a club where all the players would hang out, and when he saw her, he grabbed the hand of another woman he was with and left without saying one word. Lee's actions only put more fuel on the fire. Kelly became upset because her weak reasoning told her that this was how she would be treated if the baby really was his. Consequently, she didn't feel guilty for taking him to the bank. She threatened Lee, saying that she was dead serious about the situation and that she was going to tell Linda if he didn't do the right thing.

"Kelly, the shoe store is four blocks the other way. Where are you going?" I asked her.

"I have to take care of some business first."

"What kind of business?"

"I'm going to meet Lee."

"You're what! . . . For what? I thought you two already met and that's why you've been so quiet, because you were upset about the outcome."

"We did meet, but he was trippin', talking about how he wasn't giving me anything, so I'm bringing you as a witness to scare his ass."

"The hell you are. Kelly, you might as well forget about this whole thing and just turn the car around, because I'm not getting myself involved in this shit."

Kelly just kept driving.

"Look, Cece, this is what I'm going to do. I'm going to tell him that ten thousand a month is what I want. Do you think that's enough for a man that has a twelve-million-dollar guaranteed contract? Or should I ask for more? I told him the last time we met that if we couldn't come to an agreement, I was going to bring Linda in on our little secret. He just laughed and called me a bitch. But I'm telling you, I'll do it in a New York minute."

"Kelly, what you're doing is blackmail and I'm having none of this."

Kelly pulled into the parking lot of a small restaurant. "Come on, Cece. Just go in with me. You don't have to sit with us. Just come in and sit inside . . . Please."

"Damn it, Kelly. Come on, but I'm telling you I have nothing to do with this," I told her. When we walked into the restaurant, it was completely empty. I stayed behind Kelly and sat down in the first booth that I came to where I could face the front door.

"Come on back, Cece, it's okay," I heard a lady's voice say. "I know you're not involved in this foolishness."

I slowly turned my head and there was Linda standing at a table while Lee sat pouring himself something to drink. Kelly stopped and looked at the situation. "Come on back, you two. I think it's time we all talk," Lee said.

I got up from my seat and walked with Kelly over to their table. "Hi, Cece," Linda said, then she looked Kelly up and down. Lee didn't even look like the situation was affecting him. He sat his bottle down and looked at us with a businessman's grin.

"Welcome to my new restaurant. I just bought it yesterday. How do you like it? So, what is it you want to talk to me about, Kelly?" Lee asked, sitting there as though he had nothing to hide from Linda. Kelly looked a little confused about Linda being there, but she didn't back down one bit.

"You know what I want to talk to you about, Lee. We've already talked once, but you act like you don't want to be bothered with our situation." Kelly tried her best not to look at Linda, but Linda was looking at her dead in the face.

"Kelly, say what you have to say. I don't have much time," Lee said.

"I don't have to say much. Look at me. I'm pregnant and the baby is yours."

When Kelly said that, I didn't feel one thing for her. She was out of control and wrong as hell. Lee began to shake his head, then turned to Linda and smiled as though he'd been right about something for a long time.

"You see, baby, that's why I did it. Because of stupid bitches like her," Lee explained to Linda.

"Kelly, you should be ashamed of yourself. I thought you were different," Linda said.

I was as perplexed as Kelly now, because Linda grabbed Lee's hand and then kissed him on his cheek. "I'm sorry, baby, I'll make it up to you," she told Lee.

What the hell is going on? I thought to myself. I know if someone told me that they were carrying my husband's child, I would go off. But Linda was sympathetic toward Lee for some reason and looked at Kelly like she was calling all the shots now. Lee just sat back and watched with a smirk on his face.

"Look, Kelly, I've known about you and Lee before you two ever went to bed together the first time. As a matter of fact, I knew when I met you at the game and went shopping with you. All I was doing was checking you out to make sure that you were right for Lee."

Kelly was in shock and stood silent. "That's just the kind of relationship we have. I know you can understand that. I do want to thank you though."

"For what?" Kelly asked her harshly.

"For letting Lee take his frustrations out on you during the season. I never let him abuse my body like that when he's under all of that pressure. He just weighs too damn much." Lee started to laugh and moved his eyebrows up and down at Kelly.

"I'm just not into letting anyone, not even my husband, get as filthy and freaky as Lee wants to get during the season," Linda continued. "But I thank you dearly, because I hear you're nasty, too." Linda smiled. Kelly acted like she couldn't comprehend what she was hearing even though she had always told me about people who get married for different reasons. These two were definitely not married for love.

"Look, I don't know what the hell you're talking about, Linda, but I'm having Lee's baby. So all I want to know is how are we going to resolve this?"

"No. You look, bitch." Lee pressed his shoulders back into the booth as Linda took the floor. "You don't get it, do you? Lee is not the father of your child and you will resolve this when you find out who the father is. Lee had a vasectomy four years ago, So, who's the daddy now?"

Kelly was paralyzed. She was more embarrassed than anything else as she stood there silently, watching all of her money go down the drain. She was almost in tears. Linda and Lee whispered to one another and began laughing again as Lee poured her a drink.

Kelly turned around and started to walk out. I was right beside her.

"Oh yeah, Kelly, I don't want you to have another surprise when you get home today because I don't want it to disturb your baby. But your friend Deric. That's his name, right?" We both turned around. "He called me a while back to let me know that my husband was cheating on me and I told him that I knew all about it. He was a little surprised, but I told him it was just a phase he goes through every season. Anyway, he left me his number and I called him about half an hour ago to let him know about your plan. I advised him to go get a blood test so he could make sure the baby was his."

I didn't know what the hell Linda was talking about because Kelly knew the baby was Deric's in the first place. I looked at Kelly strangely.

"And, Cece, my sista, I'm glad you came because it will save me a phone call to you. I know you might want to hear this bit of information up close and personal, girlfriend. Ms. Thang here slept with Scooter while he was trying to talk to you, so it's a very strong possibility the baby is his. Isn't she a trip! Just straight nasty. Tell me, how long have you two been friends anyway?"

Linda looked at Lee and they both shook their heads. "You ladies have a safe drive home. Maybe I'll call you, Kelly, so we can do some shopping some time." We heard them laughing as we walked out.

Who would have thought that things could have gotten any worse? My house, even though Kelly still lived with me, was solemn and cold. Not much different than my feelings for Kelly. I believed in Kelly and I thought she respected me. It's going to be hard to forgive her. She was my closest friend but I started to watch her every move. When the mail came, instead of hollering through the house that the latest Coach advertisement had arrived I just laid it on the table. If she saw it, fine. Instead of talking about how good Malik Yoba looks on TV and sitting on the couch, talking to each other about any and everything that comes to our minds, I watched TV in my own room without Kelly. She was wrong, so wrong that I don't even want an apology. Our conversations have been reduced to simple pleasantries. Our friendship was left at Lee's restaurant, right in the middle of the floor.

I got tired of living like that and asked Kelly to move out. She told me in passing that she'd decided to marry Deric. I'm not surprised. She tried the same money scheme on Scooter. This time she was going to get her money because the baby turned out to be his anyway. But after she found out that his knee injury was career-ending and that his wife and three kids in Aiken, South Carolina, needed him badly, she decided that her chances with Deric were looking better.

When Deric came over to help her move her things, I can't explain what I felt. Bitterness and betrayal were fighting inside me because of the many years of friendship that I had believed had always been genuine. Not that I wanted Scooter. I just couldn't understand why she would want to have sex with him when she knew there was a slim chance of us getting together. I didn't care if he was the only man on earth. Best friends don't give in to the pressure in my book.

I sat on the couch and watched Deric take Kelly's last box out to the car. Kelly stood by the front door, then came over and sat down next to me. We sat still for seconds. I know she was wondering how the hell things ended up this way. Myself, I felt worse than when I left Kahlil for good. This was the end of our bond, which I believed to be stronger than anything in the world. I was determined not to cry. I had cried enough. Kelly exhaled and then tried to smile.

"Cece, no matter what you think, I hope you know that I'll always love you." We looked into each other's eyes for the first time since the restaurant. "You've been like the sister I have never had, and I hope, in time, we'll be able to get over this. I'm so sorry." She bent her head down, but never moved her eyes away from mine, ashamed, afraid of what I was going to say. I couldn't speak. "I have wished so many times that I would have taken your advice. Cece, I really do respect you. I know that you probably don't believe that right now, but I want to make it right."

There was nothing Kelly could do for me, but I had been wondering. "Kelly, when did you sleep with Scooter?" I asked her.

"When he came over to show you his new car. It just happened, Cece. It didn't mean a thing. But I want to make it right," she said again.

I was still concerned about her. "Are you going to be okay?" I asked.

"I'm going to try my best. I'll still see you at work and we'll talk, maybe we can go out to lunch sometime." She smiled sadly, knowing that we wouldn't. Not anytime soon anyway.

"Cece, there is something else I have to tell you." Kelly grabbed her index finger and twisted it slowly. I was ready for anything. "When I told you that Kahlil tried to sleep with me, I lied." Anything except that, I thought to myself.

"That's all that I'm saying. It was all on me," Kelly said, as her tears began to flow. "But I wanted to make it right for you. Baby girl, you go get that man, because I have to tell you this. He is true to you, and loves you very much." Kelly got up from the couch. I stood next to her, trying to hold back my mixed emotions.

"Kelly, tell me, is that the reason you couldn't hold my hand when you told me about Kahlil?" Kelly nodded her head yes, then reached out for me. I tried to move my arms toward her, but I couldn't. She stood there with her arms extended. Deric's horn saved me from trying again. Disappointed, she dropped her arms by her side.

"See you around. I'll call you," she said.

"Okay . . . be careful," I told her.

I thought I was crying, feeling pain and sorrow. As Kelly walked out my door, I attempted to wipe my eyes. It surprised me when I touched my eyes and found them dry. My mind, body, and soul were fed up and wouldn't let my tears go. Kelly shut the door almost without a sound and I walked to the phone, praying to God as I dialed Kahlil's telephone number that he would forgive me.

Show Time

It was seven in the morning and I'd just dumped my fourth cup of coffee into the sink. I was a nervous wreck. "Mommy, I want some water," Octavious said as he tried to reach for his cup that was on the counter. I opened the refrigerator, grabbed the pitcher of ice water, and poured some into his plastic Michael Jordan cup as he tried his best to hold it steady. When I finished, he turned around so quickly that half the water in his cup spilled out and he was off to his bedroom like he hadn't spilled a drop. "Stop running in my house, Octavious," I said to him, at this point not really caring what he did because he was hyped about being on TV with his daddy. I looked at the pitcher of water still in my hand and gulped some straight down as I tried to counter the awful taste lingering in my mouth from the coffee.

My entire morning had been a series of phone calls and I could feel time slipping from me, so I decided to leave the phone off the hook until I was ready to go. My father called me twice, giving me advice on how to answer questions and to remind me that he and all of his retired friends were going to be watching the show. Before that, Sonje called to find out if Octavious and I were getting ready and to let me know that she couldn't stop thinking about me. She talked nonstop, not knowing I had Demitrious on call waiting. He was excited about how much fun we were planning to have in the Big Apple. To top it off, my son got out of bed one hour before I did and woke me up to ask me if he could look through one of the television station's big cameras when he arrived at the studio. And I couldn't forget about the night before when Kahlil had called to see if I wanted a ride to the studio. How our conversation got on Cece and Sid I really don't know but I listened as he seemed to be carrying a heavy burden. My only saving grace was that I'd packed everything during the week that I was taking to New York. We were leaving directly after the show and thankfully my baby-sitter's house was on the way to the airport.

We arrived at the studio and it was as hectic as Sonje told me it would be. The audience had begun to file in and take their seats. Sonje came out from behind the set to do some promotional commercials about her upcoming shows. Some of the audience members and faithful viewers began to applaud her so she stopped to sign autographs and to say hello to some of the national media there covering the show's debut. I'd never seen Sonje at work before. For the first time I saw her take over in public like she did with me when we were alone.

Sonje noticed me and Octavious when we were being seated on the set by the floor director and walked over to greet us, along with all of the other guests on the show. She quickly finished her promos, waved to the audience, and disappeared behind the stage down the hallway to change her clothes for the show. Kahlil, Demitrious, Police Chief Parham, and another gentleman I'd never met walked into the studio together. Octavious forgot that we were already wired for the show and pulled his microphone out of its place when he tried to get out of his seat to hug his father. Demitrious and Chief Parham took their seats right next to us, while Kahlil and the other man took their assigned seats in the first row of the audience. The production crew ensured that all of the microphones were working properly and finished some last minute light adjustments.

"I hope you know I'm really doing this for Octavious . . . look at him," Demitrious said to me. His big black eyes were glued on the large cameras and the floor director as they prepared for the opening shot.

"I know. I've never seen him so excited," I realized.

"I just hope I don't let him down when that big-ass camera gets all up in my face," Demitrious muttered.

"You won't. He adores you. By the way, Demitrious, who's that with Kahlil?"

"Oh, that's Mr. Robinson, a good friend of ours. I'll tell you about him later. So, are you ready for the big city?"

"You know I am." I bent over to straighten out O's tie for the umpteenth time. The audience began to applaud again, as Sonje came out onto the set and began to tell jokes to loosen everyone up. Suddenly, "Quiet on the set," the floor director yelled to everyone. He signaled to Sonje and the *Women Only Show* theme music began to play. I was impressed with how calm Sonje was when I could feel everyone else's nervousness. She took a sip of water from her cup and positioned herself in front of the camera. The red light on top of the camera came on and immediately the floor director pointed to Sonje and she began.

"Good morning and welcome to the *Women Only Show.*" The audience applauded. "Today we are discussing a dilemma that is, quite frankly, all too often ignored in our society. It is a problem all across the country. Today, in our urban communities, statistics show over seventy percent of African-American children grow up in single-parent households."

Sonje pointed to the monitors in the studio and we could all see a tape showing small black children walking to school with their mothers and playing ball by themselves in the park. "Way too many times these statistics breed false innuendos, many of them heard on other nationally televised shows that don't tell the real story, which I have here for you today. For the first time in the history of the *Women Only Show,* and because I believe children should be raised properly, we have as our guests Detroit's most powerful grassroots organization that, I am happy to say, I sit on the board of—the Urban Coalition." The audience began to applaud. "Coalition members are here to discuss this growing problem in our community and also to share the secrets to the success they've had with the If Man Be Man program," Sonje explained.

It was very exciting. The audience began clapping again and the cameras swept over the panel guests and many of the audience members from the community who had come to support the show.

"Now, let me get started with the director of the If Man Be Man initiative, our very own chief of police, Donald Parham. Tell me, Chief Parham, why did the Coalition come up with this program in the first place?"

The chief cleared his voice. "First of all, Sonje, during our weekly meetings, it came to the attention of the Coalition in almost every meeting we held that mothers were concerned by the crimes their children were committing. They didn't know how to handle the situations they were confronted with alone. They needed and wanted direction. They all felt something was missing in their children's lives, and that's why they came to the Coalition for help. After doing a thorough investigation and reviewing the information from each household, we came to the conclusion that in all of these homes there were no fathers present for the boys and girls who were committing terrible crimes in the community. So what we did first was sit down and think about how the black community has always dealt with our problems. In the days of slavery everyone was held responsible for their family's actions by the slaves themselves on the plantations, where the men played an important role in the discipline. And it's important to point out that the majority of these men were not the real fathers because families were split up. It didn't take the master to keep order in the households—our forefathers did that on their own initiative. Fathers who lived with their families took great pride, even though they were enslaved, in making sure that the children were respectable to other slaves on the plantation. This gave us the premise of the If Man Be Man program. Our program recognizes that mothers in our community should never have to shoulder the full burden and responsibility of rearing children. Now, the Coalition works with mothers who don't want to handle the responsibility of raising their children alone. Upon their request, the Coalition will locate the fathers of the children, counsel them, and let them know that they have a personal obligation to take care of their responsibilities. Then we make sure it is being done by constant review."

The audience began to applaud and Sonje took over.

"Okay, fine . . . but let me play devil's advocate. You know that we have people out there right now saying, Well, the police chief is using taxpayer's dollars to locate these men and that's not right."

Police Chief Parham acted like he was waiting for the question and quickly responded. "Sonje, let me say that, yes, I am using my assets, as chief of police of this city, to track and hunt down fathers in our community who will not, for some reason or another, take care of their children. I call that a terrible crime. Secondly, I say to all of the upset taxpayers and Monday-morning quarterbacks out there, we have located over two hundred and fifty fathers in the last six months and there will be more to come. So what they

276

should consider before attacking the plan is how much money it's saving the city on welfare and Medicaid allowances that these mothers would otherwise be forced to use if we didn't find these men."

"That's a very good point, Chief. Now let me go to one of the fathers who was found by the Coalition." Sonje stood in the audience and pointed to one of the guests on the stage, who was sitting to the far left of me. "Ronald, would you please tell us your situation and your connection to the Coalition."

Ronald was surprised that she called on him first and his eyes lit up. "Well, Sonje, when my wife and I graduated from college, I looked for an entire year for a job, something which for some reason I could not obtain . . . that's another show. My wife was pregnant during the entire time I was searching for a job. She had the baby and I still had no job and I needed to provide for my family. She recuperated and within three weeks she went out to the same streets where I had searched for a job. She found an excellent position. She brought in enough money to support the baby, pay all the bills, and put food on the table, while I continued to look for my first job. It was now going on a year and a half.

"To make a long story short . . . I became expendable. I didn't feel worthy of being . . . quote, unquote, the head of the household and making decisions for my family when I wasn't making any money. My manhood was stripped from me. I felt like all my life I had to prove myself to others and when I finally show that all black men aren't criminals or dope dealers by obtaining my degree, how am I rewarded? By waiting in the unemployment line for a year and a half, with people who didn't even have a high school diploma. So I left. I stayed away for nine months. Then the Coalition located me and not only have I come back home, I've taken classes at the Coalition on starting your own business. Courses, I might add, that are not taught in college. Thanks to their help, I've started my own computer repair company. I signed a huge contract with the city last month and hired my first two employees just this week. So, the Coalition is doing it all."

The audience was applauding for Ronald and I could see everyone on the set begin to relax, including Octavious, as he watched Sonje make her way through the audience.

"Intriguing, very intriguing," she said. "Now, Mike . . . my brother, my brother. I just have to come to you next, sir." Sonje smiled and so did Mike. "To say the least, you've been getting busy . . . why don't you tell us what's been going on in your life and how the Coalition got involved."

"Well, first of all, you have to understand. I am a product of what we are trying to keep our children from becoming. I grew up without anyone in my life and I have six brothers and sisters and we have never seen any of our fathers. When I was eight years old, I started hanging out in the streets and getting into trouble . . . you could say I was very wild." Sonje looked at Mike and nodded her head vigorously in agreement with him, getting a few laughs from the audience. "But, uh . . . I have five kids myself. I had the first one when I was fourteen years old. They range from eight and a half months to ten years old. To keep it plain and simple, I wasn't doing anything for them. Basically, even though I knew deep down inside that I should have been in their lives, I didn't know how or what to do. I never had an example to learn from."

Sonje made her way up on the stage and looked at Mike. "Fine, Mike, now tell us how you were located by the Coalition after the mother of your youngest asked for their assistance?"

"Well, one day, I was talking to this young lady friend of mine at the bus stop, on my way to pick up my welfare check. Every time I saw her, I would ask her out—I mean time and time again. And finally she said yes. When the bus arrived, we took one step on the bus and not ten seconds after we sat down, she looked up at a poster that was on the bus and *BAM!* There was my picture. Sitting right dab in the middle of one of the Coalition's posters they place everywhere in the community. She turned to me and said, 'Hell no, I'm not going out with you. You have other things you need to be taking care of.' Then she pointed at my picture on the poster, which embarrassed me. James, the bus driver, gave me the card of the Coalition as I was getting off the bus, and told me to give them a call. On my way home I thought about what she'd said and how bad my picture looked on that poster so I called the Coalition up. Now I takes care of mine and have gotten off welfare, too." Mike bent down and kissed his eight-month-old baby, who was sitting on his lap. The audience applauded.

"We'll be back in a moment," Sonje said.

During the commercial break, Sonje and the floor director were in a deep conversation and I spotted Kahlil looking at Chief Parham, giving him the thumbs-up signal. Parham winked back. They were both elated at how well the show was going. When the camera light came back on, Sonje had changed her demeanor and poise somewhat. She seemed more inquisitive and she paused for five seconds after the floor director gave her the cue that she was back on the air.

"I would now like to introduce Demitrious, who also has a story to tell. Demitrious, the floor is yours." When she said that, my son's face lit up with pride for his father. He looked up at Demitrious when he began to speak. I even felt good, just by sitting next to the father of my child.

"Well, Sonje. I left my son and wife, because I just flat out didn't think I was going to be a good father to my son. I mean, things had happened in our lives between Dewayna and me. So much, in fact, that I couldn't stand the pressure of it all, so I left. My good friend, who sits on the board of directors of the Coalition, took it upon himself to locate me and he convinced me to get involved in my son's life again. I did and I will never leave him again because I love him so much." Demitrious looked down and rubbed Octavious on the head. Sonje was sitting directly in front of Demitrious now, on the steps of the stage, but facing her audience with her back toward the guests on the stage.

"Now, Demitrious, are you sure that's the reason why you left your son and wife alone?" Sonje asked.

I could tell by her voice that Sonje was being sarcastic. I'd grown to hate it when she sounded that way. I looked at Demitrious with concern.

"Yes, why do you ask?" Demitrious looked at Sonje's back, waiting for her answer.

"Well, Demitrious, some talk show hosts would say, 'I'm glad you asked me that,' but not me. I would have a hard time saying that."

I looked into one of the monitors in the studio, because I couldn't see Sonje's face. The camera began to zoom in on her face in a rehearsed manner, while she began to cry. I didn't know what the hell to think. Everyone in the studio had become still and silent and I grabbed my son's hand when he looked up at me with confusion in his eyes. He wanted to ask me what was wrong.

"I have to admit that . . . audience . . . excuse me," Sonje said, "but this is going to hurt me as much as anyone to do this. And to do this in front of my first nationally televised audience hurts even more."

The floor director came up to Sonje and gave her a tissue and she paused for a moment. "First of all, I have gone undercover at the Urban Coalition and have unraveled a terrible, hideous crime that has not only been covered up by the Coalition, but by our police chief himself, the board member to whom the problem was brought initially, and Mr. Robinson, Demitrious's counselor. Not only has this crime been kept from this child's mother, but it would have been glorified here today, if I had not looked into this matter myself. I want to give Demitrious one more chance to tell the nation why he left his child without one word to anyone."

There was mumbling in the audience as they wondered what

was going on. I looked at Demitrious, who was visibly shaken. He began to tremble. Octavious let his hand go and looked at him, confused. He didn't know why his strong daddy was shaking the way he was. Kahlil looked at Demitrious and he acted as though he had seen him this way before. He stood up.

"Don't say anything, Demitrious, she set you up."

Sonje looked at Kahlil as if to say, "Don't you dare fuck with me." She pointed to him and the security guards, who were dressed in suits, surrounded Kahlil and escorted him out of the studio. Immediately after that, two Detroit police officers entered from the side of the stage. Police Chief Parham looked at them. "You two better not move," he shouted and they stopped where they stood. I was still unaware of what was going on and grabbed Octavious and sat him on my lap. He was scared and began to cry.

"Go ahead, Demitrious, this is your chance," Sonje said. Demitrious wiped his eyes and tried to speak several times, but nothing came out of his mouth. He turned to me.

"Dewayna, I had no intention of telling you something like this on national television, but it looks like she gives me no choice. You remember, I told you I had something to tell you when we got to New York? I swear to you, I had planned on telling you this when we got there." Demitrious cleared his throat of the tight knot, which appeared to be choking him. I began to tremble, when Sonje came up to where we were sitting and put her hand on top of Octavious's head. Demitrious squeezed Octavious's hand and then wiped his own eyes. Octavious tried to look right back into his father's eyes, which he had never seen so red. Demitrious turned and looked at me. "Dewayna, when I was younger my father abused me. He beat me more times than I care to remember. Something in me wanted to start doing the same thing to Octavious, but before I laid one hand on my son, I packed my bags and left. The Coalition helped me to get over the aggression that was put into me by my own father."

Sonje looked at Demitrious. "Now, Demitrious, be honest. I have records right here saying that your case at the Coalition is an abusive parent case and we would all like to know in what way you have harmed this child."

No one in the studio was more bewildered than I was. After all, why would Sonje lie like this on her special show? What she's saying must be true. Maybe I rushed things with Demitrious, maybe somewhere inside I knew there was a reason I was apprehensive about us ever getting back together. I am not going anywhere with him and he will never see Octavious again, I thought. I began to feel a hot fire burn inside of my body. I just wanted to get out of my seat and wanted to begin to shout, in hopes that someone would just please help me put the damn fire out. I could see all the cameras focusing on my face, while all of the other parents on stage held their children close to their bodies. Octavious didn't know what was going on, because he didn't understand. He knew that, whatever it was, it was bad and clutched my hand with all his might. The audience stood and looked at our family in silence, they were all shocked. Then I heard Sonje say, "Back in a moment."

During the commercial break, the police walked up on the stage and told Demitrious that he was being charged with child abuse by the state of Michigan. They began to read him his rights and escorted him off the stage.

"Don't worry, Demitrious, I'm on my way down to the station, along with Kahlil. It's nothing but a big mistake," Parham assured him. Mr. Robinson, who had been sitting next to Kahlil, ran up on the set.

"Sonje, what records are you talking about? Have you lost your mind?"

"The files I got out of your cabinet," she snapped back.

"That file was not complete when you saw it. You read the wrong information."

Fed Up with the Fanny

"Sure. Just sit down before I have you tossed out of here," Sonje shouted back at him.

I tried to get someone to tell me what was going on but the floor director once again told everyone to be quiet, and Sonje began to give her last statement for the show.

"You now realize why this has been, and will continue to be, called the *Women Only Show*. It's indeed a shame that on the national debut of this, my very first show, I had to expose such information. Men, particularly black men, constantly say that they never get a fair chance in the media. Here was a chance to show some great efforts, but once again they were unable to prove themselves. My heart aches most for the family of this young victim and his mother, and we are willing to pay for counseling for both of them. But you better believe it won't be at the Urban Coalition, which stands up for the disrespectful black men that we have become accustomed to in our society. Not only will they hurt the people we care about, but their own as well. Thank you for watching and I'll see you next time on the *Women Only Show*."

The members of the audience who were not affiliated with the Coalition cheered and applauded as Sonje put down her microphone and walked quickly off the set. I grabbed Octavious's hand and ran after her. Thoughts ran through my mind. I was now worse off than when I first went to Kahlil for help—now my son's father had been taken to jail. I didn't know what to do, but I ran to Sonje because I knew she would talk to me. She promised me that she always would.

"**Sonje,** what's going on?" I said, trying to catch my breath. "Why didn't you tell me anything about this? What am I going to do now? My baby doesn't have a father again. Shit, let's go somewhere and talk. I feel like I'm going to pass out."

Octavious started sobbing louder. He looked up at me and began to say my name over and over again while Sonje looked at me very coldly, undisturbed by the show's events.

"Dewayna, look, I don't think I can talk to you right now. I'm very busy. As a matter of fact, I think it would be best if we ended this now."

"What?" I was in shock and I just stood there while my son began wiping his eyes. The most exciting day in his life had turned into a nightmare.

Sonje looked down at him, then bent down to his level. I didn't have enough strength to pull him away from her, but he knew that she was an evil person because he turned his head and put his face into my legs and held me tight. My son was smarter than me.

"Bye, Octavious," she said touching his shoulder. "I hope you had a nice time." Then she got up, gave me a piercing look, and strutted down the hall to her dressing room like she was on top of the world.

Paid

◇

I was stunned when Waydis called on my cell phone and said, "Kahlil, I want to see Sid tonight." Waydis was flying back to Boston for an emergency business meeting in the morning. He said that he was about an hour outside of Detroit and I told him that I would meet him in the lobby of his hotel as soon as I could.

His call couldn't have come at a worse time. It was raining like crazy outside and I had just finished at the police station with Parham, straightening things out with state officials concerning Demitrious and Sonje's outlandish allegations. At the beginning it was rough. Parham was in his office, because the Mayor was on the line on a conference call, wanting to know if what Sonje said was true, breathing heavily on the chief's back trying to find out what he had to do with the whole situation. The FBI, on the other hand, had Demitrious so mixed up, putting words in his mouth, that he didn't know his right from his left.

Demitrious decided he would talk to the investigators without a lawyer present, because he had nothing to hide, but I sat in with him as he answered questions. They tried their best to confuse him and I finally told him not to answer another question without a lawyer.

They took him into the waiting room, and it saddened me that a brother who tried to do so right could be treated so unfairly. I wanted to stay and wait for Demitrious to finish talking with his lawyer, but I had to find Sid. I promised Demitrious that I would call to make sure things were okay. Mr. Robinson expressed concern, saying that in these situations a large group of people become suicidal because the information they'd held back for so long came out when they weren't ready to discuss it. So I asked Parham to make sure someone kept an eye on Demitrious. Sonje really fucked up and there was no way she was going to get away with her nonsense.

I opened the door to my mother's house and decided that I was going to bypass Leandra and talk straight to Sid. The way my mind was going, I knew that I'd blow up at Leandra. I'd say things that probably needed to be said, but I'd already wasted enough time talking to her. Now, it was all about Sid and Waydis. The house was quiet and it seemed like everyone was already asleep. I walked through the kitchen, opened the basement door and walked down the steps.

"Sid, you come down here right this minute and tell me what's going on!" Leandra demanded from below. I walked down the steps and found her with a very worried look on her face, holding a wad of money and a loaded pistol in her hand.

"Oh, Kahlil, I was about to call you. Look what I found under Sid's mattress. Where the hell did he get all of this? There must be at least fifteen thousand dollars here, and what is he doing with a pistol?" she whined. "When I heard that he was running with the GPC, I didn't think much of it. But now he has got me scared, with all of this."

"You knew? You knew he's been running with the GPC?"

Leandra nodded her head yes. "Well, a girlfriend of mine told me she heard Sid was stealing cars, but I didn't think they were carrying guns and hurting people."

"Well, did you ever think he was hurting himself, Leandra? Damn, I swear. Look, I have to go. I don't have time to be talking with you." I turned around and began to walk up the steps. Leandra followed me.

"Kahlil, listen. I'll talk to him tonight. What brings you over here so late anyway?"

Leandra's misplaced priorities got the best of me and I couldn't hold it back any longer. "I wanted to talk to Sid about something," I told her.

"About what?"

"About how you've been lying to him all of his life."

"What the hell are you talking about, Kahlil?"

"I'm talking about Waydis," I shouted at her.

She was speechless. I was expecting her to lie, maybe I even wanted her to. I still couldn't believe how she'd lied to all of us, all these years. Leandra looked at me like she was exposed and stripped before the whole world. The look on her face was full of shame. I turned around and began to walk out the door as my mother came from the hallway.

"Who is Waydis?" she asked, looking at both of us.

"Ask her. I have to go find Sid."

We were sitting in Rashaad's old 1974 Impala that he always drove when he didn't want to draw attention. I was in the backseat, nervous as hell and rocking back and forth, making the seats crunch and squeak.

"Damn, Sid, you sound like you got a bitch back there or something. Nigga, quit moving around so much and drink one of these brews and chill your ass out," Rashaad said, as he gave me a beer. "You made your decision, so be a man." I sat it on the floor, I didn't want it. I just wanted this shit to be over with, so I could go home and forget about the whole fucking thing.

"What's up, brutha? You nervous or something?" Difante asked from the passenger's seat. "Fuck that, this is what it's all about. Get ready, because I feel like we are about to run up on our car." He was cool and collected.

"That's right. Just do 'em like I've done in the past and just pull the mothafuckin' trigga," Rashaad said, pretending he had a gun in his hand. Difante looked back at me and tried to reassure me things were going to be okay.

"We've been through this shit so many times, Sid, don't even sweat it. We've been out here for two hours now, looking for this car, and when we run up on it, just do what you have to do and we'll be back home before you know it."

I tried to agree but I started to think of all the reasons why I should point the fucking pistol I had in my hand at someone who hadn't done shit to me, someone I didn't even know, and pull the trigger. I thought long and hard and I couldn't even come up with one. Even when the thought of the fifty thousand dollars we were going to split came to mind, it didn't seem like it was the right thing to do. I even thought about what Rajanique told me, about the type of nigga she wanted to be down with and what Kahlil told me in the car just the other day. Why did I have to tell these Negroes that I would do this? I knew if I did this shit, neither Rajanique nor anyone like her would ever want to be with me and if Kahlil ever found out, he would kick my ass. I leaned forward to the front seat, to tell those crazy fools that I wasn't shooting anybody, and Difante started clapping his hands in excitement.

"Look a here! Look a here!" he yelled, then pointed to a smoke black, four-door Lincoln Town Car that was pulling up at the stop light. Rashaad pulled up and stopped behind the car and Difante turned around and looked at me with blood in his eyes.

"All right, Sid. At the next stop, get out and run up to the car. Tell 'em to get out, do 'em, and then jump in the car and start driving like the motherfuckin' car is yours. We'll be right behind you."

I looked at Difante, wanting to tell him that I didn't want to do this shit, but everything was final. It was too late now. I had to do what we'd come to do.

Rashaad was tapping his fingers on the steering wheel in excitement and as the light turned green, he followed closely behind the car. We went through two green lights and Rashaad screamed, "Catch a light. Just catch a light." I sat still and quiet as hell, hoping with my fingers crossed that the damn car would never stop. Suddenly, I saw the light up ahead turn yellow and the brake lights of the car in front of us lit up. "Yes, baby, yes," Difante said. "Get ready, my brother."

I wanted to drop the pistol and run. The car came to a complete stop and I didn't want to get out of the car, but Difante looked back at me.

"Go, Sid, hurry up."

I hesitated for a half a second and then jumped out of the car with the nine by my side. I quickly approached the driver's side of the car and banged on the hood.

"Get the fuck out of the car," I said nervously, nothing like I meant what I said. All of a sudden I became excited and I began to jump up and down as the motherfucka in the car looked at me with fear and surprise all in his face. He tried his best to hurry up and take off his seat belt. I opened the door and he stepped out of the car. He didn't know if he should put his hands up or what. I just pointed the pistol directly at him.

"Please, don't shoot me. Go ahead and take the car, but I have a family," he pleaded.

"Shoot him! Hurry up and shoot him!" I heard Difante and Rashaad scream, then Rashaad flashed his bright lights on us. It happened all so fast and without thinking I pumped the first round directly into his chest. No one told me that I would feel the pain of the bullet as he fell to the ground. I pointed the pistol at him again and fired two more shots into the defenseless man. The sight of him, on the ground with the rain washing his blood away under the car lights, would not allow me to move. He twitched and squirmed. I shook and tried not to throw up. I was in shock. I stood there helpless, unable to take my eyes off the flowing blood. I began to gasp for air, along with the man on the wet pavement.

Difante ran up to me. I began to reach down for the man, something told me to help him.

"Come on, Sid. You did good. Now let's get the fuck out of here!"

I bent down lower, feeling a need to touch his hand. He reached for mine and I touched him, then Difante grabbed me and pushed me into his car. I sat in the passenger side, stunned, as Difante drove the car off into the city lights, screaming, "It's time to get paid," as Rashaad followed behind us.

I went back to my house, hoping Sid was there. When I found out that he wasn't, I began to ride around in the neighborhood, scanning the front of the barbershop, where I knew he sometimes hung out. I didn't know how he was going to react to the news that his father was finally here after all this time, and that he wanted to see him. I looked at the time and called the hotel to leave a message for Waydis that I was running a little late.

Deep down, I was happy as hell for Sid. Maybe it would let him see how his father did care for him. As I turned the corner I passed the shop and saw Rashaad who was standing with a hood over his head trying to stay dry. I pulled over to the curb.

"Yo, Rashaad. Let me speak to you."

Rashaad walked over and put his hands in his pockets. "What's

up, Kahlil? What brings you out here? Checking up on the brothers?"

"Yeah, I guess you can say that. Listen, have you seen Sidney?"

Rashaad wiped his mouth and looked down the street. "No, not
since yesterday."

He was lying and I knew it. My cell phone rang. It was Parham.
"Kahlil, I need you back down here," he said. I hung up and
looked back at Rashaad who backed away from the car. "Look,
Rashaad . . . if you see him, tell him to call me as soon as possible."
Rashaad nodded his head as I drove off.

When I walked into Parham's office, the chief was sitting at his
desk, talking on the phone. He motioned for me to sit down and
then hung up the phone.

"Kahlil, I'm sorry to bring you back out here tonight," he said.

"No problem, Chief. Is Demitrious okay?" I asked.

He looked at me sternly. "Yes, he sure is. He went home about
ten minutes ago." I was confused.

"The reason I called you is, well, we just picked Sid up."

"What?"

"Just about a half hour ago, in a stolen car. Two of my cops
stopped the car that was speeding minutes after they found a
body laying in the street. He was found in the car with a gun that
had just been fired, with a guy named Difante. As you know, Sid
took the rap for Difante last year on the gun charges."

"But he didn't do it?" I hoped.

The chief lit his pipe. "No, he hasn't said. But that Difante is a
real smooth mothafucka. He's down the hall right now, singing
the blues and making a deal with prosecutors as we speak, blaming the shooting on Sid, along with seven other robberies. It looks
like Sid is going to be charged with all of them plus tonight's jacking and attempted murder." I turned around and walked to the
door.

"Let me see him, Parham. I want to see him now."

I sat in Parham's office for about twenty minutes, while Sid was being fingerprinted and photographed. Leandra and Mama had arrived and came into Parham's office. All my differences I had with Leandra didn't seem to matter anymore. When I saw the pain and confusion on her face as she hesitated before reaching out to me, I grabbed her, along with my mother, and held them tightly as they began to cry.

"You can go down and see him now," Parham announced in a quiet voice.

We walked down the cold and brightly lit hallway. It seemed colder than when I went to see Demitrious. We walked into the room that was surrounded by concrete walls. Sid was sitting in a chair, flanked by two police officers, and Parham told them to leave. When Sid saw us walk in, he dropped his head. Leandra ran over to her son, placed her trembling hands on his face and stood there, rubbing the sides of his face as though he were an infant. I sat my mother down in a chair across from Sid. She couldn't stand to look at her first grandchild in handcuffs. I could see her trying to look at him but failing.

"Sid, what happened?" I asked. "I know you're not involved in this, are you?"

He didn't respond.

"Sid, answer me, so we can get this straightened out," I pleaded with him.

Leandra, who couldn't take her hands off Sid, bent her knees as she leaned beside him and tried to look at his face. Sid would not look at her.

"Baby, what happened? Are you okay?" Leandra asked.

I had flashbacks of the first time he fell off his bike and we all rushed to his side. Sid still did not respond. My mother got a burst of energy and, despite the handcuffs that frightened her to death, she grabbed Sid by his arm.

"Sidney, look at me, boy. Tell me you didn't shoot anybody tonight." She waited for him to answer. She shook his arm once, twice.

Sid slowly lifted his head. It looked like he wanted to say that he didn't do the shooting. He glanced at all of us, then slowly dropped his head and began to cry. We were all silent, jarred by his confession to us. The echoes of my mother's cries, along with her daughter's and grandson's began to really get to me, as I realized this grandson, son, and nephew had committed a terrible crime. I felt a tear begin to run down my own face. I couldn't stand strong any longer. I was fed up, truly fed up. I turned my face toward the concrete wall and rested my head.

Parham walked back into the room with the two officers. We all turned to him, with hopes that he would say this was all a misunderstanding, that we could leave and take Sid home. The gloom that covered his face discouraged any such possibility.

"I have more bad news," he said.

My mother took a deep breath and Leandra took Sid's head and placed it against her womb, from which he had come.

"The victim . . . the victim who was shot, died five minutes ago. He was a forty-year-old businessman named Waydis Thomas. And his last words were, tell my son I love him," Parham said, trying to hold his composure.

I felt like I'd been shot and my mother and Leandra screamed out loud. "Oh my God. Oh my God." Sid raised his head, with tears coming down his face, and Parham walked over to me.

"Kahlil, what's wrong?" he said. I could not answer.

"Mama, what's wrong?" Sid asked.

Leandra stood still, now crying hard, as she trembled all through her body. She looked at my mother.

"Go ahead, baby. Go ahead and tell him!" she screamed out.

Leandra took both of Sid's handcuffed hands and gazed right into his eyes. I walked over to my mother and held her as she began to cry louder, much harder, waiting for the shock waves to erupt.

"Baby . . . Waydis Thomas . . . Waydis . . . Waydis Thomas was your father," Leandra said, as she tried to touch Sid's shocked face.

Sid jumped out of his chair and started to shout so many things that had been on his mind all of his life. He began cursing Leandra and I rushed over to him, along with the guards. Leandra grabbed Sid first and tried to hold him.

"Baby, I'm so sorry. I should have told you. Baby, I'm so . . . sorry," she cried.

Sid realized why he'd felt the pain as he pumped the rounds into his own father. He finally stopped walking back and forth and looked down at his mother hatefully, as she tried to bury her head into his chest.

"I'm so sorry, baby . . . It's all my fault," Leandra cried out.

"Get me the fuck out of here," Sid said in a trembling voice.

"Oh, Sid," my mother cried.

We all stood silently as the guards escorted him to his cell, and there was nothing that I could do except listen to Leandra and Mama crying.

Deep into Thought

Sid is locked up for at least twenty years. The judge had mercy on him and viewed the murder of his own father as a special circumstance case. He stated as he sentenced him that he was involved in a "horrific tragedy at best," which he never wanted to see happen again in his lifetime. Sid is at his lowest point now, one that I could never imagine myself ever reaching. He hasn't said a word to anyone in or out of prison, and it's been six months since his incarceration. I've made a promise to myself that I will help him get through every day that he is locked up behind those cold metal bars. I've been sending reading material to him to lift his spirits, and my connections have assured me that they will keep an eye out for Sid in prison. I even have someone overseeing my lookouts to ensure that is exactly what happens.

My mother finally broke out of the sadness she fell into after she yelled out "I love you, grandson," at the reading of Sid's verdict. She realized that there was a strong possibility she may never see her first grandchild again without metal bars between them. Her pain spilled over to the rest of my sisters but especially Pam, as they all had to explain to their own children what Sidney had done and where he was going to spend the next twenty years of his life.

I sat down with Leandra and she surprised me when she told me about being a manic-depressive and how her medication affects her. I began to understand her unwillingness to put things in the proper perspective when it came to dealing with her life. I could tell she was having a hard time accepting what had happened to Sid and Waydis. She is so full of guilt and shame that I worry about her condition getting worse. As I spoke with her she confessed that she wished that she would have told us all so that we could have kept Sid from getting into trouble. She wants to get some help. I'm sure she now realizes that family is the most important thing in life, and that everyone has the right to know who their parents are no matter what the circumstances. I just wish it didn't have to happen this way. I know it's God's will, but this whole terrifying ordeal has changed all of our lives and all of those close to us. I can tell you one thing, though, this situation really proved that each decision we make affects others, too, sometimes more than ourselves. I learned that we should think thoroughly before we make any decisions at all.

I'm glad to see Dewayna and Demitrious back together again. I think the tragedy in my life, along with the bullshit that Sonje pulled on them, inspired them to make a stable home for Octavious. Dewayna realized the hard way that a woman will hurt you in a relationship just as bad as, if not worse than, a man.

Sonje became desperate in her attempt to win ratings and decided to let her viewers know she was bisexual on a show where bisexual women confessed their sexuality to their male partners. I'm very glad to say that she thought wrong. After the Coalition sued her for defamation of character and demanded she admit to the public that her show about the Coalition was a complete lie, her show went downhill with the quickness. Now she is doing a live show on Sunday nights at three in the morning. No one ever sees her on TV now. It serves her right.

In no time after I had deposited my thick check from Nachi and made sure it cleared, the president of Nachi called me and offered me a position with the company. I guess the accounts I handled were really upset to see me go and were causing problems. Of course I told them hell no. I am putting all of my time into the Coalition because there are just too many things that need to be done in the community. I decided my first project would be an attempt to reach young black males. They're in trouble and something has to be done.

Cece and I are trying to work out our misunderstanding. Communication and trust are the foundations of any relationship, and I guess we just lost sight of one another. With Kelly out of the picture we are talking about marriage again. Love as deep as ours cannot be denied; together she and I are one. One thing is for sure, we all learned a hell of a lesson.

Acknowledgments

To the entire family: Carl and Sue White, Richard and Ann Griffin, Clarrettae Allen, Sandy, you know you're my girl, we were put here to make a change on the same day, so do your thang—always Twin I, C.K. Cheek-ums, Karla, Lil' Qleo, Bidea, Deanna, Puddin, Erin, Kaloa Hearne, Chaka Chandler, James and Carol Brown and family—Anthony (Prime-Time) Dan, T-man and baby Aaron—aunts and uncles who taught a brother right! Emma Moore, Reva Walker, Danny, Tyke, Amos, Phil and Jerry White, Warner K. Parsons. New York City Connection, Reggie English, Bill Bolden, Ernestine Callender, Wilton Cedeno, Vaughn Graham, Pam Mason, Joann Christian. Partners in crime Randy Clarkson (Ham), David Dungy (Wham), Lamonte Waugh (Lam), and Alvin Dent (I'll be Damn), Ronald Steward, Garland Williams, Lee Craft and family, Toni Jones, Tonya Anderson, Saqaula Jones, Chris and Mel Carter, Frank Tatum, Mark Stinson, Poindexter clan, whaz up Terrance, Ziggy, Patrick, Mr. and Mrs. Jackson, Buddy, Nel, Danny, Deris, Teddy Briggs, Eric and Adam Troy, Deric Russell, Clyde Smith, Durroh family, Rosita Page, Tina Bates, Chuck Ragland, Michael Washington, Joyce Gregory, Dr. Lois Benjamin, Ike Henry, Eddie Managult, James Black, Eddie

Acknowledgments

Rhodeman, Debbie and Donna Turner, Dewayna Chambers, Nate Beach, Joy Eubanks, Kathleen McQueen, Tonya Clark, Tressy Murray, Charles Baker Photography. Those who read it first, much thanks. Darryle Melson, Yvonne Daniels, Jacqueline Daniels, LaTonya Beavers, Hope Boyd, Joan Niesmith, Regina Larkins, Angie Wilkens. Special shout out to Mark and Latina Anthony, SFC Boxton and family, James Allen rest in peace.

Those in the business telling stories and portraying characters as never before—thanks for keeping a brother constantly motivated: Nikki Giovanni, Walter Mosley, Toni Morrison, J. California Cooper, Bebe Moore Campbell, Nelson George, Alice Walker, Terry McMillan, April Sinclair, Tananarive Due, Octavia Butler, Spike Lee, Bill Duke, Mario Van Peebles, Hudlin brothers, John Singleton, Martin Lawrence, Matty Rich, Wayans, Miea Allen, Wesley Snipes, Nia Long, Robin Givens, Leonard Lee Thomas, Conrad Cozy, Laurence Fishburne, Jada Pinkett, Angela Bassett, Giancarlo Esposito, Paula Jai Parker, Larenz Tate. Music that put me through: Maxwell, Mary J. Blige, Babyface, TLC, Tupac, X-scape, Marcus Miller, Anita Baker, Foley, Angela Bofill, Najee, Bob James, George Howard, Randy Crawford, Puffy Combs, Carol Raines-Brown, Fugees, Toni Braxton, Rahsaan Patterson, Kirk Franklin's Nu Nation.

About the Author

This is Franklin White's first novel. He is a graduate of Central State University and has published *Accent Magazine* along with working as a consultant with the Black Film Makers' Foundation in New York City. He is active in the National Urban League "Beep" Organization and is currently working on his second novel, along with writing for television and music lyrics. He resides in Atlanta, Georgia.